Golden Fleece

Mine-Finding and Adventure in the Pacific Northwest

A Novel
by

K.C. McTaggart

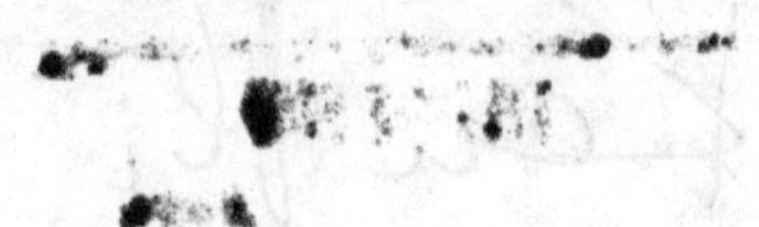

Editing by Suzanne Bastedo and Paul Vanderham
Text design and layout by Warren Denny
Cover painting by Katharine Dickinson
Cover design by Warren Denny
Illustrations by the author

Published by Elton-Wolf Publishing
Vancouver, BC

First printing February 2000

Canadian Cataloguing in Publication Data

McTaggart, K.C., 1919-
Golden fleece

ISBN 1-58619-078-4

I. Title.
PS8575.T345G64 2000 C813'.6 C00-910183-7
PR9199.3.M34212G64 2000

ELTON-WOLF PUBLISHING

Vancouver • Seattle • Denver • Milwaukee • Portland

Suite 212 - 1656 Duranleau Street Granville Island
Vancouver, BC V6H 3S4 (604) 688-0320 Fax (604) 688-0132

Email: jblackmore@elton-wolf.com
Internet: http://www.elton-wolf.com
Printed in Canada

Contents

Prologue

He went to the far corner of the barn, emptied a large canvas bag onto the work-bench and stuffed weighty fist-sized chunks of copper ore into his pockets until they would hold no more. He positioned a box, lifted a coil of rope off a nail, fashioned a noose, threw it over a beam and fastened the bitter end to the leg of the bench. He climbed awkwardly onto the box and adjusted the noose around his neck. He tied a loose clove-hitch in a piece of heavy cord, slid the hitch around his wrists, tightened it and looped the free ends around his belt, knotting them once, twice, five times, savagely tightening. He looked once more around the old barn and kicked the box away.

His ten-year-old son, Ben, found him half an hour later.

John F. Kennedy was shot the next day, November 22, 1963.

CHAPTER 1

GUS AND BILL

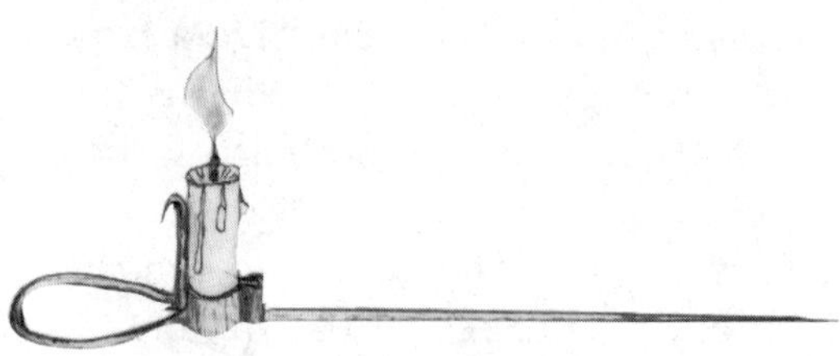

"Drop it, you stupid son-of-a-bitch!" Gus squatted, applied a head-lock and prised open the dog's mouth. The jaws yielded reluctantly, King's eyes puzzled, reproachful. He shook the dog's head and dislodged the offending horse bun.

"Now go." The dog trotted off, licking his chops. Gus groaned. Why does he do that? I wish Jack would keep his damned animals fenced.

He straightened up, wiped his hand on his pant leg and looked around. The landscape was typical of the interior dry-belt region of southern British Columbia. Pine-filled gullies criss-crossed the nearby grassy slopes. Beyond, the backdrop of densely treed mountains had been dusted by an early snowfall. A cold white peak could be seen through a notch in the hills. The sun, low in the west, broke through the clouds and an aspen exploded in a dazzling yellow flame. An echoing rifle shot was answered by hysterical shrieks from a pair of loons patrolling a shallow lake which lapped the lower slopes. A mile away, a logging truck growled to the top of Jorgenson's Hill, cleared its throat and roared towards the bridge at Piebyter Creek.

Gus crossed the upper meadow, stepping around

scattered aspens and ducking under brittle limbs. A diamond-backed bull snake, disturbed by his passing, slithered under a rotting log. He inhaled deeply as he waded through foot-deep pine needles under a giant ponderosa, its orange-red alligator-hide bark smelling sweetly of cinnamon. King ranged ahead of him, tacking through the coarse brown grass like a schooner beating to windward, sniffing at gopher holes, picking up and rejecting sticks and following mysterious scents.

Gus swerved to his right, towards the lake and picked his way through scattered underbrush. Wild rose shoots snagged his elbows as he made his way down a narrow draw which cut back into the bench. With a wide sweep of his arm, he broadcast grey sand across his path, replenishing his hand from an ancient army sling-bag which hung by his hip. He emerged from the draw and picked up the old trail at lake level.

He now became aware of a musical, high-pitched whispering or hissing which, as he approached the lake, became louder and finally seemed to envelop him. It sounded as though the air were full of twittering birds or rustling insects or perhaps a million tinkling fragile glass bells. He was not startled by these sounds—he had heard them a few times before. They were made only when the temperature was a little below freezing, generally on very still October or November evenings. Near the shore the surface of the lake was just freezing, forming a paper-thin layer of ice. At the same time, the glassy surface was being rippled by a tiny zephyr which caused the ice layer to fracture and the edges of the fragments to rub together. The continual breaking of the ice film and the rubbing together of the wafer-thin shards produced the bell-like tinkling which filled the air.

Gus continued on the trail, stepping over and around

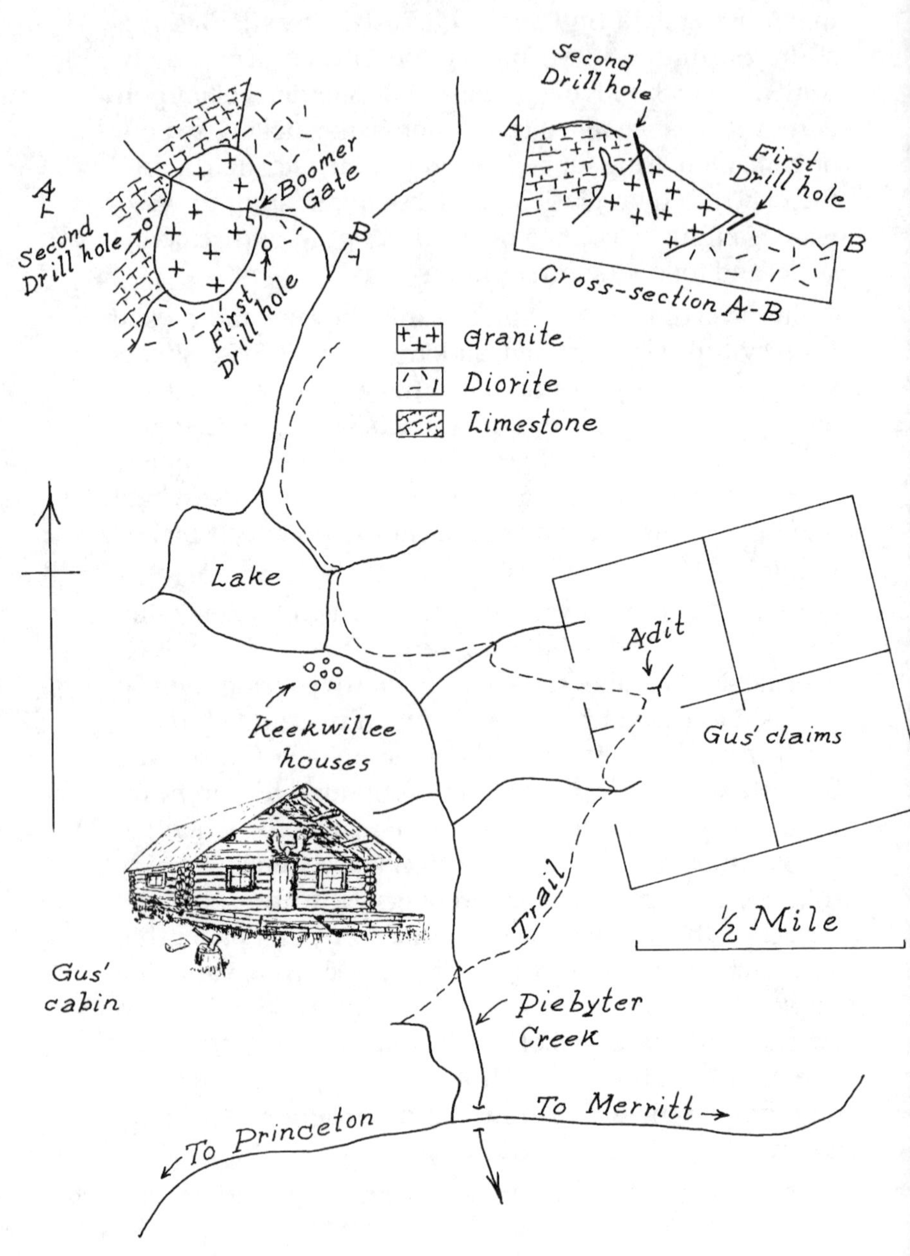

A
Second Drill hole
Boomer Gate
First Drill hole
B
Second Drill hole
A
First Drill hole
B
Cross-section A-B
Granite
Diorite
Limestone
Lake
Adit
Keekwillee houses
Gus' claims
Trail
1/2 Mile
Gus' cabin
Piebyter Creek
To Merritt
To Princeton

aspens that had been cut down, cleared of branches and partly peeled by beaver. Here the path climbed a couple of hundred feet to the waste dump of an old mine adit.

The adit, a tunnel drilled and blasted into the hill some twenty years before Gus had come to the area, had seen better days. The first 10 feet passed through overburden. Here the supporting timbers had all but rotted away and soil and gravel had fallen through the planks of the overhead lagging, partly blocking the entrance. Beyond, where the adit penetrated solid rock, little had changed since the days when it had been driven by a hopeful miner. Month after month he had swung a five-pound sledge hammer, turning the drill-steel with his left hand to keep it from jamming, drilling holes for his explosive charges. Month after month he had sharpened his 3-foot drills in a forge sheltered under a lean-to at the portal. The miner had hoped to find the source of the pale green copper stain that smeared the nearby outcrops. About 50 feet from the portal, he had given up.

As Gus walked across the mossy dump he heard a scuffle in the adit. He assumed that he had alarmed the resident pack-rat whose nest was just inside the portal. King barked and raced into the adit to investigate. Gus continued down the side of the dump where the trail led into a stand of pines. He stopped short, startled by frantic barking behind him. A second later he saw King racing towards him, now not barking but yelping. A black bear appeared over the edge of the dump and the next instant was tearing down the trail after the dog, both of them coming directly towards him. King obviously expected Gus to save him from this monster.

Gus turns and selects his tree—probably not the best tree but he hasn't got time for picking and choosing. This one is only feet away and has branches not far above the

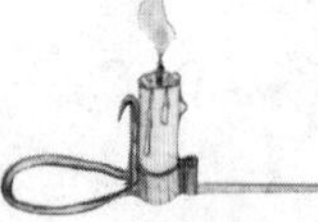

ground. He climbs frantically, hands clawing and feet thrashing. He's about 15 feet up when the bear, snorting and puffing, abandons King for bigger prey and leaps squirrel-like onto the trunk. Gus is able to keep ahead of the scrambling bear, but the higher he climbs the smaller the trunk becomes. Now he's clutching a tree only 3 inches in diameter. The puny limbs bend in his hands. He dares go no higher.

Gus has no weapon. He looks down at wrinkled snout, yellow teeth and two-inch claws. He desperately rips off his haversack and, as the jaws snap at his feet, empties a cloud of sand and dust in the bear's face. The bear pauses and tries to brush the sand from his eyes. By now King has come to the base of the tree, barking and yelping, telling the world that he has successfully treed his enemy. The bear, blinking and pawing, hesitates, then decides to tackle the noisy dog once more. Sliding and falling, claws gouging furrows in the bark, the bear reaches the ground and races off after the yapping dog. The sounds dwindle and finally cease.

That was bloody close. He slowly picked his way down the tree. He was brushing himself off and trying to unstick his pitchy fingers when he heard a distant yelping. He listened intently as the sound grew louder. Then he saw King reappear and his heart sank. The dog was racing up the trail towards his saviour, the bear in hot pursuit.

Up the tree again. The bear, tired of chasing the dog, decides that, after all, the object up the tree offers better odds, and mounts the tree once more. Gus climbs and the bear climbs. He is soon clutching a spindly trunk and dares climb no higher. The bear, red-eyed and slavering, is again snapping at his feet. He frees a leg, and timing his kick, manages a glancing blow. The bear snorts and inches higher. Gus pulls up his legs—at this height the tree is a flabby sapling and starts to bend under his weight. He shouts obscenities at the bear. King has returned and is barking hysterically, dancing and leaping, attempting to climb the tree and finish off his enemy. The bear ignores him and, getting a fresh grip, lunges at Gus' foot, catching a boot heel and wrenching it off. Gus knows that in a moment he is going to be pulled from his perch. The bear braces himself and lunges.

A shot. The bear's massive head sways, its limbs relax and it falls, bending and breaking branches until its limp carcass thumps on the ground. King approaches it cautiously, growling and sniffing.

"What are you doing up the tree?" A familiar voice.

"It's you, Jack." Gus paused. "Took your time."

Gus climbed down awkwardly. His arms were tired and his ankle sore. He hobbled around the tree, looking for his sling-bag.

"I guess you heard the dog. Was that your shot I heard a while back?"

"Yeah. Missed. A nice six-pointer. Where'd you find this fellow?"

"He was up in the old adit. Probably looking for a place to hole up for the winter. King flushed him."

Jack looked up the tree and grinned. "Probably shouldn't have climbed the tree. Guy down at the pub the other night claimed that a fellow can always outrun a bear because he will have better footing." Gus smiled sourly.

They abandoned the crude wagon road for a shortcut, and descended the steep grassy slope directly towards the cabin, stepping from one cow contour to the next. Cow contours? Scores of miles of bunch-grass-covered

hillsides in the dry-belt are marked from top to bottom by arrays of amazingly regular horizontal paths lying one above the other and spaced less than 3 feet apart. They have been formed over the years by the hooves of grazing cattle and deer. Sweeping around hills and disappearing into draws like contours on a topographic map, they are commonly referred to as cow contours.

At Gus' cabin, Jack left, heading for his own farm a quarter of a mile distant.

Gus' log cabin was of a design found all through the northwest. The pitched roof of hand-split shakes extended forward to keep the weather off a large porch area. A set of moose antlers was nailed above the door. A screened cooler hung on the outside wall in a shady spot.

Gus hooked his sling-bag on a nail near the plank door and used the boot scraper before entering the cabin. He cut feathers on a couple of pieces of kindling and soon had a fire roaring. He filled a bowl with a patented special vitamin- protein- mineral- fibre-rich dog food, added water and condensed milk, and placed it outside. Then he set about preparing his own dinner of beans, bacon and coffee.

Gus was of medium height and slim. His right eye was permanently closed—destroyed when a splinter flew from a block of quartz as his partner cracked it with a sledge hammer on the 400 level at the Pioneer gold mine. The loss had turned out not to be a great handicap. He quickly learned that small sideways head movements allowed him to gauge distances, the successive views giving him adequate depth perception, and he got along almost as well as his binocular mates. Luckily, the bridge of his nose had been flattened in a logging accident so that he had a reasonable view to his right. He was completely bald.

His face was tightly muscled, no slackness or extra chins, and covered with a greying stubble. He shaved on Saturday morning, before his regular trip to town. His hands would have been considered remarkable by city folk—large, fingers like bananas, powerful, nearly immune to hammer blows, slivers, thorns or wasp stings.

Gus had been brought as a child from Norway and raised on a farm in Saskatchewan. At age sixteen he had left home and hitch-hiked out to British Columbia. He had worked in the mines, on fish-boats and in the woods. He had never married. He was now sixty-four years old.

His unfenced 320 acres were some 120 miles northeast of Vancouver and his nearest towns were Merritt and Princeton. About half of his property was lightly timbered with pine and fir; the rest was natural meadow with scattered aspens. His small lake, about half a mile from the cabin, fed Piebyter Creek which chuckled a few feet from his door. He owned four mining claims, one of which included the old mine adit.

As he washed his few dishes that night he planned his next day. Gas up the tractor. Cut up that windfall near the northwest corner of No. 1 claim. Dump a little more sand in the upper side creek while I'm there. He looked up at the saucy hip-sprung damsel with the wide open mouth and at least eight extra gleaming teeth. Should have kept the 1980 calendar—the girls were much prettier. Got to get to the mining recorder's before the end of the week and record my trenching.

◊ ◊ ◊

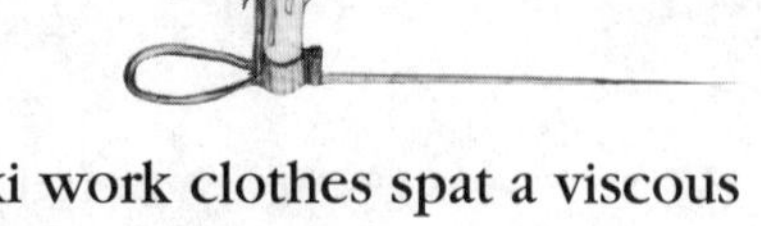

The man in the dirty khaki work clothes spat a viscous gob into the widening canyon between the rusty hull and the mussel-encrusted planks and pilings.

"Tlingit Bay is the asshole of the world and the Casco mine is 25 miles up it."

Bill Trelawney silently agreed with his morose, hungover companion as they leaned on the teak rail and looked down at the receding dock: muddy pick-up truck, piles of mining machinery, yellow tractor, stack of 8 X 8 timbers, a drunk sleeping against the open-sided shed, a grubby wharfinger, his job done, lighting a cigarette.

Bill looked at the swirling water under the stern: oily whirlpools, grey plastic twisted into obscene shapes, ragged pouches of orange peel. Rain pocked the filthy water. An average day at Tlingit.

In the near distance was Tlingit Bay village with its three muddy streets, slippery plank board-walks, bent rank grass emerging from heaps of dirty snow. It was only one o'clock but the beer parlour in the clapboard hotel was already busy.

Half a dozen new arrivals, just off the boat, resigned, grim faces, carrying cheap suitcases, climbed into the makeshift bus, and sat facing each other on mud-encrusted plank seats. This battered and rusty crummy would grind and jolt for 25 miles through devil's-club-infested canyons back and forth across the river on narrow bridges made of bundles of 2-foot-through logs bound together by wire cables, to the Casco Silver mine.

Bill's only regret on leaving Casco Silver was the food. At home, when he was growing up, his family had eaten meat once or twice a week and dessert was a special treat. But at the Casco mine dining hall, there was a choice of several main dishes every night and it was expected that young fellows would have seconds. A shy return for thirds raised no eyebrows. Motherly ladies pressed cakes and ice-cream on him. Why, he could take a whole pie to his room in the bunk-house if he wanted to. He thought of what it would be like living again in Vancouver where he would eat in greasy spoon cafes or fix tasteless meals in his room. For a moment he considered climbing up to the wheel-house and demanding that the skipper put him back on the dock.

After graduation in the class of '81 Bill had found a job as assistant geologist at the Casco mine in northern British Columbia. He had looked forward to spending much of his time tracing the geological formations through the virgin forests in the bracing alpine air. Instead, he had been sent down into the mine. There, encumbered by inflexible rubberized pants and coat, a stiff leather belt carrying a heavy battery, an uncomfortable helmet, and awkward boots sucking through the fetid mud past stinking "honey boxes", he traced veins and faults and tried to identify minerals and rocks in the yellowish lamp light. Not fun.

But Bill had another reason for leaving Casco Silver. It had happened in a section of the mine being explored for a new vein. That morning the shift boss had met him by the mucking machine.

"Have a look up the raise just across from the ore-pass on 240," he said to Bill. "Nice showing of native silver. They're timbering up there right now but they'll come off for lunch and you can go up and have a look."

At noon, Bill made his way to the raise and started up the 50 feet of ladder. When he was about half way up, a light appeared at the foot of the ladder. Someone shouted: "Fire!" Bill scrambled down as fast as he could and a miner

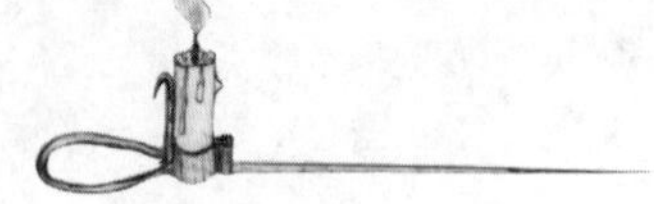

dragged him along the drift and around a corner as the dynamite went off. He had missed death by about thirty seconds. The lunch-bound miner, slower than his mates, had seen Bill's light stop at the raise and had run back to warn him. It turned out that the miners had decided to blast out a small shelf to hold some timbering and had not been told that Bill would be prowling around. Bill didn't have his usual appetite for lunch that day and he found that he had lost his already scant enthusiasm for underground geology.

The following winter the snow had built up to a depth of 58 feet. The men travelled like moles through wooden tunnels to bunk-house, dining hall, office building and mine portal; they rarely saw daylight. A crew worked continually, shovelling the heavy snow off the roofs of the vulnerable buildings.

Bill had stuck it out for nine months. Now, having saved his pay (there was precious little to spend it on), he had given his notice and, armed with a couple of good references, was on his way to what he hoped would be a better job in Vancouver.

CHAPTER 2

KINGFISHER EXPLORATIONS

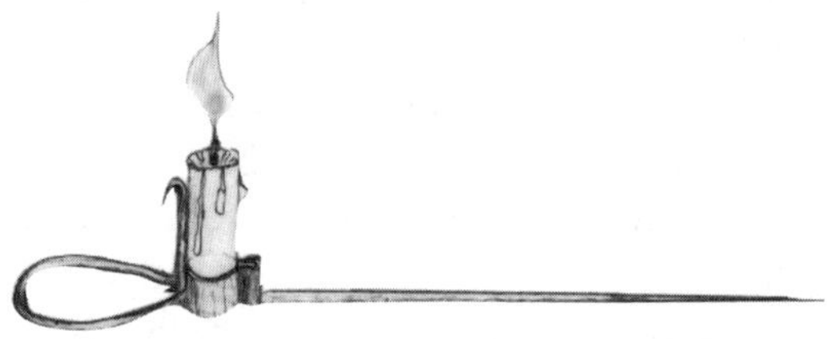

Chris Bancroft worked for Kingfisher Explorations, a subsidiary of the Toronto company Magnalode. One of the best features of his job was the view of Vancouver from his fourteenth-floor office in the MacDonald Building. His windows looked north, over the harbour, with its derricks, wharves, fish-docks, sheds, and freight cars. Beyond the harbour, the North Shore mountains still retained patches of last winter's snow. Directly below, ferries crossed the inlet to North Vancouver, dodging stately freighters plodding eastward to grain elevators at the Second Narrows. To his left Chris could see Stanley Park. At its northern edge, the Lion's Gate bridge, hanging on its spider web, provided access to the north shore of the inlet. The bridge carried commuters to the residential developments gradually expanding up the mountainside and along and above the shore to the west. Beyond, to the left, he could see the open expanse of English Bay. And, beyond the bay, the mountains of Vancouver Island showed faintly across Georgia Strait. This morning Chris could see six cargo ships at anchor waiting for their turns at the docks. Seeming nearly motionless, sailboats tacked north or west against the fair-weather breeze

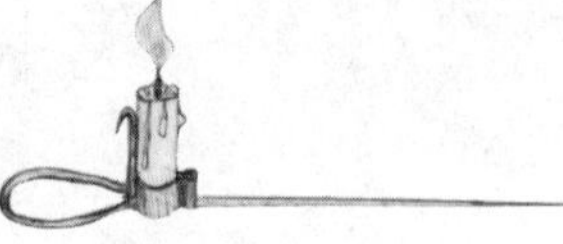

like white moths pinned to a blue-green board.

A descending twin-engined float plane swooped silently over Stanley Park. Chris watched it cross above the forest of sailboat masts towards its landing area in the inner harbour. His eyes followed it until it had ploughed a white furrow, slowed, and turned, its engines roaring. He generally kept an eye on planes. Occasionally, somewhere, one would explode in the air or sputter and cough before diving into the ground. It would be a pity if he were to turn away and miss the burst of flame and smoke or the sudden loss of control and the terminal black plume. He turned back to his desk, putting behind him vague feelings of disappointment and guilt.

The Kingfisher suite consisted of a dozen different rooms. A visitor would be struck by one feature that distinguished the offices from any others in the building: the abundance of maps. Every surface except the floor and ceiling was covered by maps, in some places two or three deep—highly coloured geological maps, contoured topographic maps, claim maps, mine maps, magnetic maps, gravity maps, geochemical maps, tectonic maps, interpretive and highly speculative maps, maps in preparation, maps complete. They were on all scales, from regional maps at several miles to the inch to detailed mine maps at 10 feet to the inch. Highly coloured cross-sections showed geological interpretations, generally fantastic, of what lay far beneath the earth's surface. The walls of the private offices of the technical people were also papered with maps. Every room had a large chest of map drawers and a drafting table.

Chunks of interesting or puzzling rock, spectacular pieces of ore and cylindrical lengths of drill core lay on top of bookshelves as book ends, on desk corners as weights to hold maps flat, or on the floor as door stops.

A computer hummed in its own corner in the large outer office and a secretary sat at another.

Besides Chris, who was a mining engineer, the office personnel consisted of Isaac McLean, the boss, two geologists, Jay Bateman and Bill Trelawney (Bill had been hired just a couple of weeks before), a geochemist, Carl Costello, and a secretary, Julie Muller. They were now assembling around the large conference room table, two to a side, leaving room at one end for Isaac and Julie. Julie kept the minutes of the meeting and supplied information about past decisions taken, budget, schedules and other essentials while the others indulged in fanciful geological speculation and expounded unprovable theories in their attempts to find new ore deposits.

Chris slouched near one end of the table where he could easily keep an eye on his fellow workers, his head bent forward, dome flashing, chin multiplied, and rolled-up brown eyes peering over the frames of his reading glasses. Tall, overweight, and slow moving, he was draped over, rather than sitting in his hard-seated chair. His clothes were a trifle shabby; he looked as if he had just come to the meeting from weeding and mulching his garden.

He was older than the rest of the office people. Chris had early come to terms with the fact that he was not going to set the world on fire or even produce much smoke. He was relaxed in his work, which he performed competently but without undue enthusiasm. At these meetings he watched his striving associates with good-natured tolerance.

Chris studied his assembling co-workers through half-closed eyes. He enjoyed categorizing faces. He had a half-formed theory that most people belong to one of a few dozen facial types and that these facial types were clues

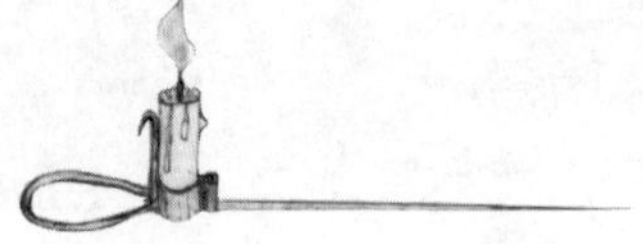

to their ethnic origins. He had been playing this game for years, although realizing, when good sense momentarily gained the upper hand, that there was a complete spectrum of facial types and that people had genes from so many sources that most of his attempts were doomed from the start. Still, he thought that he could classify certain faces, those of people whose dominant genes had somehow survived relatively unchanged, as though the melting pot had been incompletely stirred. He looked across the table at Bill Trelawney.

Chris ticked off Bill's salient features: light blue eyes, large head bounded by irregular planes giving the impression of a badly made or slightly broken box, close-cropped red hair, freckled face, turned-up bony nose, and a mouth full of slightly misaligned large white teeth. He was big, angular and bony. Chris had found him easy to categorize—Scottish, probably with a large genetic contribution from Norse marauders. Chris had missed the boat. He should have known that most people with names starting with *Tre* were of Cornish origin. He noticed that Bill's attention seemed to be concentrated towards the far end of the table: Bill was watching Julie.

She was worth watching. Large brown eyes set a little slanting, snub nose, dark brown hair. Slightly sepia skin. Dark red lipstick but no other makeup. Hair naturally wavy and cut short. Teeth startlingly white against her darkish skin. Her face was never at rest: she mock-frowned at Chris, raised her eyebrows in admiring astonishment at Jay's new necktie and winked at Carl.

Today she wore a simple skirt and jacket of beige cotton, the sort of outfit favoured by female big game hunters: epaulettes, lots of pockets, broad fabric belt. Brown and white shoes. The suit, simple and expensive-looking, showed off her slight figure.

She welcomed Bill with an uninhibited smile, thinking: Isaac must have scraped the bottom of the barrel for this one. Where does he find them? Big but skinny—looks hungry. Blue eyes go nicely with his red hair. And those eyelashes! White skin, freckles; cuts himself shaving. Not much clothes sense. Keeps an eye on me but doesn't say much.

Chris, in his genealogical speculations, had decided that Julie was probably of North African origin—Egyptian, Moroccan, Algerian? As usual, he was wrong. She had been christened Juliana Muller. Her family had been planters for generations in the Dutch East Indies and her parents, having barely survived in a Japanese concentration camp, had managed to make their way to Canada in 1946.

Chris sniffed and stole a sideways glance at Jay Bateman, the senior geologist. Dark brown, nearly black eyes. High bridged nose. He was aware of Jay's cologne, and sneered inwardly at his heavy gold ring and pin-striped suit. His black hair, short except for a fashionable vestigial pigtail, formed a dramatic widow's peak which complemented the curves of his carefully tended close-cropped dark beard and moustache. These covered about half of his face and were bounded by a complex pattern of swooping curves—some circular, others parabolic. Jay's judiciously pursed lips were framed in a hairy ellipse.

Jay, a snappy dresser, was an impressive sight as he arrived at the office each morning, ten minutes later than the rest of them. Square-shouldered formal navy blue overcoat, white silk scarf, leather gloves. His fedora perhaps two and one half degrees off the horizontal—angle enough to show that he was human but not enough to encourage familiarity. Jay was an able geologist, up-to-date and at ease with the latest scientific jargon. Chris had gained the impression that Jay was a little puzzled

that he hadn't been made president of the company but was willing to give the board of directors a little more time to come to its senses.

Chris looked across at Carl Costello. Straight black brows nearly met over deep-set round blue eyes usually concealed, as they were today, by opaque dark convex sun glasses which reflected tiny images of the assembled group. When talking to him, Chris could never tell whether Carl was taking his remarks seriously, rolling up his eyes in amusement or, out of the corner of his eye, cannily gauging the boss' reaction. Chris associated opaque sunglasses with the dead-faced members of the Tonton Macoutes. Or with the beefy traffic cop, eyes invisible (threatening? bored? enraged? amused?), who had the other day given him a ticket for making an illegal left-hand turn.

Geochemists, like Carl, use the chemical make-up of soil and rock in their attempts to find ore deposits. Most of their efforts are spent in collecting hundreds of samples of soil or stream sediment (hence the nick-name 'dirt-bagger'). They analyse the samples for a dozen or so different metals and apply statistical tests in an attempt to find a chemical anomaly, that is, a departure from the fairly constant background metal values found in soils all over the world. In Vancouver, garden soil may contain fifty parts per million of copper. Much higher copper values might indicate the presence of a copper deposit in the underlying bedrock, the copper, having been leached from the rock, contaminating the overlying soil. Or high values in mud from a stream might point to a metal deposit in its headwaters. In their search for geochemical anomalies, geochemists have used many approaches as well as the common one of analysing soil and stream sediments. Knowing that living things may absorb and become enriched in metals that are present in their environments, some geochemists analyse the metal content of plant or tree leaves, trout livers and even bee pollen brought to the hive, in the knowledge that unusually high values might lead them to a nearby mineral deposit.

Isaac was late. Chris couldn't waste such an audience, so he launched into a story about marimbas. He and his wife had spent a couple of weeks in Mexico in January. There he had learned that the sounding keys of primitive marimbas were made of bones rather than slats of wood, that the bones of the jaguar were especially resonant, and that the collar-bone of that feline could be depended upon to produce a slightly sharp E-flat. This acoustic peculiarity allowed a uniform tuning of instruments between families and villages, facilitating marimba ensembles. That was why this particular E-flat bone was known as the well-tempered clavicle.

Chris looked around to gauge the effect of his story. A snicker from Carl. Puzzled looks from Julie and Bill. A frown from Jay. Then Isaac slouched in and dumped a pile of folders and a battered pair of reading glasses on the desk.

Black eyes; when he blinked, lower and upper lids met half-way, lizard-like. Coarse greying black hair. A broad, heavy face, a little too large for his head. Regular large white teeth. His skin, which fit him very tightly, was slightly olive. He was a big man, fiftyish, running to fat, his tight shirt outlining a modest belly which overhung his belt. His legs seemed too short for his massive torso.

Isaac, Chris knew, had come up the hard way. From driller's helper to driller to company prospector. By hard work, uncommon good sense, and practical know-how, Isaac had worked his way up to the position of head

prospector, camp manager and valued jack-of-all-trades. In 1972 the geologist in charge of one of Kingfisher's exploration parties had been asphyxiated in a long unventilated exploratory adit, where, over the years, rotting mine-timbers had used up most of the oxygen in the stagnant air. Isaac had managed to haul the third member of the team to the portal before passing out. After the inquest, the company, short of staff, had left him in charge for the remainder of the field season. Shrewdly sizing up an abandoned mineral showing, he proved up a small but profitable silver-lead-zinc mine. Impressed, Kingfisher persuaded him to take a business management course, and within a few years he was in charge of the Vancouver office.

Puzzled as to Isaac's genealogical origins, Chris had concluded tentatively, largely because of his first name, that he was Jewish. But McLean didn't fit. Chris considered the fact that there were few Jews among the scores of exploration engineers that he knew and speculated sourly that they were probably too damned smart to pick a job where one is often away from home, wet and cold, flitting around in dangerous helicopters, eating badly prepared food and sleeping alone on uncomfortable cots in draughty tents.

Isaac spoke with a slight accent, a guttural underlay, which Chris could not place.

"Toronto has been bugging me as usual. The usual complaints. Money's scarce. They set up this office eleven years ago and we've been sitting out here, enjoying the balmy weather and spending money, but we haven't yet found a decent ore deposit. They closed the Newfoundland office last month. I get the feeling that this time we're really under the eight ball. They're getting pretty serious about the Cougar Lake copper deposit and want a big sampling project started this summer. As most of you know, Magnalode has a one-half interest in it and we are going to have to make a decision whether to go ahead with it or back away." He turned to Chris. "Chris, you'll be going up to the property pretty soon and meeting with engineers from the other owners. It'll be a big project and will keep you busy off and on for months."

"Not much point in going up there 'til June," Chris answered. "The trenches will be full of snow 'til then." Chris was referring to exploration trenches dug by bull-dozer or back-hoe to expose the bedrock. "Perhaps not full but it lingers in the trenches. Can't see through the snow. May's too early—maybe late May."

Jay's loud voice interrupted. "Not keen to leave the fair Elaine? Or do your tomatoes need attention?"

Jay's laugh rang out above the general sniggering as he looked around at each of the others to make sure his sally was appreciated. Chris ignored them all.

Isaac continued. "Carl, how is the geochemical prospecting going?"

Carl's green lenses turned towards Isaac.

"We've got four parties out," said Carl. "Two of them are involved in continuing the systematic coverage of the area centred on Highland Valley—dirt-bagging. The country's been covered in a haphazard way several times but it's elephant country and worth a thorough going-over. It stands to reason that there are more mines to be found there. The third one is stream-sediment and soil sampling, checking the area between Princeton and Merritt. The northern crew, in the Sustut area, is delayed by bad weather and late snow but should get going soon."

Isaac took over. "Each of those parties costs us about $5,000 a month. That's adding up and that's just the thin

end of the iceberg." He looked around the table. "Do you have any idea what this office, all of us, costs? Somebody back in Toronto is adding it all up. The longer we go without finding a mineable deposit, the more vulnerable we are. We're riding a paper tiger. Jay. Anything to report?"

Jay smiled confidently, the circular curves traversing his cheeks becoming noticeably hyperbolic.

"I agree with Mel that our future is in gold," Jay said. Mel was Dr. Melville Cassidy, the extremely successful chief of exploration for the parent company in Toronto. Everybody but Jay referred to him, with awe, as Dr. Cassidy.

"As you know, I've been concentrating on those two properties in the Bridge River area. A couple of quality showings that have been overlooked. Totally awesome. At this point in time the area's pretty well dormant and we should keep our mouths shut about them. These deposits show the exhalative features characteristic of the Japanese sub-type and the rare-earth ratios are seductive." Chris was sure that no one had a clue as to the meaning of Jay's last statement, but no one ventured a question.

"I'll have a definitive report to you in a couple of weeks," Jay added. "We may have a mine, or maybe two on our hands."

Julie glanced casually at Chris and sent him a barely perceptible wink.

After a long silence, Isaac resumed his monologue on the difficulties of dealing with the Toronto people who expected great things of the Vancouver group but were reluctant to fund new ventures. Then, without a pause, he outlined in his unemphatic voice his plans for Bill, the newest member of the group. Sensing towards the end of his remarks that perhaps he hadn't had Bill's full attention, Isaac raised his voice a little, and asked: "Any comment, Bill?"

Bill, not familiar with the current projects and lulled by Isaac's monotonous drone, had been daydreaming about life, sex, and in particular, Julie, whom he found very attractive. He had been watching her covertly, wondering if she had a boyfriend, when he was jerked out of his daydream by mention of his name.

Isaac, frowning over his reading glasses, asked again: "Any comment, Bill?"

"No, no, sounds good to me."

"Then it's settled." Isaac pushed his chair back from the table. "Shouldn't take you much more than a couple of weeks. Meeting's over."

Back in his office, Bill considered his problem. He had no idea what he was expected to do or where he was expected to go. He'd have to ask someone and try not to appear a complete fool. He decided that his best bet was Chris, who seemed to be a friendly and helpful type. He knocked on Chris' open door.

Chris sat at his desk behind an unstable rampart of books, folded maps, small items of field gear, sample bags, pieces of ore, unwashed coffee cups, mummified apple cores, crumpled lunch bags, and junk mail. The slope on the left- hand side of the pile had exceeded the angle of repose and a couple of books, lubricated by glossy advertising leaflets, had slid and fallen, forming the nucleus of a new and growing pile on the floor. With his hand-lens almost touching his eye, he was peering at a chunk of quartz. As Bill came in, Chris tossed the specimen to him.

"That's what you'll be looking for," Chris said, "but

you'll be damned lucky if you find anything as good as that."The quartz was seamed with bright yellow gold—the sample would run thousands of dollars to the ton. "Doctor's sample."

Bill looked puzzled.

"You don't know about doctor's samples? Well. I thought everyone knew about doctor's samples. Well, nearly everybody. Several of the local prospector-promoter types carry this sort of specimen around in their pockets.They've found over the years that the easiest people to sell worthless mining stock to are medical doctors—maybe because a lot of them have more money than they know what to do with. Or perhaps making life-and-death decisions in their dealings with worried and frightened people all the time gives them god-like confidence. For whatever reason, these promoters show their flashy samples only to doctors, not wanting to waste their valuable time on ordinary folk. Hence the name."

Bill found this interesting but had something else on his mind. After expressing his amazement at the richness of the specimen and learning that it had been picked out of the soil near one of the new finds in northern British Columbia, Bill ventured:"Say, Chris—I'm not entirely clear on what Isaac wants me to do. Could you fill me in on the details?"

Chris grinned. He had relished Bill's violent recall to the real world and had been wondering how he was going to solve his quandary.

"Well, what Isaac wants you to do is go up to the Cariboo, to Wells. About 500 miles north of here. Ever been there?"

"I was there five or six years ago. Had a look at Barkerville. Beautifully restored ghost town. But that was before I was into geology."

"Well, our interest there is in the lode mines. Gold-quartz veins. The powers that be think that the price of gold is going to rise. Two or three mines near Barkerville have produced a few million bucks. You've seen the area—low mountain country, mantled with deep drift and there's no outcrop. Well, anyway, not much. In some places there's a fair amount. There are more veins to be found and you're going up there to try to figure out some new approach."

Bill didn't look too sure of himself, so Chris continued. "Now if I had this assignment, I'd spend the next couple of weeks in the library." He nodded to his left towards the small library where federal and provincial government geological reports and scientific journals dealing with economic or mining geology were stacked to the ceiling.

"There are lots of reports dating well back into the 1800s and there's a recent top-notch account of the regional geology, with great maps, put out by the provincial geological survey. If I were you I would spend the next three weeks in our library, down the hall, going through the various federal and provincial geological reports on the Cariboo district. Make lots of notes and photocopy the best reports and maps."

"I suppose Isaac'll want some kind of a report?" Bill asked.

"He will want a report from you outlining the current state of exploration activity in the district. You'll hand your report to Jay—he'll look it over and make recommendations to Isaac. Isaac's not a geologist.

"But the most important thing, what he really wants you to do, is to figure out how we can find us some new

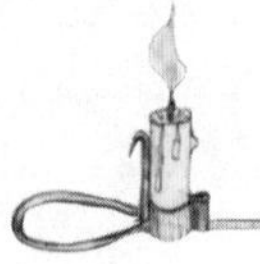

veins, a mine. Try to give us some sort of a target. You'll need a new approach. A new angle, a bright idea. Something we could base a small trenching and drilling program on. Keep in mind that at least one other outfit is sending scouts into the Cariboo to do exactly the same thing. You'd better stay in the hotel in Wells. You'll have a four-wheel-drive pick-up. Go around and look at all of the properties. Don't neglect the placers—the placer gold has to come from somewhere. Talk to the old-timers."

◊ ◊ ◊

Late that afternoon Chris heard a tentative knock at his office door. He looked up from his cluttered desk and saw a stranger. Short but sturdy, tidy clothes but not much worn—a whiff of moth-balls. Unblinking large grey eyes. Why do these guys always arrive at quitting time?

"Mr. Bancroft? I'm Ben. Ben Richards." Surprisingly loud high voice. Small mouth, almost lipless, bad teeth. "A friend of mine said you were a good company—make a good deal with guys who bring you mining properties. I've got a mine for you—2 miles from tide-water. High grade aluminum. Whole mountain of it."

"Where exactly is this deposit?"

A knowing smile, "Ah, that would be telling."

"Well, O.K. What kind of rock is it?"

"Got a sample right here." He bent and reached into a dirty canvas sample bag. Thinning black hair plastered over a white skull. Dirty collar around a creased brown neck. Most of two fingers missing on the left hand. He extracted a plum-sized sooty lump streaked with runlets of black glassy material.

Chris sighed."What have you done with it? This isn't a natural rock."

"Oh, I tested it.Welding torch.Test all my rocks."

The specimen had been partly melted and any useful physical properties obliterated. Chris didn't know what this pyromaniac had been testing for in his basement laboratory, nor, he suspected, did the tester.

"What makes you think it's valuable?"

"I had it analysed. Look at this." He extracted a certificate of analysis from his wallet.

"Twenty percent aluminum oxide. O.K.? That's about 10 percent aluminum metal." He fixed Chris with a steely glance to make sure that this demonstration of his mastery of analytical chemistry had registered.

"That's 200 pounds of aluminum in each ton of rock!" He unfolded a newspaper clipping and waved it under Chris' nose. "And each pound of aluminum is worth fifty cents."Triumphantly,"That rock is worth one hundred dollars a ton! And that doesn't take into account all these other metals." The man's horny finger jabbed at the certificate. "Iron, magnesium, titanium, silicone, all the rest. Why, my mountain's worth billions." He paused, his eyes narrowed."What kind of a deal can we make?" He waited, apparently confident that a large cheque would be in his hand within the hour.

Chris sighed again. He knew that he wouldn't be able to reason with this would-be tycoon.

"What you say is true," he said calmly."The rock probably contains a hundred bucks worth of aluminum per ton. The trouble is, it's going to cost you two hundred bucks to get the aluminum metal out of the rock.You'd lose your

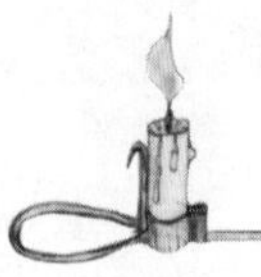

shirt trying to extract the metal. There's no technology known to science that would allow you to get the metal out and make a profit. Lots of ordinary rocks have about 20 percent aluminum oxide. You need about 50 percent aluminum oxide to allow a profit. So I'm afraid your rock is not worth very much."

His visitor refolded his certificate and newspaper clipping, pocketed his specimen, and now, his voice rising:

"All you big corporations are the same: keep the little guy out. Prevent competition. Maintain your monopoly. And as soon as my back's turned, get up there and stake it for yourself." He was now shouting. "Damn good thing I didn't tell you where it is."

Chris tried to reason with him. "Look, Richards, I'm not lying to you. Magnalode, that's our parent company, has a big aluminum mine in Jamaica. Their ore runs about 55 percent aluminum oxide."

At the mention of Magnalode, Ben Richard's face twisted and his eyes bulged. "Magnalode!" he screamed. "Magnalode, the big Toronto outfit? You're part of them? Why I wouldn't deal with you people if you were the last company on earth!"

He snatched up his bag and whirled through the door. Julie and Bill, having heard the commotion, stood watching as Richards blundered through the outer office. Julie touched a finger to her forehead as Bill grinned at her. Richards turned at that moment and stared at them, his face contorted by rage and hate. He snatched up a chunk of glistening copper ore and hurled it just as Chris emerged from his office. It missed Chris' head by a foot, crashed into the door frame and ricochetted across his chair. Richards disappeared through the outer door. Bill ran after him.

Chris was shaken. "What got into him? I didn't say anything."

Julie, white faced, asked, "Should I call the police?"

Chris shook his head. "He needs a doctor—he must be around the bend. I don't think we'll see him again."

Bill reappeared. "He ran down the stairs. Must be nuts."

CHAPTER 3

CHRIS AT HOME

Another day. Chris locked the deserted office and took the elevator to the parking level. He climbed wearily into his car and edged into the thick traffic.

He pulled into a parking space on Tenth Avenue, looked in his rear view mirror to see whether he was going to scoop up a cyclist, opened the door and headed into the shopping mall. A young woman, a stranger, smiled at him and he surreptitiously confirmed that his zipper was in the up position and stealthily checked his glassy image. In the drugstore, he examined the newspapers on the stand, and, after looking around to make sure that there was no one he knew in the vicinity, bought a $1 lottery ticket. Since he had no reason to believe that one number had a better chance than any other, and since he refused to pick numbers based on his wife's birthday, the number on his license plates, or the number of green apples on his Spartan tree, he let the machine pick his numbers. In fact, he knew that the array of numbers 1, 2, 3, 4, 5 and 6 had as good a chance of winning as any other, but he couldn't bring himself to tell the clerk that he wanted these, knowing that she would immediately categorize him as mentally deficient. And he had to admit to an uneasy feeling, completely contrary to common sense, that the numbers

12, 17, 19, 32, 39 and 46 were more likely to win than 1, 2, 3, 4, 5 and 6! He felt foolish about his purchase, realizing that he had a much better chance of being struck by lightning than of winning the lottery.

As he left the store, Chris speculated that if one takes into account the total effect on all of the participants in a lottery, one sees that the mere buying of lottery tickets produces far more happiness than does the winning of the lottery. Each ticket holder is exhilarated by the knowledge that he has as good a chance as anyone else of becoming a multi-millionaire. Each plans a new life. Chris planned a new life. Move to another city? No. A few wooded acres in West Vancouver, on the waterfront. Big house. Couple of gardeners. Greenhouse. Move Elaine's sister into a decent apartment close to the hospital. Perhaps a Mercedes. Or two. Travel a lot. Cruise ship. See Europe. A yacht. Sail or power? How large? Small enough to be handled by two. No point in having a permanent paid crew. But Elaine doesn't really like boats. Well then, there would be enough money to allow each of us to have a hobby. We could go our separate ways. On holidays. But we'd never separate. Never. Well, who knows? Julie winked at me this morning. I wonder if she has a boyfriend. Pah! I'm far too old for her. Well, not much. And on and on. He realized that he had already had two dollar's worth of pleasure from his purchase.

Chris turned from Greenall Road into the driveway which ran beside his split-level bungalow and parked under the fruit trees. The cherries were developing nicely and the Gravenstein promised a decent crop. He frowned at his plum tree. Probably another bumper crop on the way. He wasn't looking forward to the next campaign in the Great Plum Wars. The trouble was that some of his neighbours had similar trees. In August, laden with the

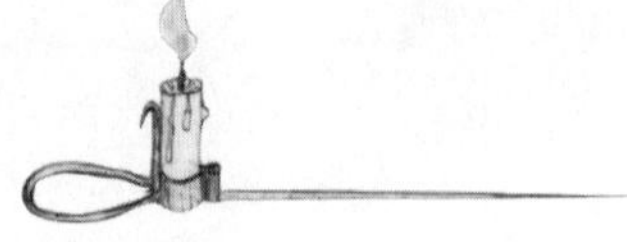

juicy yellow globes, he would knock on doors, half the time to be rebuffed: "Bobby Benson (or Billy Simes or Mrs. Gaspard) gave us all we can use." Or worse: "Thank you. Lovely. But you must try this year's zucchini—take six big ones—a great crop this year."

The neighbourhood, some blocks from any main thoroughfare, was very quiet. Chris told himself once more how lucky he was to live in such a peaceful area. He stood in front of his house, inhaled deeply and leaned back, stretching and easing his lower back which always bothered him after a day spent leaning over the map table. He watched a bald eagle repeat its disappearing act as it slowly drifted to the east. At a lower level an elegant grey seagull, like a sleek jet, winged its way towards the municipal garbage dump. Still lower, an exultant crow flapped to its home tree carrying a naked baby robin in its beak, pursued by frantic squawking parents. A few feet away, a dozen sooty-coated starlings advanced across the grass like medieval monks searching for a lost crucifix. He scowled as he saw a new mole hill on the lawn.

As he entered the side door he looked at the nest under the eaves. An apron of swallow droppings expanded down the wall. Three stumpy bandits peered hopefully over the edge of the nest as their mother scissored by.

Elaine was chopping salad makings in the kitchen. He tip-toed up behind her, slipped his arms around her, squeezed her breasts and kissed her neck, his recent lottery-inspired infidelity forgotten. She leaned forward and, raising her rump, dealt him a blow to the mid-section. He danced to one side and snatched up a stick of celery.

"Hi, what's new?"

"Bought a new spring coat," she said. "Marty's had a big

sale. I'll slip it on—tell me if you like it." She wiped her hands and disappeared into the bedroom. She reappeared, the coat distinctive with large green-and-white checks, wide belt and standup collar.

"Do you like it?" she asked.

"Well, we'll be able to see you coming. Isn't it a little um . . . overstated?" He meant garish, but didn't dare say so. He knew he wasn't the best judge of colours.

"It's the style. And I got 40 percent off."

Chris said, "I like it."

He yawned and turned towards a cupboard. "I'm beat," he said. "Where are the boys? I see the moles have been at it again. I'll open a bottle of Red Tide." Chris made this wine from grapes imported from California. It was high in alcohol and would not win any prizes for bouquet or clarity, but cost only a few cents a glass. He carefully decanted the nearly opaque wine from the black precipitate which lined one side of the bottle. After he had filled two glasses, he held one up to the light and scanned the surface.

"Slight oil slick. It's that olive oil I used to prevent oxidation." He handed a glass to Elaine.

"Thanks. Anything more about the crazy that threw the rock at you last week?"

"No. Nutty as a fruitcake. He's probably back out in the bush, scaring bears."

He settled down with the evening paper. The crash of bikes against the house announced the arrival of the boys.

"Hi Dad."

"Hi Dad."

Rufus the spaniel walked across section B of the paper, muddy paws wiping out the weather synopsis and, as

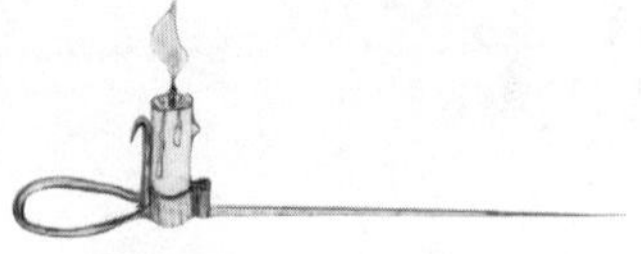

Chris swiped at him, twisted out of reach, destroying half of the obituaries. Chris leaned back in his chair and inspected the boys.

"Well, what have you been up to today?"

"Rufus has got the blue shits again," the younger one replied.

Rufus would chew up and swallow almost anything and had recently found a secret and seemingly inexhaustible supply of blue plastic. Chris suspected that it was the neighbour's inflatable swimming pool but was afraid to investigate. "Fort's almost finished," the older one said. "Need some stove pipe and a couple of boxes and we're in business." Chris was afraid to ask what business. The boys and two friends were building a shack somewhere over in the bush across the street. Having been through this phase himself, he hoped that the worst crimes committed in this secret retreat would be a little tobacco smoking, eating of half-burned, half-raw potatoes, and the trading of dubious information about girls and sex.

After supper Chris went out to inspect the newest mole hill. He had been carrying on a battle with the moles for several years, but the moles still flourished, their hills spoiling his lawn, dulling his lawn mower, and their tunnels channelling his irrigating water to depths and locations unknown. He had tried chemical warfare, pouring a couple of bottles of ammonia into their runs without effect. A dose of gasoline had killed his bedding plants. He had buried a radio tuned to a twenty-four-hour hard-rock station in a flower bed. This seemed to keep them out of that particular area, but he would have needed half a dozen radios to clear his yard. Taking advice from an old gardener, he had tried inserting moth-balls into the mole runs.

These were returned contemptuously to the surface.

His latest effort had also ended in disaster. He had read in a gardening magazine that another victim of these subterranean terrorists had, by luck, managed to kill one. Having no particular place to dispose of the corpse, the man had stuffed it down a handy mole hole. To his pleasant surprise, the moles disappeared, probably moving to a neighbour's yard, apparently distressed by the body of a dead relative. Chris had analysed the situation: Since a dead mole probably didn't smell very different from any other rotting animal, he reasoned, why not stuff some kind of meat down the holes? He would have to find a cheap substitute—he wasn't going to bury sirloin steak in his garden. The solution was obvious. For a modest sum he had obtained 10 pounds of fish heads at the local fish market. He stuffed a couple of heads down each of a dozen holes and sat back to wait for developments.

For two days—nothing. On the third morning, he let Rufus out the front door and half an hour later went out into the back yard. Rufus appeared—looking as if he needed a good brushing, his hair curiously matted. As Rufus got closer, it became apparent that he had been rolling in rotting fish. With a sinking heart Chris walked around the yard. Fish heads were everywhere—sunken eyes staring at him from the deep grass and peering at him from among the forget-me-nots. A strabismic halibut stared with clouded eyes simultaneously at the top of the cherry tree and at the rhubarb along the back fence. Chris never learned whether it was Rufus, the neighbour's cats, the moles, or the numerous raccoons from the bush across the street that had dug them up. Perhaps it had been a team effort. Chris had spent his Saturday morning picking up fish heads, washing the dog, and assuring Elaine that the stink would disappear in a few days. The project had had no vis-

ible effect on the moles.

After inspecting the newest mole hill, Chris walked across the street and into the woods. His house faced a tract of undeveloped parkland, part of the University Endowment Lands, now thickly forested with alder, second-growth fir, cedar and hemlock. Dozens of walking trails wound among giant cedar and fir stumps. Many of these relics of the original forest were 8 feet tall and 6 feet or more through at ground level. All were rotting, slabs of the outer skin crumbling or gone and the core reduced to a soft red-brown powdery chalk. In some stumps, a chopped out slot survived in the original sapwood into which the faller had jammed his spring-board, the narrow plank on which he balanced with his axe above the tangle of limbs and underbrush around the expanding buttressed trunk. Fungi as big as dinner plates, creamy above and brown below and almost as hard as horn, were platforms for scolding squirrels. Almost every stump was crowned, this one with a dainty huckleberry bush, that with leathery-leaved pink-beaded salal, another with a drooping hemlock sapling.

Rufus surprised a foraging squirrel and looked back at his master for approval.

Chris sniffed and inhaled deeply. The spring smell of the woods was an irresolvable blend: bitter spice of rotting wood; aromatic pollen from cedar, fir, and hemlock; bland bark scent of alder and maple; nectar from elderberry flowers; and the smell of last year's leaves and of the earth itself. The occasional whiff of corruption—a last trace of the previous winter's kill. Chris had inhaled these comforting, reassuring aromas with pleasure for forty years.

He ducked under the vine maples with leaves like half-opened umbrellas. Small white fungi spiralled up decaying alder trunks decorated with tiny rectangular windows left by foraging woodpeckers. On one such trunk someone had painted in white, neatly, professionally: "Jesus the light of the world," and on another: "Jesus died for your sins." Chris had seen such phrases painted over an area of several square miles; they were especially numerous at bushy dead-ends of lanes and along the beach a few miles to the north. All done by the same brush. Maybe a desperate attempt to reduce fornication in the sylvan glades? The signs were now fading and peeling and had not been touched up recently—perhaps the painter had gone to his reward.

Chris turned back towards home. The core of a giant first-growth cedar log had rotted out, leaving a shell, a partial cylinder which resembled a dugout canoe. Did a ruin like this inspire the great war canoes of the Haidas? he wondered.

On his return, he stood in front of his house, inspecting his various shrubs and trees. Most of them were now getting too big. There must have been one day when they were just right, but now he could look forward to major pruning or, more likely, digging out and replanting. He glumly watched Rufus defecating on his front lawn—a little Kremlin turret with scattered blue tiles.

Later that evening, the paper finished, pleasantly relaxed in his easy chair, having put away three glasses of Red Tide, Chris realized he was humming a tune, a piece he hadn't heard for weeks or months. Why this bit of music and not some other? He wondered if his subconscious had been humming that music, going along about its own business, and if somehow the tune had leaked across to his conscious mind. Then suddenly he realized that he had not been humming at all. He had been thinking the music. He was thinking the tune, not whistling or

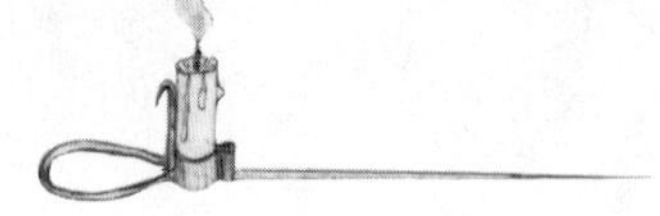

humming it. He realized that he could think a tune and rhythm, enjoy a few themes or whole sections of one of dozens of pieces of music. In fact he could think them more accurately and with more virtuosity than he could hum or sing them.

How is it possible to carry a tune in my brain? How can my brain tell me that I'm thinking the wrong note? And does this mean that music does not necessarily involve sound at all? Maybe sound is merely a means of illustrating the music that I hear in my brain.

But is there anything remarkable about all this? I can imagine colours, different wavelengths in the electromagnetic spectrum, so what's so remarkable about imagining sound? Aren't the notes just different wavelengths of vibrations in air? But colours are visual—I can call up a mental image of a traffic light with its three colours easily enough. Sounds offer no visual clues. I can relate the quality of sound to a visualized instrument—the ripe sonorities of a trombone or the cry of a violin, but I can't visualize G above middle C.

Chris yawned, struggled out of his chair and turned on the TV.

Chapter 4

Bill and the Prof

On his way to the Cariboo on his first assignment, Bill called on Professor Wegner, who lived some 50 miles east of Vancouver, not far from the village of Agassiz. Recently retired, the Prof, as Bill called him, had supervised Bill's senior-year thesis project. In the course of many discussions and arguments, they had become good friends.

The Prof's house, about 100 yards from the main highway, was framed by a pair of giant weeping willows. A small garden contained a few rows of vegetables and half a dozen apple and pear trees. His nearest neighbour was a couple of hundred yards down the road. The Canadian Pacific Railway ran between the Prof's house and the Fraser River. As the trains rolled past, the house rocked, the bed shook, the crockery rattled, and the brass light fixture over the kitchen table became a stately pendulum. The Prof was so used to the trains that he never noticed their passage; he would look questioningly whenever a visitor flinched or looked for the nearest exit, fearing that a killer earthquake was at hand.

A widower, the Prof lived alone except for Newton, a large unfriendly mongrel. Why Newton? Because, the Prof liked to explain, his obedience diminished sharply as his

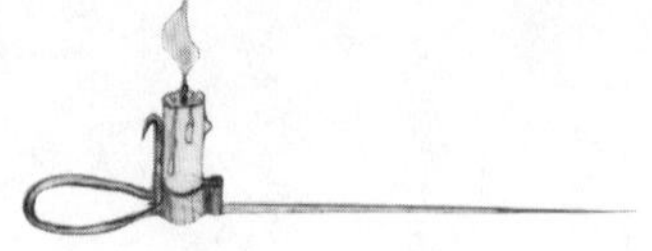

distance from his master increased, apparently governed by the Inverse Square Law, as is Newton's law of gravitation.

Bill parked and strolled over to the open front gate. Newton barked, charged, and stopped a few feet from Bill, chest down, hind end in the air, lips curled back from glistening canines. A low wavering growl, like distant thunder.

The Prof bustled over, restrained Newton with one hand and fished a biscuit out of his pocket with the other. "Give him that and he'll be all right."

Bill took the biscuit and cautiously, like a referee dropping a hockey puck between two bellicose forwards, flipped the morsel to Newton. The dog snapped the biscuit out of the air and quickly munched it down, then closed on Bill who stood like a statue, uncertain as to Newton's next move. Newton, muttering all the while, sniffed Bill's crotch, wagged his tail, then padded over to inspect the sweet-peas. Bill was half convinced that this whole performance was played out for the sake of a dog biscuit—this was not the first time he had had to bribe his way into the yard. He thought of the Prof's grim-through-clenched-teeth advice: "Never, never own a dog that's smarter than you are."

"How's it going?" Bill asked. The Prof looked the same as ever. His tiny twinkling eyes were shaded under thick and abundant eyebrows, their outer ends forming well defined antenna-like points. A few white tendrils straggled across the top of his long blotchy skull which resembled the roof of a camouflaged Greyhound bus. Red bulbous nose and a mouthful of large teeth flashing with gold fillings. He was short and stout.

"Surviving. Getting older. What brings you here? You're

supposed to be up at Tlingit Bay."

"I stuck it out through the winter but I decided I wasn't cut out to be a mine geologist. I've got a new job with Kingfisher."

"Oh. They're a good outfit. Come inside and tell me about it."

They walked through the garden, admired the green apples and entered the house. The livingroom was furnished with simple old-fashioned furniture, much of it acquired at local auction sales. A stone fireplace was centred in the long outside wall. Windows on each side of the fireplace looked down towards the river.

Bookshelves filled with mining and geological works lined most of the remaining walls. Some of the lower shelves were covered with mineral specimens, rocks and other mementos of field trips and expeditions. One shelf held a collection of miner's lamps, including dull brass carbide lamps with circular nickel-plated reflectors and shrouded cylindrical coal-miner's safety lamps. A pair of miner's candleholders, stabbed into the wall above, completed this collection. Each was about ten inches long, made of steel rod, sharpened like an ice pick at one end, formed into a handle at the other. In the middle, a sprung band held a candle. In use, the sharp end was driven into a mine timber or the device was hooked into a crevice in the rock wall where it would provide a dim and flickering light. These had been used until the early part of the century when carbide lamps took their place.

"So you're headed for the Cariboo, eh? I worked at the Cariboo Gold Quartz mine years ago. You would see some nice high-grade once in a while." He pointed, "There's a nice specimen near your elbow there. The miners would sneak the gold out in their lunch buckets. You could often

see where they'd been high-grading—their carbide lamps would blacken the white quartz where they had been digging and prying at the gold. It's a nice country for walking around in—underbrush nothing like as bad as the Coast."

At the university, the Prof had been popular with his students. He worked them hard and managed to impart to most of them his own enthusiasm for mineralogy and mining geology. He was left-handed and would write on the black-board with his left hand and erase ahead with his right, never pausing in his progress across the board, keeping well ahead of students trying to copy his formulas and diagrams.

Now that he was retired and relieved of the pressure of preparing course work, lecturing, marking exams, editing theses and writing the occasional technical paper, he had ample time to brood over the world's problems. Most of his forecasts were gloomy and pessimistic. Living alone, he had no opportunity to debate or defend his dismal prophecies. As a result, many of the startling conclusions he inflicted on his infrequent visitors seemed extravagant and wild. Bill often tried to interrupt the Prof's rambling tirades, but his tentative objections were generally brushed aside. This visit resembled many others. After making his polite enquiries and showing some interest in Bill's project, the Prof turned abruptly to the matters that really concerned him.

"You know, human beings are finished. They are animals whose primary instincts are for self-preservation, procreation, greed, and lust for power. When living is easy and these urges are largely satisfied, they indulge themselves in certain altruistic or artistic aberrations. But when times are hard, they revert to their animal natures. Look at the steepening population curve. In a few years, as food, water, land, and decent living conditions in general have to be shared, man will revert to his true nature. And then bloody fighting and chaos.

"And what are the clever people of the world doing about it? Are they working out ways of persuading the fertile masses to limit their progeny? To better conserve our shrinking resources? To reduce pollution? No. They are fiddling around trying to prove Fermat's last theorem, fussing about black holes, trying to determine the frequency of earthquakes on the moon, the life cycle of the lesser wombat." He paused. "No, it's not their fault—the solutions are simple. It's the people who pay attention to demagogues and who are unable to shake off the chains of custom who are to be blamed."

Bill butted in. "But people have improved—they're getting kinder, wiser, more generous."

"They are certainly not becoming kinder," growled the Prof. "Troy was sacked 3,500 years ago; Constantinople in 1453; Nanking and Lidice yesterday. People haven't changed in thousands of years: for every atrocity of ancient times, you can find a parallel in the last hundred years. Hasdrubal's head was lobbed into Hannibal's camp in about 200 B.C.; Ares' head was passed from one mountain fighter to another in the Pindos in 1945.

"And on average, human beings are not getting any wiser, either. In 1700 B.C. at Knossos, penitents were begging at the feet of the statue of the mother goddess; nowadays, four thousand years later, you see penitents crawling the length of a cathedral begging for health or wealth or revenge at the feet of a statue of the Virgin.

"The fact that man is not evolving into a wiser animal is the best evidence for creationism." The Prof smiled wryly.

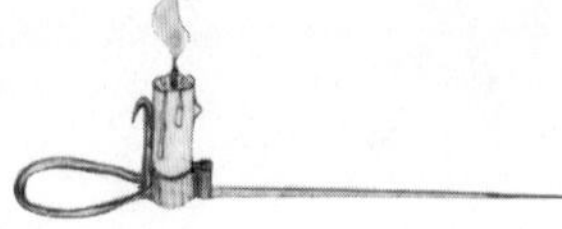

Bill protested: "Surely we're not all evil. Most of us, many of us, do some good. Or don't encourage evil. Most people have some sense of morality." At the word morality the Prof's eyebrows quivered.

"Morality! There's no such thing as morality. Morality is 98 percent custom. Infanticide, pederasty, slavery, and torture were considered normal and moral during the Golden Age of Greece. To the Eskimos, before the white man came, adultery came under the heading of hospitality. And in India, only a few years ago, suttee was the accepted practice. Clitoridectomy. At this moment more than one hundred million women in Africa have been mutilated, and it still goes on. Bah!"

"Then is there no absolute morality, goodness?" Bill asked.

"I subscribe to the idea that you can condense the whole moral code into this: That which results in a net gain in pleasure is good; that which results in a net increase in pain is evil. The difficult part is the net, and sometimes it is not easy to make up the balance sheet." The Prof paused.

Bill considered asking how a sadist, whose pleasure in torture might be more intense than the pain felt by his victim, would fit into the code but thought better of it.

"Surely the church does some good, gives us rules for behaviour," he ventured.

The Prof was getting red in the face.

"How can man, who has dissected the atom, dated the beginning of the universe, and explored the moon, seriously entertain the notion that some mysterious intelligence supervises his actions and answers his prayers? I predict that the time interval 10,000 B.C. to 2,100 A.D. will be known by historians of the distant future as the Age of

Religion. If there's anyone left in the distant future." The Prof regularly revised the second date upwards as he marvelled at religion's staying power.

Abruptly, he changed the subject.

"Married yet? Serious girlfriend?" His eyebrows rose to the top of his forehead.

Bill was always a little embarrassed by this question—he knew that he was a little slow in the girlfriend department and mumbled that he was working on it.

Later, after a cup of coffee, the Prof walked him out to the road. He watched with envy as Bill hopped the low gate and slipped into the truck.

He hadn't been feeling well lately and, like uncounted thousands before him, considered whether there wasn't some way of defeating his enemy—time. A fellow engineer with whom he had worked on several projects, instead of asking: "What's the time?" would habitually ask: "How's the enemy?"

The Prof knew that he lived in a veritable soup of electromagnetic waves and was being bombarded by all sorts of particles. Most of the waves and particles passed unnoticed through his body. But the odd one, perhaps a particle having travelled for a billion years through the cosmos, might score a direct hit on some vital cell or perhaps on the critical bit of DNA whose function it is to prevent a cell from wildly multiplying to form a tumour. Are accumulations of such direct hits the major cause of aging? And if he could find relief from them for a while, could his damaged systems repair themselves?

Suppose he spent a month in the abandoned Britannia Copper mine, a few miles north of Vancouver, where the rock roof is about a mile thick. Thus insulated, would his tired cells repair themselves, his wasting muscles thicken,

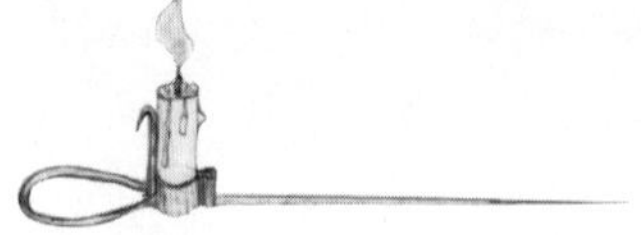

his skin unwrinkle, his liver spots fade, his vertebral discs inflate, and his scalp twitch as new dark hair sprouted on his mottled scalp?

Awakened from these grim speculations by the sound of Bill's horn as he drove away, the Prof waved, then walked slowly back to the house.

◊ ◊ ◊

A few days later, back in Vancouver, Chris was enjoying a warm Sunday morning. He was in the front garden relaxing in a canvas deck chair beneath his grape arbour. The area was paved with slabs of dark grey slate separated from the lawn by a bed of scarlet geraniums. Bright circular discs, like silver dollars, danced on the slate as a breeze stirred the grape leaves. He was sitting inside a giant pinhole camera and each bright disc was an image of the sun projected from a random small opening in the foliage.

He raised his eyes to look beyond the geraniums. An inch-high bulge was advancing across the freshly cut grass, leaving behind it a low serpentine ridge—a mole was forcing its way along the interface between turf and soil. Chris leapt from his deck chair, ran to the head of the advancing bulge and placed his foot on it. He could feel a definite hump under his sole. His face lit up with a diabolical smile—he had his enemy pinned. He considered his next move. He needed a weapon—a pitchfork, a screwdriver, a jack-knife, a sharp pencil, a nail file, a toothpick. His pockets were empty. Elaine and the boys had gone to visit her sister.The neighbours seemed to have gone into hiding.

Chris stood there for about five minutes. A dirty pick-up slowed, the driver peering at him from under a broad-brimmed hat, apparently intrigued by Chris' asymmetric, awkward stance. Chris stared at the top of a nearby cedar, hoping to be taken for a dedicated bird-watcher. Or perhaps a student of bark diseases. Anything but an outsmarted, defeated mole hunter. He made his next hopeless, doomed move. He ran to the carport, snatched a digging fork from the rack, raced back to the ridge's head, stabbed it, and then worked back towards the tail, thrusting madly and inaccurately as he went. He was not rewarded with any sign of success—no mole screams, no bloody tines. The pick-up moved on down the street.

That evening Ben Richards, now wearing a baseball cap, slouched in his pick-up truck. He watched from half a block away as Chris and his wife, wearing her new checked coat, took their regular stroll around the neighborhood. Ben, clutching the steering wheel in a strangler's grip, silently cursed those Magnalode crooks.

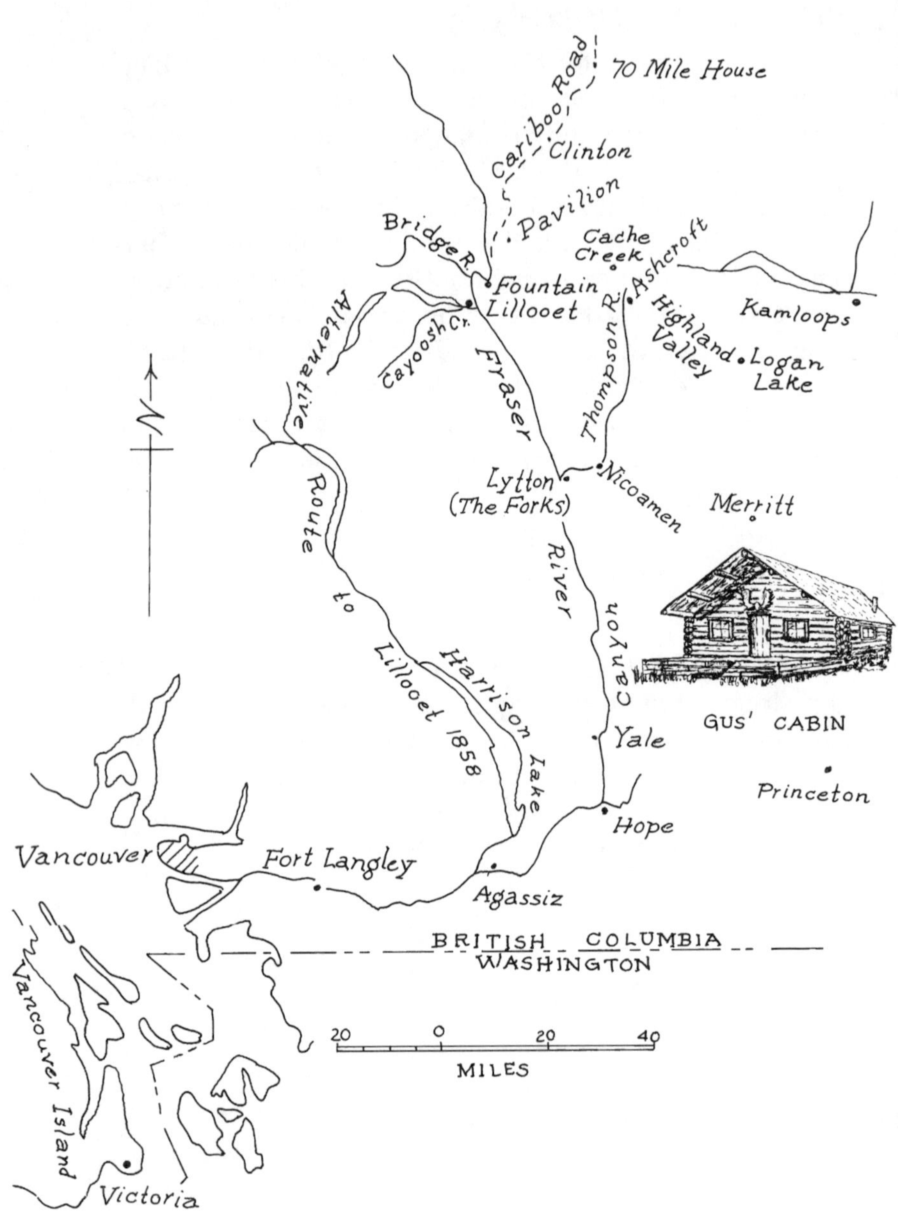
70 Mile House
Cariboo Road
Clinton
Pavilion
Bridge R.
Cache Creek
Ashcroft
Fountain
Lillooet
Kamloops
Alternative
Cayoosh Cr.
Fraser
Thompson R.
Highland Valley
Logan Lake
N
Route
Lytton
(The Forks)
Nicoamen
Merritt
River
to
Canyon
Lillooet 1858
Harrison Lake
GUS' CABIN
Yale
Princeton
Hope
Vancouver
Fort Langley
Agassiz
BRITISH COLUMBIA
WASHINGTON
20 0 20 40
MILES
Vancouver Island
Victoria

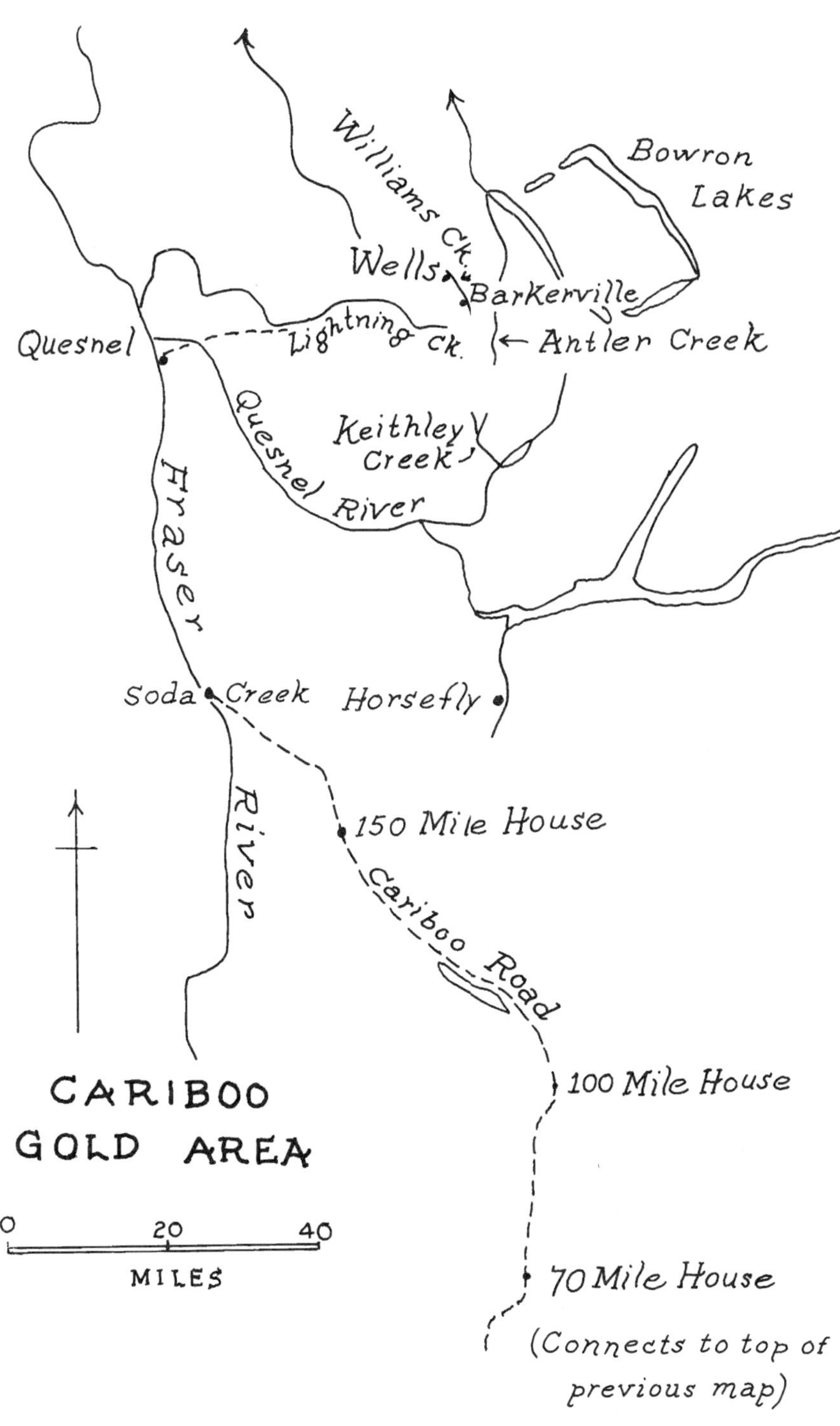
Williams Ck.
Bowron
Lakes
Wells
Barkerville
Quesnel
Lightning Ck.
Antler Creek
Quesnel River
Keithley
Creek
Fraser
Soda Creek
Horsefly
River
150 Mile House
Cariboo Road
100 Mile House
CARIBOO
GOLD AREA
0
20
40
MILES
70 Mile House
(Connects to top of
previous map)

Chapter 5

Cariboo Gold Rush

In the late afternoon of the next day, Bill threaded his way down the canyon of Devils Lake Creek, swept around the end of Island Mountain, past Jack of Clubs Lake, and entered the town of Wells.

He was now about 3 miles from Barkerville, the centre of the Cariboo gold rush. In 1862, when the rush was in full swing, Barkerville was the largest town in what was to become the province of British Columbia. The town lies along Williams Creek, the richest gold creek ever found in the province.

He rented a room in the sixty-year-old Golden Cache Hotel which was to be his home for the next couple of weeks. He unpacked his suitcase, hung his work clothes in the musty closet, and placed his rucksack and boots in the corner. He was relieved to see a wooden table beside the window—he would need a working area for his maps and papers. The bathroom was some distance along the hall.

After a late supper in the hotel dining room, he explored the town. Not a lot to see. He admired the monument to promoter Fred Wells, after whom the town was named and who brought the Cariboo Gold Quartz mine into production after years of frustration. He returned to the hotel as it became dark.

In his room he could hear the occasional shout or laugh from the pub directly beneath him. Spreading a map on his table, he began to work out a rough schedule for the next few days. A few hours later, having familiarized himself with the local geography and made some tentative plans, he got up, stretched and prepared for bed. It had been a long day and he looked forward to a good night's sleep. But once in bed, thoughts of his project crowded his mind. Is that really the best way to tackle the problem? Maybe first I ought to look at some of the abandoned mines. Then hike up into the hills and see if I can sort out some of these formations. But not much outcrop in those rounded mountains. Got to get some sleep. He turned on his sagging mattress. Maybe I should visit the operating mines before I check out the regional geology? Are the backcountry roads shown on the old maps still usable? Find out tomorrow. Chris warned me not to neglect the placers.

Hours later he was still wide awake. He turned on the light and looked at his watch. Two AM.

He got up, dressed, and went down the creaking wooden stairs in the semi-darkness to the lobby. Nobody behind the desk. A bell on the counter for late comers. He looked around the lobby. A fireplace made of blocks and chunks of vein quartz—probably from one of the local mines. A chair in the corner beside a table and reading lamp. He switched on the light and examined a pile of dog-eared paperbacks. Nothing of interest. On a dusty lower shelf an out-of-date road map, some leaflets, and a yellowing government publication on placer mining, dated 1925. From the bottom of the pile he retrieved a slim volume of *The Wells Historical Society*, the 1970

issue. He flicked the pages. An article caught his eye—*A Brief History of the Cariboo Gold Rush,* author unknown to him. He made himself comfortable and started to read.

The year was 1852. England, France, Turkey and Russia were about to become embroiled in the Crimea. Britain had won the first Opium War and had been ceded Hong Kong. The Mutiny would break out in India in five years. In Washington there was fierce debate over slavery and in a few years bloody civil war would settle the issue. The Australian and Californian gold rushes had peaked. The fur trade, controlled by the Hudson's Bay Company, prospered in the peaceful wilderness extending for hundreds of miles north and east of Fort Victoria, the principal British settlement on the northwest coast of North America.

An Indian of the Kamloops band was about to stir things up. He had noticed pebbles and grains of a yellow stone as he bent down to drink from the Thompson River. Days later, he shyly placed his find on the plank counter at the Hudson's Bay trading post at Fort Kamloops. Chief clerk Murdock poked at the lustrous grains.

He questioned the Indian in the Chinook jargon, a lingua franca used in trade between whites and Indians. Chinook had originated at Fort Astoria, at the mouth of the Columbia river, where commerce between English-speaking fur traders and the Chinook Indians had become established shortly after 1800. As its use spread, it incorporated words from various Indian dialects, as well as English, French, Spanish and Hawaiian. Such Chinook words as salt-chuck (the ocean), and skookum (strong) are familiar to most northwesterners.

He called over to the other clerk. "Look at this, Antoine. He says he found them in the bed of the Thompson River, near Nicoamen."

Nicoamen Creek is a few miles northeast of the confluence of the Thompson and Fraser rivers. This junction, where the clear water of the Thompson mixes with the muddy Fraser, was referred to in the early days as the Forks. The town of Lytton was established there a few years later.

"Could it be gold?"

"Fool's gold, no doubt. There's no gold in this part of the world."

"Yes. But it looks like gold. How can you be sure?"

"Fool's gold is iron pyrites and it's hard and brittle. Tap it with the hammer." Antoine took it over to the rough stone fireplace and made the test.

"It flattens but doesn't break. It's soft—look, I can cut it with my knife. Could it be brass?"

"What would wee bits of brass be doing in the river, miles from here or any other habitation? Better ask Mr. McLean."

Chief Trader McLean was called from his account books. They went through the same arguments, the Indian smiling or grave as the white men tried to reach a decision. The upshot was that the Indian was given a blanket for his trouble and instructed to go back to the river and get some more yellow pebbles. In the meantime, McLean read everything he could find about gold and made casual inquiries of those known to have done some mining before coming to the settlement.

Indians brought a larger sample. McLean knew enough now to pound the particles into a single slug from which he was able to get some idea of the density of the metal. It turned out to be much higher than that

of iron and measurably more than that of lead. It seemed to be immune to such acids as he could obtain. Concluding that it was gold, McLean informed the Indians that he would buy their yellow stones and equipped them with iron spoons for scraping the gold from crevices in the riverbed. Soon gold was being brought in regularly and some of McLean's French-Canadian employees began panning gold. In a year or two, gold was found in the gravels of the Tranquille River, just northwest of the Fort.

News of these finds spread and by 1857 miners, mostly American, working their way north along the Columbia and Okanagan valleys and then overland to the west, arrived at the Forks. They found gold in the Thompson and in the Fraser above the Forks. By the end of the year, a total of some 1,400 ounces of gold had been recovered from the area and sold to the Hudson's Bay Company traders. It was shipped to San Francisco to be refined.

By this time, the California gold rush was in decline, the easy pickings gone, and a large population of miners was looking for the next adventure. When news of the gold shipment from the Fraser River spread through San Francisco, the rush was on. In early 1858, ships from San Francisco disembarked more than 20,000 miners, adventurers and entrepreneurs at Fort Victoria. They crossed by boat to Fort Langley, near the mouth of the Fraser River, to be joined by another 8,000 who travelled overland from the south. Many of them arrived when the Fraser was in flood. Before the river level fell, thousands of would-be miners, finding the gold-bearing bars under water, no roads, no accommodation, and food and supplies scarce and expensive, had left the country. Those who stuck it out made their ways along the lower stretches of the Fraser and, as the river level dropped, found enough gold in the bars to entice them upstream. At Yale, head of navigation, where the swift flowing Fraser escapes from its mountain canyon, loses speed and drops its entrained gold, the bars were especially rich. Hills Bar, at Yale, yielded half a million dollars in gold that year. Pure gold was worth $20 an ounce, but like almost all natural gold, Fraser River gold was alloyed with silver, so the miners were paid as little as $16 an ounce. The bars near and below Yale were soon worked out.

There were only primitive trails through the canyons north of Yale, impossible at first for horses and mules, and supplies had to be carried on men's backs along the cliff-sides on narrow ledges and over Indian paths. These trails were improved and mule-trains reached the Forks in September. Before the season ended, all of the bars between Yale and the Forks were occupied and some miners had ascended the Fraser as far as the Indian village of Fountain, a few miles above Lillooet. By January 1859, however, all but about 3,000 miners had lost hope of a quick and easy killing and had returned south, mainly to California.

An alternative route to the upper Fraser gold fields, longer but easier, was established in late 1858. From the head of Harrison Lake, relatively short wagon roads connected several long mountain lakes, allowing travellers using barge and wagon to reach Lillooet in as few as five days. The short stretches of road along this route were built mainly by miners when the Fraser was high and the river bars could not be worked.

The names given the river bars tell something of the times. The lowest productive bar on the Fraser was Maria Bar. Who was Maria? Many of the mining claims recorded in British Columbia in the early days were named after popular whores. Did Maria arrive in one of the first boats from Victoria and entertain her cus-

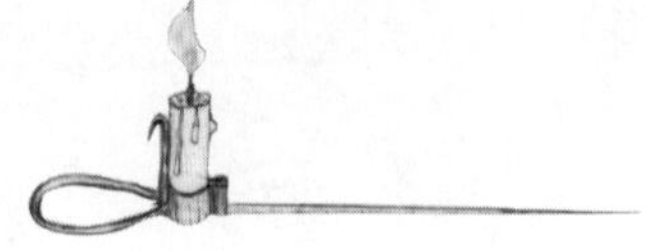

tomers in steamy tent or mosquito-permeable hastily-thrown-together log cabin?

Bill got up and stretched. Never heard that before, he mused. I wonder if the Kootenay Belle mine was named after a hooker. He wandered over to the fireplace and inspected the pyrite crystals which filled fractures in the quartz. He returned to the history of the gold rush.

Upstream from Maria Bar was Murderer Bar, 4 miles below Hope. The criminal for whom it was named is unknown. Most miners carried leather pokes of gold dust and it is easy to imagine theft and violent reprisal. Perhaps a quarrel over Maria's favours? Or perhaps the body of a miner, murdered upstream by Indians, cartwheeled down the swollen river and was swept into a back eddy at this bar. Although Indians north of Yale resented the white intruders, there were only a few ambushes and skirmishes. In general, the invasion was a peaceful one.

Above Hope, the names of many of the bars have an American flavour—most of the miners were San Franciscans. Fifty-four Forty Bar, (a reference to the boundary dispute between Britain and the United States), American Bar, Yankee Doodle Bar, Sacramento Bar and Texas Bar. The names of other gold-bearing river bars evoke other nationalities: Kanaka Bar, Dutchman Bar, French Bar, Canadian Bar, and China Bar. Most of these names are all but forgotten but Boston Bar, above Yale, survives as a prosperous logging centre.

Rich diggings were exploited at the mouth of Bridge River and at Fountain. By the end of the summer of 1859, one thousand men were working the upper Fraser, but most of the easily mined gold was gone and they were barely making wages. At the end of the year many of them straggled back to Fort Langley. But not all. Small parties, guided by an Indian, travelled north from Kamloops and others ascended the Quesnel River and that same summer, these adventurers were panning rich gravels in the Horsefly River.

Next year there was a minor stampede north to Keithley Creek, another rich producer. In the autumn of 1860, four prospectors left Keithley Creek, crossed the divide to the north and reached Antler Creek. Gold was coarse and abundant and they obtained one or two ounces to the pan. They built a cabin and two of the party returned south for winter supplies. Their large purchases, bought with coarse gold, did not escape notice and on their return they were dogged by scores of hopeful miners—the secret was out. The miners blanketed the creek with claims and, in spite of deep snow and freezing weather, worked them through the winter. Antler Creek was the first of the great Cariboo gold creeks.

William Dietz prospected northwest from Antler Creek in 1861 and staked the first claim on Williams Creek. The discovery of Lightning Creek followed soon after. From a prospect pit 8 feet deep the discoverer panned 1,700 ounces of gold in three days. Nearby a 40-ounce nugget was found.

In the winter of 1861-62, a series of letters from a Cariboo correspondent to the Times of London described the new finds and brought miners and adventurers from all parts of the British Empire. The letters didn't explain that after the long sea voyage the newcomers would be faced with a 300-mile hike! Enterprising agents in England sold stage-coach tickets for the journey from Fort Langley to the gold fields. But there were no stage-coaches. There was no road.

The news of these rich gold discoveries brought back thousands of miners from San Francisco, most of them

travelling the western route by barge and portage to Lillooet. In 1861, $2.5 million worth of gold was taken from the Cariboo.

The rich shallow gravels of upper Williams Creek were picked clean in a relatively short time. The creek was then almost abandoned, the miners dispersing to more promising diggings. Then the feckless (or inspired) Billy Barker sank shafts some 60 feet on lower Williams Creek to test the deep gravels. He struck it rich in his third shaft. The bedrock, which everywhere underlies the gravels, was mantled with the richest gravel so far found in the Cariboo. Barker took out 124 ounces in ten hours. The next claim to Barker's proved to be even richer, yielding 200 pounds of gold in one day. One of its owners swore not to leave the creek until he could take with him his own weight in gold. He quickly made good his promise and included his large dog in the bargain, leaving with 360 pounds of gold. The richest single pan of gravel ever reported from the Cariboo, from an adjacent claim, yielded 90 ounces.

The hopeful miner would sink a shaft through the sands and gravels to the slaty bedrock. He would then tunnel out from the bottom of the shaft and scrape up the gold-rich gravels that were concentrated on the bedrock. The gold-bearing gravel was hoisted with bucket and windlass, cranked at first by hand but in later days powered by giant water-wheels. The gold was then separated from the gravel by pan or sluice.

As the miners advanced their drifts, they placed supporting posts in a rectangular pattern every 8 feet, with roof timbers across to prevent the overlying sand and gravel from collapsing and filling the mine. In some workings they had to stuff spruce branches behind the timbers to stem the flow of wet clay. The weight of the overlying gravels was so great in some mines that posts 2 feet in diameter had to be placed side by side to form a solid wall and in time, even these were driven a foot into the slate bedrock.

In many places water was a problem and pumps were not always able to keep the workings dry. With water pouring through the lagging overhead, working underground by candle or lantern was like working at night in a torrential rain storm.

Shafts were sunk on dozens of claims and the gravels of a mile-long stretch of Williams Creek were riddled with vertical shafts and horizontal drifts which snaked over the buried bedrock. The town of Barkerville expanded along Williams Creek above the workings. In the heyday of mining, the pumps groaned day and night to keep the workings from flooding. The hills were stripped of their trees as woodcutters tried to keep up with the demand for mine timbers. It is said that there was more wood under the town of Barkerville than in it.

Bill, foot gone to sleep, got up and limped around the lobby. He asked himself: Did they get it all? They must have missed some of the pay-streaks. Surveying was primitive or non-existent in the placer mines of those days. They were pretty much wandering around in the dark. And they knew little or nothing about the principles of sedimentation. Probably a few million bucks worth still down there. We'll never know. He returned to his chair.

The famous Judge Begbie wrote in 1861, "the gold is a perfect nuisance, as they (the miners) have to carry it to their claims every morning, and watch it while they work, and carry it back again—sometimes as much as two men can lift—to their cabins at night, and watch it while they sleep." Getting the gold to the coast was also a problem. Much was carried by mules. Men, bent

and creaking under 60-pound loads, were paid up to $50 a day to backpack the gold to Yale. By 1865 the transportation problem had eased. A new Cariboo wagon road extended from Yale to Soda Creek and from Quesnel to Barkerville. Steamboats carried passengers and freight on the placid Fraser between Soda Creek and Quesnel. Four-horse stage-coaches now made the trip from Yale to Soda Creek in forty-eight hours. Meals, beds and a change of horses were provided at stopping places known as mile-houses, the mileages measured at first from Lillooet and later, when the road was completed, from Ashcroft. Some of these survive: 100 Mile House has evolved into a thriving town.

The early mines were financed by the miners themselves, perhaps a dozen shares being owned by miners who had combined their claims in one company. As often as not, the principal shareholders would be found down the shaft, wheeling a barrow or timbering the drift. The profits were divided weekly. According to an 1865 account: "Amongst those who went to the Cariboo in 1861, one third . . . made independent fortunes, another third netted several hundred pounds sterling and the rest returned from the mines wholly unsuccessful." Merchants, hotel owners and saloon keepers prospered. By 1874 most of the deep gravels that could be mined had been stripped of their gold. In 1876, when mining was in decline, a government geologist wrote: "Ordinary labourers receive $5 per day; mechanics from $5 to $7 per day; Chinamen and Indians, $3."

The Cariboo gold rush was a relatively peaceful one. In the early days a group of boisterous and probably drunk American miners near Yale rebelled against the authorities but their insurrection petered out a day later when a small armed force arrived from Victoria. Judge Begbie, travelling through the gold fields on horseback, meted out swift and stern justice to thieves and murderers. Tons of gold were carried by stagecoach and pack animal to Fort Langley but holdups were almost unknown. The famous Bullion placer mine, near the forks in the Quesnel River, produced more than a million dollars in gold around the turn of the century. Rumours of an impending attempt to steal a gold shipment led the mine manager to adopt a novel defence. He had the gold melted and cast into a single ingot, a smooth, rounded, 145-pound billet lacking handholds, believing that bandits would be unable to grasp it and make off. In the event, there was no attempt at robbery.

Yielding slightly less than $50 million, the Cariboo gold rush was not of the first rank. The California placers produced more than $1 billion in gold. The output of the Australian placers, which peaked in 1852, was about $600 million. The gravels of the Klondike gave up about $100 million.

At the height of the Cariboo rush, there were some 4,000 Chinese in Victoria and on the mainland. A small proportion of these were merchants—the rest mined gold from the river bars and creeks. When the Canadian Pacific Railway was under construction in 1881, more than 15,000 Chinese were recruited from California and China as labourers. When the railway was finished, many stayed in British Columbia, some to become businessmen and others gold miners working mostly along the Fraser River. The piles of boulders that the methodical Chinese moved by hand to allow the gravels to be washed of their gold stand like ancient walls at points along the Fraser river. The Chinese were patient and thorough, finding small gold-bearing pockets in the banks of the Fraser and rich side creeks overlooked by the earlier gold seekers pressing on towards the bonanzas of the Barkerville

region. Chinese discovered the gold of Cayoosh Creek near Lillooet and prospered while envious whites looked on.

The Chinese identified abundant green river boulders on the Fraser River bars as jade. It was their custom to send the bones of their compatriots back to China for burial among their ancestors and many tons of jade were shipped home in suspiciously weighty coffins. A white metal, recovered in relatively small amounts in the sluices and generally discarded, turned out to be platinum. Both jade and platinum originate in serpentine, a rock which occurs sporadically in a northwesterly trending belt extending from the Canada-U.S.A. border to and beyond the head of Bridge River.

Long before the rich gravels had been exhausted, people realized that in certain areas there were still millions of cubic yards of gravel of relatively low grade that could not be mined economically by shovel, wheel barrow and sluice. Such lower grade gravels, running only a few cents worth of gold to the cubic yard, were handled in one of two ways. Those in upland valleys or gulches were undermined and washed down by powerful jets of water and flushed through sluice-boxes where the gold was recovered. The water was brought by ditches to the heads of the gulches and piped to 6-inch-bore nozzles, known as hydraulic giants or monitors. The Cariboo area often had dry summers, and many such hydraulic operations worked for only the few weeks or months each year when water was available.

The second method of treating the low-grade gravels, by dredge, was especially suited to open, flat-floored valleys. A dredge floating in its pond was equipped with a continuous chain of steel-lipped buckets which fed a gold-separation plant occupying most of the dredge. It advanced by digging the gravel at the forward end of the barge down to a depth of 50 feet or more. After the gold was separated from the gravel, the waste tailings were dropped behind the advancing dredge. The dredge, digging ahead and filling behind, took its small pond with it across the valley floor like a tortoise carrying its shell. It left the valley floor patterned by crescent mounds of gravel tailings deposited by a swinging conveyor belt.

At the time of this writing (1969), small placer mines, found in many remote gulches, still provide a good, sometimes excellent, and always exciting living for the eternally optimistic miners.

Most of the miners were looking for the placer gold that lay in the gravels and was relatively easily mined. But always in the backs of their minds was the knowledge that the placer gold had its origin in solid bedrock—most likely in quartz veins. Were there any gold-bearing veins left or had they all been eroded and washed away to form the sand, gravel and gold particles of the placers? From the earliest days, prospectors searched the mountains that looked down on the gold-bearing river gravels, and they did find quartz veins in many places. These were sampled and assayed but most were low in grade and could not be made to pay in the days when an ounce of gold brought less than $20 and mining methods were less efficient than they later became. A mile or two west of Barkerville, the veins of Cow Mountain and Island Mountain were explored for decades by adits and shafts. Finally enough ore was proved to justify the construction of a mill for processing gold-bearing quartz. The first hard-rock mine started production in 1933. By 1966, lode mines near Barkerville had yielded over a million ounces of gold.

Bill yawned. Finish this later. He slipped the volume back into the shelf and climbed the stairs to his room. In bed, his thoughts returned to his project. He knew that his task was something like that of a detective, but rather

than looking for a murderer or a thief, he would be looking for a gold-quartz vein. Or veins. In his investigation he would consider the stratigraphy of the layered rocks, their folds and faults. He would study the nature of the known veins, their mineralogy and distribution amongst the various formations. He would look for clues that had been overlooked or misinterpreted by other geologists. Hunches and intuition would play no part in his search. He hoped that by applying a fresh and skeptical mind, by questioning the dogma set out in the older geological literature, and by discounting the accepted truths of the resident experts, he would be able to deduce the existence and location of veins concealed from view by 20 feet of soil and glacial drift.

Not an easy task and no certainty of success. But he had seen that large areas in the Cariboo District were mantled by glacial drift. And he knew that it was very unlikely that all of the veins had been discovered.

Chapter 6

Gold Veins

Bill spent a couple of days driving around the Barkerville area, maps and reports beside him on the seat, getting to know the layout of the roads, the locations of the hard-rock gold-quartz lode mines and of the placer mines, both operating and abandoned. He made the acquaintance of a few of the local mine operators and spent his evenings with maps and reports.

He then began visiting some of the properties, starting with one of the lode mines that had been abandoned some forty years before. He drove up a diminishing dirt road along one of the many deserted gulches, fording a creek several times. Small trees growing between the ruts scraped the underside of his truck. He stopped and, using his hammer handle, engaged the four-wheel drive. He cautiously nosed his way along a gullied shelf whose slumping outer edge was cradled by pines curving upwards like beggar's fingers. The road narrowed, trees crowding in on either side. A cloud passed over the sun. The dark oppressing boughs closed overhead and clawing branches scratched at the windshield. He felt a momentary panic as the truck slithered and almost stalled. The clutching smothering boughs seemed to be rasping a threat: *We are a family that extends to the tun-*

dra. We outnumber you a billion to one. You may poison us, burn us, clear-cut us and pave us over but we will outlast you. We were here before you came and we shall be here when you are gone. Bill shuddered.

The trees thinned and the truck emerged into a sunlit clearing. Before him was an unpainted, weathered building constructed of blackened rough planks, roofed with rusty corrugated iron and topped by an angular tower. He parked beneath a crude loading chute. The door was jammed, but he found an opening where a couple of planks were missing and slipped inside. The dim interior, illuminated through breaks in the roof, was crossed by diagonal rays alive with lazily swirling motes. The floor was cluttered: timbers snaggy with rusty spikes, massive castings—parts of the hoisting machinery—twisting lengths of rusty wire cable, oddly shaped pieces of corrugated iron, a square-faced gin bottle, a ladder with missing rungs. The pervasive stink of pack-rat droppings.

Bill picked his way carefully over to the shaft, dropped a chunk of rock, and was answered almost immediately by a splash—the shaft was flooded. Nothing to be done there. He picked his way out into the blinding sunlight.

Following a pair of rusty rails from beneath the loading chute through a dense growth of underbrush, Bill emerged onto a waste dump which spilled down the steep hillside. The waste from the mine was mostly hard grey sandstone of the Snowshoe Formation in which all of the gold-quartz veins of the area occurred. He now had a good view over the valley and could see in the distance several other waste dumps which marked mines or prospect adits or shafts. Making himself comfortable on a piece of timber, he started breaking pieces of quartz with his hammer, making fresh surfaces which he scanned carefully with his hand-lens. The government report had said that the quartz ran up to one-half ounce of gold per ton, but he was not surprised that he could not find any. Many visitors had examined specimens from the dump in the last forty years and they hadn't left any obviously high-grade bits for him to find. He persisted, however, and in the end was rewarded by finding a tiny seam of gold which filled a fracture in the quartz. Although one can sometimes mistake pyrite for gold, it is rarely that one mistakes gold for pyrite. Its pure colour and rich lustre immediately set it apart. Satisfied, he labelled his prize, completed his notes, and drove back towards town.

After spending the next few days looking at similar abandoned mines and prospects, Bill decided it was time to have a look at some of the dozens of placer mines.

"How do lode mines differ from placer mines?" the Prof had asked a class of first year students. He answered his own question. Gold-quartz veins of the lode mines are like ragged book-marks hidden in the pages of a thick dictionary. But of course these book-marks are sheets of quartz, perhaps 5 feet thick and extending for hundreds of feet, and the enclosing book is solid rock. To exploit the vein, the miner must drive adits or sink shafts through solid rock and blast free the quartz. Hoisting equipment, a transportation system, a mill equipped with giant crushers, grinders, and a chemical plant to free and concentrate the gold have to be provided. The cost of putting a lode mine into production can be tens of millions of dollars and once the plant is in place, the daily running expenses of extracting and processing the ore may amount to tens of dollars per ton.

In contrast, at a placer mine, the recovery of gold, found in loose sand and gravel, is relatively simple and cheap. The parent gold-quartz vein, the mother lode, and the

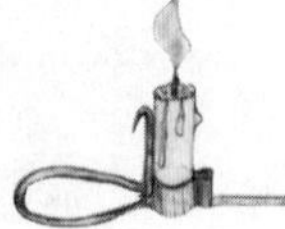

enclosing rock, exposed at the surface, over time have rotted and disintegrated, freeing the extremely durable particles of gold—like gold fillings, the Prof had said, loosening and falling out of decaying teeth. After the gold particles have been freed from the enclosing rock and quartz, they may be concentrated by running water in layers or pay-streaks in the gravels of a river bed. The gold can then be recovered by shovel and pan. Mining, crushing, and concentrating, which are expensive for lode mines, have been done free of charge by nature. The attractions of a placer operation, where only relatively simple and cheap equipment is needed and the retrieval of the gold is easy, are obvious, the Prof had said . . . .

In the Cariboo it has taken millions of years for weathering and erosion to disintegrate and disperse the cubic miles of country rock that contained the auriferous veins.

The concentrating of indestructible gold in a river gravel depends largely on the fact that the density of gold is much higher than that of any of the common minerals and metals. It is nineteen times as dense as water and almost twice as dense as silver. Its density is exceeded only by that of platinum. Because of their high density, gold particles find their way down between the river boulders, escape the force of the current and move only slowly downstream.

High density, the Prof had continued, has been used since ancient times to confirm gold's identity and test its purity. In 250 B.C., Archimedes, using his new understanding of the principles of buoyancy and density, was able to determine whether a goldsmith had made King Heiron's new crown of pure gold or of a less dense alloy of gold and silver. A few years ago, the Prof had added, some Canadian gold buyers were swindled by crooks who encased bars of tungsten in thin skins of gold and passed them off as solid gold bricks—tungsten and gold having the same density. Now all ingots are carefully tested.

Bill began by visiting the largest placer mine in the district. He drove through a gate marked, "Private, El Dorado Placers Ltd," and wound his way along a muddy rutted road past dusty repair shops, dismantled power shovels, pumps, trucks and bulldozers to a group of trailers, one with a rough sign indicating the mine office. He parked to one side, went in and waited until he had the attention of the man—muddy coveralls, gumboots, hard-hat—behind the cluttered desk. Bill introduced himself and asked whether he could walk around and have a look at the operation. He drove up the hill overlooking the main pit where he would have a good view.

A giant shovel was cutting into a 30-foot-high bank of layered sands and gravels and loading them into a waiting truck. The gravel would be taken down to the sluices where the gold would be recovered and the waste sand and gravel added to the growing tailings pile. As the shovel undercut the bank, it caved, forming a small landslide. What looked like a door, framed by rough timbers, appeared in the newly exposed cliff-face. The mine had advanced into ground that had been explored by shaft and drift one hundred years before, and the shovel had exposed a set of rotting mine props. Some poor devil had struggled to keep the gravels from flooding in as he dug towards the sloping bedrock floor.

An hour later, Bill returned to the office and asked if he could see some of the recovered gold. He was shown into a trailer where a bored fellow was swirling concentrate in a large gold pan. Bill's guide led him to a small plastic bucket and handed him a large spoon. The gold particles, mostly flat, like scabs or fish scales, about the size of uncooked rice grains, were a strange silvery colour.

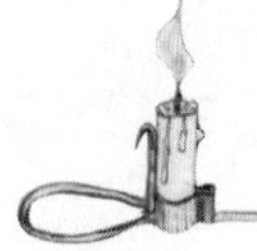

"Why is it white?" Bill asked. "Doesn't look like gold."

"It's coated with mercury. Contaminated. They used tons of mercury in the old days. And they recovered very little of it."

This was news to Bill. Perhaps he had slept through the relevant lecture.

"What was the mercury for?"

The foreman explained patiently—he'd been through this before. "If you drop grains of gold in mercury, the two metals will combine to form a pasty amalgam—like silver-coloured putty. In the old days they would put mercury in the sluice boxes and the fine particles of gold would stick to it and form this amalgam."

"How much mercury would they have used in the old days?"

"I don't have any figures for the Cariboo," said the foreman, "but I've read that in a typical large California placer mine of the 1850s 2 to 4 tons of mercury would be in use at any one time and since it was constantly being lost into the tailings, more was added daily. At cleanup time they recovered only 85 to 90 percent of the mercury. Right now, hundreds of pounds of mercury are lost every day into the Amazon drainage."

"How would they handle the amalgam?"

"To recover the gold, it was squeezed in a canvas or chamois skin to get rid of the excess mercury and then heated in a retort to vaporize the mercury part of the amalgam. A dangerous business because mercury fumes are deadly poison. The mercury was condensed in a water-cooled pipe and returned to the sluice. The spongy gold, left behind, was melted and poured into a mold to make a brick. Our old workings are thoroughly contaminated with mercury lost by the old-timers. So are nearly all of the creeks in the Cariboo mined in the early days."

As Bill drove away from the hotel next morning he mulled over what he knew about gold. It was not a very useful metal. Its value was largely psychological. Its valuable properties included its durability—it was not attacked by tarnish or rust or most acids—its attractive colour, and its malleable, easily worked nature. It was also scarce. All of the gold so far mined in the world could be contained in a cube about 70 feet on an edge. He had read that natural gold ranged widely in composition, being alloyed with silver, copper or mercury in amounts up to several percent. As the proportion of silver, which in nature could range up to more than 40 per cent of the total, increased, the gold-silver alloy lost its yellow colour and became nearly white. The industrial uses of gold were few: in special electrical circuitry, dentistry, coinage, and jewellery. The ratio of the cost of an ounce of gold to the price of a loaf of bread had not changed much in the last one hundred years.

He knew that gold has been mined from earliest days, probably first from river gravels and sands. Jason's golden fleece was probably a sheepskin held down by boulders on the bed of a river emptying into the Black Sea, left there to entangle gold particles being swept along by the stream.

Next day Bill took the road east to Antler Creek and followed a partly washed-out side road up Nevada gulch. The gulch was a man-made gash in the overburden cut along the course of what had been an inconspicuous creek. The gash, about one-half mile long, 100 feet deep over most of its course, with flaring sides, ended in a theatre-like headwall. The gulch had been cut in the 1920s by a hydraulic monitor which directed a high pressure jet against the gravel banks and flushed the gold-bearing gravel down through sluice boxes. The sluice boxes used in these

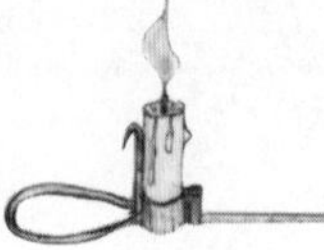

operations were troughs about 4 feet wide and 2 feet deep, made of heavy planks. Slats, known as riffles, were nailed across the bottom and as the gravel was washed through the box the dense gold particles lodged behind them.

Bill knew that there were many such placer gulches throughout this part of the Cariboo. Great quantities of water were needed to feed the monster nozzles. Commonly enough, certain gravels, known to be rich, could not be mined simply because large flows of water could not be economically supplied. In many places, miles of ditches or canals drained lakes and diverted rivers and creeks to feed into the pipes and hoses that led down to the nozzles.

Such methods of operating are no longer tolerated because the uplands become deeply scarred and the downstream valleys overwhelmed by thousands of cubic yards of gravel tailings. Some gold-rich gravels, mainly at great depths under the broad flats of the main rivers, have never been mined—shafts were flooded by volumes of water which giant pumps could not clear.

Bill switchbacked up the side of the gulch, beyond its head, and came out into a clearing in which sat a house-trailer. He parked in the mud and strolled over to the trailer, hammering on a rock as he came to give warning of a visitor. A curtain twitched and a middle-aged woman was dragged through the door by a powerful, amiable-looking Alsatian.

"Looking for Henry?" the woman asked. At Bill's nod, she pointed up the hill where Bill could hear the intermittent roar of an earth-moving machine. Bill thanked her and followed the muddy track up the hill. From a high point he could look down into the draw and see the whole operation.

A crude earth and timber dam confined a muddy pond. At its lower edge, a diesel-powered pump sent water by pipe and hose to a bench above the pond. Here a back-hoe was dumping gravel into a bin which fed the gravel into a slowly revolving, gently sloping steel cylinder, 4 feet in diameter and 20 feet long, perforated by hundreds of 2-inch holes. The cylinder and gravel were washed by torrents of water pumped from the pond. Boulders passed along and through the sloping cylinder and were finally discharged as tailings. Material smaller than 2 inches was washed through the holes into a bank of sluice boxes. Bill was astonished at the volume and speed of water cascading down the steeply sloping sluices and marvelled that any gold could be caught behind the riffles. The water from the sluices ran down a ditch to the pond whence it was recirculated by the pump back to the machine. No muddy water or tailings escaped to the lower valley.

Bill wandered up the hill to where the gravel was being mined. About 100 yards higher up the draw, he found a back-hoe clawing at the gravels. After studying its actions for about ten minutes, Bill could see that the pay dirt was a 6-foot layer of white gravel which was underlain by brown-weathering gravel and overlain by about 4 feet of glacial drift and soil. This upper layer was being removed and dumped to one side. The white gravel was being loaded into a dump truck which took it down to the washing and sluicing machinery.

Spotting a stranger, the back-hoe operator pulled the machine off to one side, lit a cigarette and climbed down as Bill walked over to introduce himself.

"I'm Bill Trelawney—geologist. I work for Kingfisher, down in Vancouver. I'm looking around at the various

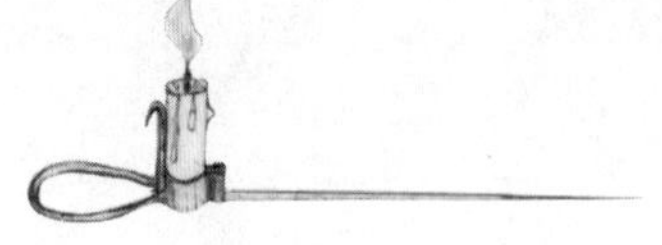

operations. How's it going?"

"I'm Henry. Well, you'll be able to see for yourself. You're just in time for the clean-up."

"Great, I've never seen one. I've worked mostly around hard-rock mines."

"Well, don't expect too much. We clean up every two days and sometimes it's pretty exciting but other days we don't get much." They walked back to the gold-separating machine, where the last load had been processed and Joe, Henry's helper, was getting ready for the big event.

The woman from the trailer, Henry's wife Martha, joined the group amid a general air of anticipation and suppressed excitement. Henry and Martha now attacked the sluice boxes, removing the big pebbles by hand. Bill lurked behind them, trying not to get in the way but watching closely for giant nuggets.

"What's that?" he asked, pointing to a grey lump behind a riffle.

"Lead bullet," said Henry. "We find all sorts of stuff: horseshoe nails, bullets, birdshot, coins, gold teeth, copper or platinum nuggets, chunks of tungsten ore or lead ore and grains of magnetic black sand. Any heavy stuff will lodge behind the riffles along with the gold. We often find little round things, like fine bird shot. I was told that they're meteorites. They're found in lots of the placers."

The remaining contents were carefully washed with a hose and brushed into buckets, Martha keeping an eye peeled for large nuggets. Then the buckets were carried over to a sluice-box about 6 feet long in which corrugated rubber matting formed the riffles. The concentrate was fed slowly into this small sluice. Martha held a small jar in one hand and a pair of tweezers in the other. As nuggets appeared, most of them less than a quarter of an inch across, she speared them and dropped them into her jar.

This process was repeated until the contents of all of the primary sluices had been reconcentrated and the obvious nuggets captured. The corrugated mats were then removed from the small sluice, inverted, and washed in a large gold-pan. The sluice box was carefully hosed, washing any remaining concentrate into the pan. Henry squatted and immersed the half-filled pan in a square galvanized washtub half full of water. He swirled the concentrate a few times, roughly scraped off the larger pebbles and then with a few rotary movements reduced the load to about a cupful. A few more swirls and it was done. Bill was amazed at Henry's quickness—he did in a few minutes what would have taken Bill half an hour. Martha seemed satisfied with what appeared to be a few tablespoonfuls of sand-sized gold particles. She carried the pan back to the trailer to dry the concentrate so it would pour easily and so the black magnetite grains of high density, which accumulated with the gold and made up about one-quarter of the concentrate, could be removed with a magnet.

Henry announced that he could use a cup of coffee and invited Bill to join the rest of them. They sat at the oilcloth-covered table under the awning in front of the trailer, drinking coffee and sampling Martha's cookies.

As he accepted a second cup of coffee, Bill said: "I've been wondering why you prefer a steel pan to a plastic one."

"Well," said Henry, "I guess the main thing is that the steel one can take a certain amount of battering."

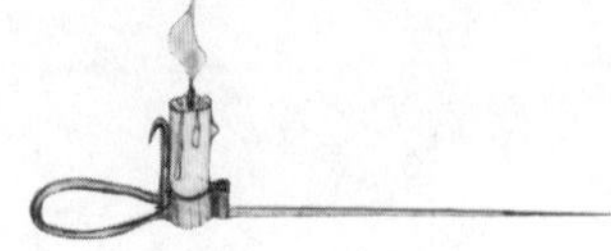

"I haven't done a lot of panning," Bill said, "But I've got one of the plastic pans and I think I like it better. It doesn't rust and it doesn't rattle all day in the back of the truck. It's black, so the gold is easy to spot, and non-magnetic, so I can run my magnet around it and get out the magnetite. It's also got a couple of riffles molded into it, which makes panning a little easier."

"You've got some points there," nodded Henry, "But I can put my steel pan on the stove or on a fire and dry my concentrate and you can't do that. Or fry up some bacon and eggs. But a plastic pan is sure easier on the hands in freezing weather."

While Bill and Henry were talking, Martha had returned to the trailer. She reappeared with a pickle jar which, a little shyly, she passed to Bill. Henry and Joe watched in silence a performance they had seen many times. Bill tipped the jar and a few score of nuggets, mostly about the size of grapes, spilled out onto the table. Martha was obviously very proud of her nuggets and knew the dozen or so large ones as well as she knew her own fingers. She pointed out their unusual features and recounted their histories. She sold nuggets to visitors, mainly tourists, and charged, as did all of the nugget sellers, nearly twice the value of the gold. The nuggets were mostly ugly lumps, like small scabby potatoes. Bill found it hard to understand why people cheerfully paid prices higher than the going price of pure gold for the natural, unrefined genuine nuggets.

"Where do you sell your gold?" he asked Henry. "Apart from the nuggets, that is."

"A gold buyer from Vancouver comes around to the various creeks quite regularly. He seems to have a pretty good idea how pure the gold is—it's different in every creek. He weighs the gold and pays on the spot."

Henry asked Bill a question. "What do you think about these giant nuggets you read about in the papers? They've found several 50-pounders and the world record, Australia, I think, is more than 200 pounds. The biggest one from the Cariboo is only about 3 pounds. My theory is that the really big ones are fakes—stolen gold that has been melted and cast into nugget-like shapes. Once you melt the stuff nobody can say where it came from. Lots of gold bars have been pinched and never seen again."

Bill, the great explainer, was happy to oblige.

"To account for large placer nuggets," he began, "some geologists maintain that gold seams, plates, crystals and wires form a connecting network extending through many cubic yards of vein quartz. These gradually collapse, coalesce, and are compacted into a single giant nugget as the enclosing quartz is dissolved away. This takes thousands or millions of years. Others argue that as boulders crash together in turbulent streams, small gold particles are pounded or welded together to form large nuggets. And still others think that in certain hot climates, gold is dissolved in natural waters and is later precipitated as new gold, forming large nuggets in places favorable for deposition. It's like limestone that gets dissolved away, leaving giant caves, and later comes out of solution elsewhere to form stalactites and stalagmites. And, just recently, somebody has proposed that certain bacteria are able to precipitate gold from solution, forming spongy nuggets in sands and gravels. Myself, I don't believe it."

Henry, having received more information than he had bargained for, moved on to a pet subject.

"You know, you geologists ought to able to find the

veins that supplied all this placer gold."

He went into the trailer and returned with a couple of pill bottles and two sheets of paper. He spilled sand-sized gold into two separate piles.

"Now look at this sample from Joshua Creek. The gold is mostly nicely formed little crystals and sharp-edged crack fillings. It hasn't travelled very far from the mother lode. But look at this one, from lower Lightning Creek. They're like fish scales—pounded flat, scratched and bent and some of them folded. Look at this one—it's been folded twice. These have travelled a long way from the quartz vein. Now if you guys took these differences into account, I'll bet you could track down the source of the gold."

Bill examined the gold with his hand-lens and had to agree that Henry's argument made a lot of sense.

Now Henry and Joe were becoming restless and Bill could see that they wanted to get back to work. He gulped his coffee and, explaining that he had two more properties to look at, took his leave.

That afternoon, as he drove back to Wells, his thoughts returned to a concern that had been growing in his mind as each day passed. This was the nagging awareness that Isaac expected him to come up with a proposal, probably involving trenching or drilling, which had a chance of leading to the discovery of some gold veins. There weren't many days left and he was no closer to a proposal for Isaac.

Bill spent the next few days visiting small placer mines and talking to their owners. One of these was the Wild Rose placer operation. As he pulled into the clearing at the end of a twisty road, he was surprised to find a shiny new Cadillac parked beside the expected muddy pick-up truck. He followed a path to a cabin. Empty. He looked around. In the distance three men were rebuilding a sluice box. Beyond them, another fellow paced slowly and deliberately across the valley floor, turned where the ground began to rise, and continued towards the other side of the valley, veering around excavations and tailings piles. His path brought him within a few feet of Bill.

A perfectly levelled stetson was pressed down on the man's short grey hair. Gold-framed spectacles. Formal dark suit. Well-pressed trousers were folded neatly into the elaborately tooled tops of his cowboy boots. Over his suit-coat he wore a polished leather cartridge belt supported by gleaming cross-belts. Instead of rifle shells, the belt-loops held cylindrical pill bottles. The man held the two arms of a forked branch in his clenched hands, palms up, and thumbs pointing to the sides. A pill-bottle was fixed to the fork of the stick which extended forward like a probe. A dowser, Bill thought. But what's he looking for—water, gold, what? The dowser paid no attention to Bill. Perhaps he didn't even see him. Grimly concentrating, lips compressed, forehead furrowed, he reached the end of his traverse, turned, and paced off in a new direction.

Bill shrugged and walked over to the sluice-box builders, one of whom was the owner of the claim. The dowser, now about a hundred yards away, disappeared behind some scrub alder.

"I've never seen an outfit like that before," said Bill. "What does he carry in the cartridge belt?"

"Those little pill-bottles contain samples—metals, oil, water. That pill-bottle attached to his rod has got a pinch of placer gold in it. The rod will twitch for gold and pay no attention to water or other things. If he's looking for

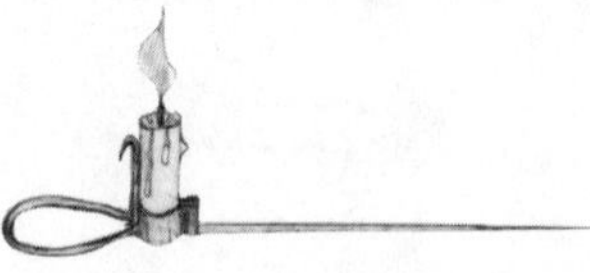

water, he hooks on a pill-bottle full of water. Or Oil. Or lead or uranium. Silver or copper. He's got samples of all of them in his cartridge belt. He's ready for anything. Seems to work real good."

"Do you use him regularly?" Bill asked.

"Whenever we lose the pay-streak we try to get ahold of him. Not always easy. Comes all the way from Fort Langley. He's terribly busy down there, witching water wells, finding lost articles, helping the police solve murders."

"Does he always find the pay-streak for you?"

"Not always. But look at that flat out there. What else can you do? Last fall we were stymied—didn't know where to dig. So we had him up here and he got a strong signal just this side of that big boulder. We saw his forked stick bending so strongly he could hardly hold it." The man pointed to a 10-ton granite monster isolated on the floor of the recent excavation. "We took 30 ounces out from under the upstream side of that boulder."

"Gee. I'd like to talk to him, ask him a few things. Lots of geologists don't understand how these witchers do it." Bill was being very diplomatic, but not diplomatic enough. At the word geologists the owner's face hardened.

"Look, nothing personal, but Mr. Arbuthnot can't stand geologists—he's had some bad experiences with them. If he finds out that we've got a geologist anywhere near the place he'll be upset. I'm paying him good money to come all the way up here and do a job and I don't want to get him riled. If you want to look over our operation, you'll have to come around next week when he's gone. Sorry."

CHAPTER 7

HIT AND RUN

At the Kingfisher office in Vancouver, everyone was assembled around the conference table.

"That damned accountant in Toronto is at it again," Isaac growled to the others. "Wants to know why we hired Bill. Knows damn well that Armstrong quit three months ago. It's beyond disbelief. Well, on to other things. Jay, what's the latest on your gold property in Bridge River?"

"We're still remapping the claims," Jay said. "We should complete the work in another month—rain has slowed us down. The old reports are all out of date—have to be reinterpreted in light of modern theory. The deposit is a dead ringer for the Japanese volcanogenic deposits. Awesome. Deposit is hosted in an accreted slab of oceanic crust rafted in from thousands of miles away some 250 million years ago."

This talk of exotic terranes made Chris uneasy—he knew that he was not up on the latest theories. He found it hard to admit that the engines that drove the world were under the oceans, where up-welling white-hot mantle splits and spreads the crust.

Chris looked across at Carl Costello's green sunglasses. He couldn't say that Carl was shifty-eyed—he couldn't

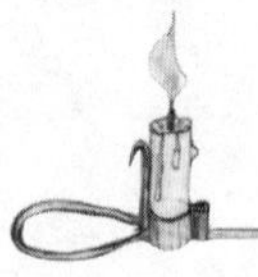

remember when he had last seen Carl's eyes. Chris studied him. Italian, Polish, Laplander? Chris was at it again. Because of Carl's black hair and Roman Catholic religion, Chris thought he must be of Mediterranean stock. But his turned-up nose, blue eyes and tall slender figure seemed to suggest more northern ancestors. Could he be a mixture of northern and southern types?

Chris for once was right but he had only a part of the answer. Carl's distant ancestor, stumbling ashore half-drowned from a wrecked Spanish galleon in a remote inlet in western Ireland, had croaked "Castile" to the questioning savages lining the shore, and he and his descendants were from that moment named.

Isaac turned to Chris. "Well Chris? Dodging any more chunks of chalcopyrite? Bought any aluminum mines?" Smiles all around.

"It's no joke," Chris complained. "The maniac's probably back in the bush by now. I hope."

"Making progress on the Cougar Lake deposit?" Isaac asked.

"I've been studying the old assays," Chris replied. Looks pretty good, provided the price of copper holds up. But sampling won't be easy—values are all over the place. Have to use gigantic samples. Big ones, anyway. Can probably get by with small ones in some places."

Carl asked, "How did we get Cougar Lake in the first place?"

"I'd say dumb luck," Chris explained."Well, this was back in the '60s—before my time—I heard it from old Browning. You've to remember that there was no Kingfisher in those days. Magnalode had a one-man, one-room office out here. It was run by a young American geologist—trained in Colorado and familiar with the big porphyry copper deposits of Arizona and New Mexico. At that time, no mining developers in the northwest imagined that anything like those giant low-grade deposits existed in this part of the world. Conventional wisdom was that they were to be found only in the southwestern States, Arizona mainly, and South America.

"A fellow in Ashcroft had held some copper claims in the Highland Valley for years. He would let the claims lapse each spring and immediately have a pal restake them as new claims. He and his pal would alternate as owners."

Julie couldn't help butting in. "Why would he do that?"

This time Carl explained. "The government requires that in order to hold a mining claim, the holder has to do a certain amount of assessment work—trenching, sampling, and so on each year—or pay an annual tax. This provision doesn't apply in the first year the claim is held, so by restaking every year the guy was avoiding these requirements."

Chris picked up his story. "He was just hanging onto the claims and not doing any work on them. Trying to sell them. This went on for years. A smart prospector-promoter, checking the records at the mining recorder's office, could see what this guy had been doing and bided his time. Finally the owner got careless—late spring, lots of snow, allowed the claims to lapse, put off re-staking. Our promoter friend rounded up a crew, snowshoed in from the Merritt side, and staked the critical claims. All perfectly legal.

"By the time the original staker discovered that his showing had been staked by an outsider, it was too late, he'd lost the claims. He was mad as hell, started a law suit, finally ran out of money. A lot of bad feelings and get-even threats. Committed suicide in the end. If he'd held onto the

 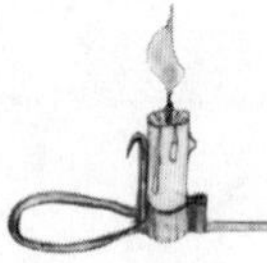

claims he would have been a rich man today.

"Anyhow, the prospector-promoter, the new owner, showed his best ore samples to the young Magnalode geologist. He recognized them as identical to ore from the giant porphyry copper deposits that he had seen in Arizona, so he immediately made an agreement to purchase the claims. He staked a hundred more claims in the moose pasture surrounding the showings.

"Magnalode wasn't pleased at not being consulted about the deal. The geologist was fired. Magnalode sold off a large part of their interest in the property. Kingfisher was set up soon after and of course now all deals have to be approved by Toronto. Finally the bigwigs in Toronto, seeing other successful mines of the porphyry copper type in the area, like Damascus Copper, are getting around to doing something with Cougar Lake. Taken long enough."

"What became of the geologist?" asked Carl.

"He went back to the States. He just retired as president of Mammoth Copper."

There was a thoughtful silence, finally broken by Isaac. "Carl. Anything new?"

"Nothing exciting. Lots of samples coming in—the labs are busy."

Isaac grumbled, "Yeah … and charging an arm and a leg.

◊ ◊ ◊

She came to one of the few blocks that had never been

built on; it was now covered with a tangle of willows, alder and blackberry vines. A few darkened houses on one side of the street alternated with vacant lots—no porch lights on. She looked right and left nervously in this almost deserted stretch and crossed onto the road where her way was better illuminated by the infrequent street lights. She passed a parked pick-up truck with its engine idling. The driver was studying a city map with the aid of a flashlight. As she walked under a yellowish street lamp, she missed a step, startled as her shadow overtook her and leapt forward.

Ben Richards waited until she was half a block ahead. That's her alright. The pick-up eased forward, lights off, then gradually accelerated. The place of impact was calculated to be the dark area between lights. At the last second she realized that the pick-up was closing on her but she had no time to scramble out of the way. It hit her and sent her flying. Only a muffled thump. No scream. He slowed and stopped. No lights came on. No doors opened. He rolled the body and peered at her in the dim light. Glass or plastic crunched under foot. Damn, I've broken something—can't leave her here—they could trace the car. He dragged the slight figure to the pick-up. A moan. She's still alive. He squeezed her throat until she was finally still and silent. He threw back the lid of the plywood tool box, folded the slight body into the box and leaned on it, compressing it so the lid could be secured. He checked the bumper and radiator. If there were any new dents he couldn't see them. But he would have to replace the turning signal lens.

He drove to the nearby shopping mall, sat and watched. A newish station wagon turned in and parked beside him, nose-in against the concrete retaining wall. Its driver disappeared into the supermarket. After glancing around, Ben

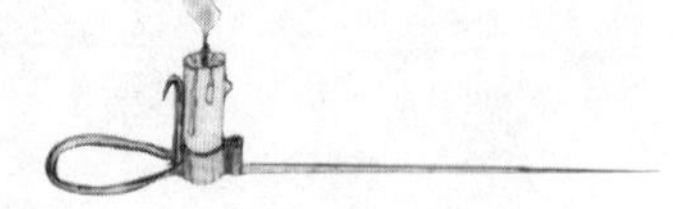

squatted at the front wheel of his pick-up as if to check the tire. Using pliers, he twisted off a protruding bit of the plastic trim surrounding the headlight of the adjacent station wagon and put it in his pocket.

At about one AM he drove to Greenall road, moving slowly and quietly down the darkened street, and parked just beyond Bancroft's bungalow. He waited. All quiet. He eased out of the cab, raised the lid of the tool box and shouldered the stiffened body. He felt his way into the bush, branches whipping across his face, and dropped the corpse. He retrieved the bit of plastic from his pocket and slipped it into a fold in the coat, then raked alder leaves over the body. As he climbed into the pick-up he saw Chris Bancroft cross the road with his dog and pause to stare at the pick-up. He's seen me—I've got to get out of town.

Chapter 8

Bill's Plan

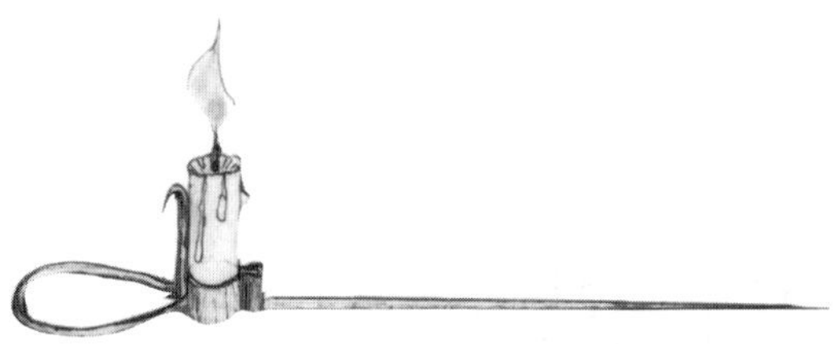

After a long and tiring day—Bill had hiked about 5 miles through bush and over the hills in the morning and later had visited a producing lode mine where he had admired their samples of high-grade ore—he slumped onto the bench against the wall in the Golden Cache pub. He loosened his boot laces as the attentive barmaid placed a sweating glass in front of him.

Most of the patrons were loggers. Blue jeans, red-checked jackets, big boots.Their stumpy figures, as thick as they were wide, could have been roughed out on a giant lathe from 6-foot logs. Several glasses in front of each. A couple of placer miners argued noisily at one table and a trio of young Indians drank quietly against the opposite wall.A pair of tourists in spotless white jackets and slacks, city shoes, flip-up sun glasses projecting forward like insect antennae, sipped their beer, conversing little, watching the regulars as children might watch a cage full of rattlesnakes.

Bill idly played with his wet glass, making a pattern of circles on the glistening table top.As usual, he was wondering what he was going to report to Isaac—he hadn't come up with any brilliant insights and time was run-

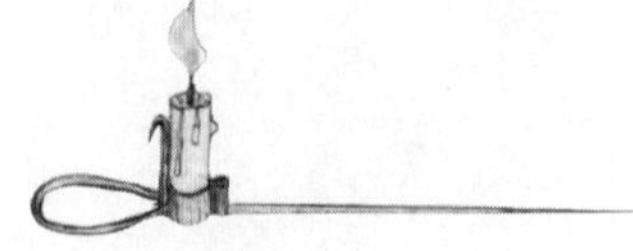

ning out. He tried to fit the day's findings into the general picture. The gold of the gold-quartz mine that he had just visited was a pale, whitish gold, high in silver. He recollected that a placer mine only a few miles from the lode mine produced two kinds of gold: particles of whitish gold, presumably derived from veins at or near the lode mine, and particles of a very pure yellow gold. Where was the yellow gold, which was more abundant in the placer than the white, coming from? He stared at the rings left by his glass on the table top.

He considered the facts once more: The gold from the mine and from all of the veins in its immediate vicinity was white. At the placer operation northeast of the mine area, the gold from the sluices was of two types—white and yellow. He had noticed also that the white gold particles of the placer, presumably originating in the mine area, were more worn and flattened than the yellow, many of the latter being only slightly worn garnet-shaped crystals. Remembering Henry's criteria, he concluded that the white gold had travelled much farther than the yellow. His interest quickening, he concluded that the source of the yellow gold was much closer to the placer operation than was the mine area. In fact, the source of the yellow gold must lie well within a circle centred on the placer, its radius the distance from that placer to the hard-rock mines. Bill marked the position of the placer with a peanut in the centre of a beery circle and marked the position of the lode mine on the circumference with another. He could see no flaw in his reasoning. He realized that he was probably making lots of unfounded assumptions. Nevertheless he was so excited that he almost left without paying.

His mind racing, he went upstairs to his room and unfolded the relevant geological map. He found the position of the placer and drew a circle of radius equal to the distance from the placer to the mine area. The source of the yellow gold had to be inside that circle! Judged by the pronounced difference in the amount of wear on the gold particles, the distance from the source to the placer was not great. But the area of the circle was large. At first Bill was discouraged, but then he decided that he could probably restrict his search to the area underlain by the Snowshoe formation, its sandstone the host formation for nearly all of the gold veins of the district. The mine area was underlain by one band of the Snowshoe sandstone but a second band of the sandstone crossed the middle of his circle. The source of the yellow gold ought to lie in that second belt of sandstone and within the circle.

Bill studied the map closely. At first he found nothing, then he found a tiny map symbol that marked the location of a prospect shaft lying about 2 miles from the placer, and within the sandstone formation. The shaft, about 5 miles from the mine area, had no identifying number, and he could not find a reference to it in the various federal and provincial geological publications dealing with the area. He slept little that night.

Next morning he was up early, cursing the slow cook at the restaurant. He drove east on the main road, passed the placer that produced the two kinds of gold, and crawled up a side road towards the prospect shaft. At the end of the road he figured he was about a mile from the old shaft. He loaded a gold pan, a hammer, and a dozen sample bags into his pack.

Sliding his protractor across his map, he measured the bearing from his position at the end of the road to the prospect shaft. He established this direction with his compass, making a distant tree his immediate target, and

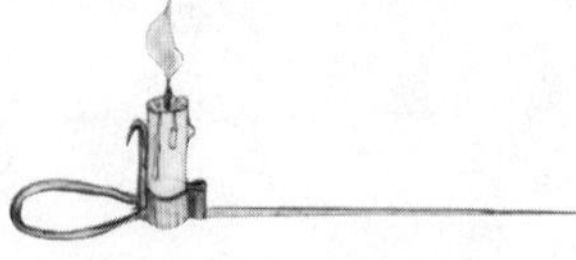

noted the angle this bearing made with the shadows of the tree trunks on the ground. He was thus able, as he strode up the gentle hill, to stay approximately on course without constant reference to his compass. After counting a thousand double paces, knowing that he had walked about a mile, he paused and looked around. Off to his right he spotted some sawn stumps. He knew he was close to the old workings.

Half an hour later Bill stumbled into a shallow slumped-in trench which someone had dug some fifty years before. From it, he spotted a slight rise which turned out to be a grown-over waste pile. Beside it, a depression marked the old prospect shaft, now completely caved in. A few rotting timbers and a rusty shovel blade were the only other signs of human activity.

Rooting around on the waste pile, he found a dozen pieces of rusty quartz. He looked long and hard at these with his hand-lens, but could see only the square openings left by weathered and rotted-out pyrite crystals. He ate his lunch and washed it down with a drink from a creek which trickled in a draw a hundred feet from the shaft. Revived, he positioned a large flat block of sandstone as an anvil, put a chunk of quartz in a sample bag and hammered it until most of the quartz was reduced to sand. He dumped the sand into the gold pan, being careful to recover all of the fine material, and discarded the now ruined bag. He repeated the process until he had half-filled his pan with angular quartz sand, then hurried over to the creek and panned the crushed quartz. Quickly he got rid of the bigger fragments and then panned carefully, reducing his sample to a handful, and finally to a teaspoonful, mostly of fine pyrite with a little quartz.

Now the fun part.

Using a gentle rotary motion, Bill gradually chased the teaspoonful of sand around the trough where the side and bottom of the pan met, spreading out his concentrate and allowing the dense pyrite to lag behind the quartz sand, forming a dull yellow pyrite-rich tail. A glint caught his eye—three microscopic specks of gold. Hands shaking, he fumbled for his hand-lens, but before he could examine the specks, he had lost them in the oscillating slurry. He took several deep breaths, made himself more comfortable, and repeated his careful panning. Finally the motes of gold reappeared at the tip of the pyrite tail. Carefully this time, he held the pan up to his face and peered at them with his hand-lens. Certainly gold. Not only gold, but the bright yellow variety!

He realized that although this vein was not necessarily the source of the yellow gold, it could be one of a group of veins that had, on being partly eroded away, supplied the abundant yellow gold to the nearby placer. The area around the shaft was mantled by deep glacial till and gravel—no bedrock in sight—and apparently had never been explored.

Isaac wanted a proposal for an exploration project. Well, Bill would propose that they explore the area around the old shaft by trenching and drilling. There was good reason to suppose that they would uncover other veins. But first, was the ground open? He'd have to check first thing tomorrow.

That night Bill couldn't sleep—his brain kept returning to scenarios in which, having found a mine, he became famous and rich, and he and a girlfriend, perhaps Julie, soaked up the sun in front of a vine-shaded villa on a Greek island.

Paranoia set in before dawn.

At breakfast, as he wolfed his flapjacks and bacon, Bill

glanced to right and left. Are they onto me? He tried to turn his face into a bland mask. How many of them have already been to that old shaft? Perhaps it's already been restaked. Was I followed yesterday? As he climbed into the pick-up, he studied the rear view mirror—nobody seemed to be shadowing him.

Bill drove into Quesnel, parked, and walked three blocks to the Gold Commissioner's office. As he entered, he risked a glance behind him—only a women pushing a baby carriage. In the office, two men examining a claim map at the end of the long counter looked up suspiciously and swivelled to interpose their bodies so he couldn't see which area they were studying. Bill asked the clerk for the map showing claims to the east of the area he was interested in. He studied this for about ten minutes until he was sure that it was safe to take the next step. He then casually asked for the map that covered the area of the old shaft.

The second map showed a few scattered claims, all cancelled years ago—the area was wide open. Bill concealed his elation, rolled up the map and went back to studying the first one. As he returned the maps to the clerk, the door swung and two grizzled prospectors strode to the counter.

"Hi Joan," they greeted the clerk.

Damn—they know her. Old pals.

Bill saw Joan replace his maps in the rack. Just in time. He nonchalantly left the office. Will that damned girl tell her pals what maps I was looking at? No coffee. I'll get the hell out of here. Rough out my report to Isaac this afternoon and head home tomorrow. As he turned off the highway onto the Wells road, he stared into his rear view mirror. He seemed not to be followed.

CHAPTER 9

BILL MEETS GUS

The Copper Mountain mine lies beside the Similkameen River a few miles south of Princeton. The mine, exhausted and closed down for many years, had produced a concentrate of copper sulfide minerals and this had been shipped to a smelter where the copper metal was extracted. Prohibited from dumping its millions of tons of finely ground mill tailings into the river, the miners had piped the slurried waste to a dyked tailings pond on the outskirts of Princeton. In the early days of mining, the process of extracting the copper minerals from the ore was not very efficient. Consequently, the great expanse of tailings, covering an area of several football fields, contained as much as one tenth of a percent of copper, much iron, and traces of other metals.

Gus was making his weekly trip into Princeton for supplies. His first stop was the liquor store, where he bought a case of beer. Then he visited the general store to stock up on groceries for the next week. As he stowed his purchases in the cab of the truck, he glanced into a bin that occupied much of the truck box. He drove through town to the edge of the tailings pile where he shovelled a few hundred pounds of the fine pyrite-rich sand into the bin. This extra weight, he would explain if anyone questioned

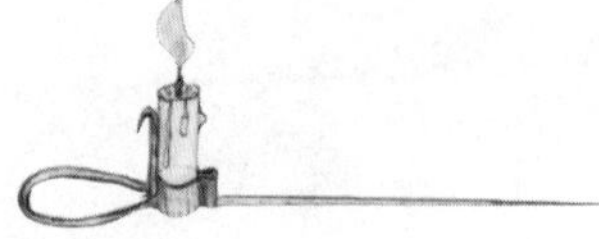

him, gave him extra traction on muddy or icy back roads.

As Gus left town, he was overtaken by a battered sedan carrying six shouting, laughing teen-agers. A beer bottle flew into the ditch. A daubed sign across the rusty doors proclaimed that Princeton Grads were Tops—a bunch of this year's graduates from high school were blowing off steam. The car slowed and, as he turned out to pass it, he glanced to his right and saw a white bum pressed against the side window. Gus was not aware that mooning is an old, perhaps ancient, act of defiance. In the 1820s, Hellenophile medical volunteers were astonished at the number of buttock wounds suffered by Greek fighters in the battles for independence. These wounds were received as the Greeks darted from behind their protective limestone outcrops, turned, dropped their drawers, and scornfully pointed their bums at the Turkish sharpshooters. Gus knew nothing of this; his only thought as he shook his head was: crazy kids.

Some hours earlier, around the time that Gus was setting out for his week's shopping, Bill was shaving in the communal washroom of the Golden Cache Hotel. A descending baritone vibrato, amplified by the plywood sound-box that was the second cubicle, echoed through the room. Bill's neighbour at the next basin lifted his razor and intoned: "Speak again, oh toothless one."

Bill grinned, nicking his lip, washed his razor and went to work on his teeth. Now he heard through the intermittent roar of his toothbrush a series of screams. He was startled, but the other fellows, at various stages of washing or shaving, seemed to be used to this sort of interruption, and carried on with their various activities. Bill was uneasy—this hotel was fairly rowdy since it housed the only beer parlour for 30 miles around, but things were usually pretty quiet after 2:00 or 3:00 AM. The screams continued, now alternating with low-pitched, indecipherable male protestations. Finally Bill could stand by no longer. After wiping the foam from his lips, he hurried down the hall.

Here he found three people grouped around a half-open door, and a gathering crowd keeping a respectful distance. The source of the screams was a middle aged woman of no great physical charms (in Bill's judgement, anyhow). Clutching together the edges of a pink garment, she was standing just inside the room. She screamed intermittently, staring up into the face of a rustic giant, probably a logger. Leaning against the doorpost, tears streaming from eyes like peeled red plums, swaying slightly and obviously drunk, he yelled hoarsely: "Nellie, I love you." His declarations alternated regularly with Nellie's screams like parts in an opera.

The third member of the cast, a smallish fellow who looked as if he had been interrupted as he was dressing, stood in his bare feet just outside the door, fists holding up his trousers. He watched the logger, obviously terrified of him, but at the same time keeping an anxious eye on Nellie.

Bill's curiosity carried him close to the door. It seemed to him that as nobody else was doing anything he could at least make some kind of a mild intercession and perhaps show these locals the power of reasonable persuasion. He tentatively approached the logger.

"Don't you think you should leave the lady alone?" The logger peered at him as if trying to penetrate a thick fog but said

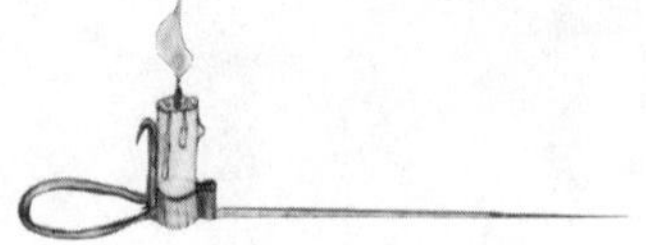

nothing. The effect on Nellie, however, was electric.

"Don't hit him," she shrieked at Bill, "he's got a glass jaw!" Hitting the logger anywhere on his anatomy, including his vitreous jaw, was far from Bill's mind. His main worry was that the logger might lose his grip on the doorframe and fall on him. The logger resumed his declarations and Nellie her responses. Bill became aware of a certain restlessness in the increasing audience—it was obviously expecting some decisive action from this intervenor. Mustering his courage, he interrupted the duet.

"They've called the hotel detective," Bill said, "and he's on his way up. You'd better get going or you'll end up in the jug."

The logger was evidently impressed by this lie and, after a heart-rending "I love you Nellie," shambled off down the hall. Bill felt rather pleased with himself at this, and, gaining confidence, addressed himself to completing the job. Turning to Nellie, who now seemed to regard him with respect, even awe, he spoke sternly to her: "Get back inside and lock the door. You'll be perfectly safe." She gave him a look full of what seemed to be puzzled gratitude and rather hesitantly slipped into the room and shot the bolt.

The third member of the troupe, who had said nothing since Bill's arrival, now muttered: "Hey, wait a minute." He was obviously displeased about something.

Bill, having seen the logger off and saved Nellie from an unknown fate, asked the fellow, seemingly only a bit player in the preceding drama, "You have a problem?" He was confident that he could straighten out any residual difficulty.

"That's my room," the man said, grasping his trousers to his sides and looking at the door.

"Well, what was she doing in your room?"

"She wasn't in my room. I never saw her before. I answered a knock on the door and she slipped in past me."

Bill wondered what Nellie might be up to in there. Had she gone to bed? Was she taking a shower? Was she leaving by the fire escape, a wallet in her hand? He noticed that they were now pretty well surrounded by the throng in the hall. Few, if any, seemed to have heard this last exchange, so he bobbed sideways and slipped back to the washroom to collect his shaving gear, vowing never again to respond to screams from strange women in country hotels.

As he got off to a late start, he was still wondering what Nellie was doing in Room 204. It was Saturday and he was in no hurry—the office would be dead until Monday. He turned east at Cache Creek, towards Kamloops, planning to drive south to Princeton. He drove along, daydreaming of his new gold mine, promotion, and Julie. The highway south of Merritt was under repair and, travelling too fast on a detour, he allowed his front right wheel to sink into the soft shoulder. Helplessly, slowly, he drove off the road and into the ditch. He suffered a wrenched shoulder fighting the wheel as he went over, but there was no serious harm done to him or to the truck. How, though, was he to get back on the road? A number of sympathetic drivers went by but could not help beyond promising to send a tow truck. After about half an hour, a rusty, slow-moving pick-up truck made a U-turn and pulled up. A scruffy old fellow with one eye climbed down into the ditch.

"Looks like you're in trouble, Red," he opined, "Maybe I can help. You're not drunk, are you?"

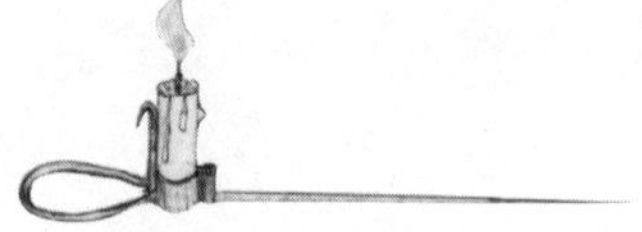

Bill, his shoulder hurting, out of patience, and not much liking being called Red, replied: "No, I'm not, and I don't think you can do much for me with that rig."

"Well, let's see." Gus moved some gear around in the crowded box of his pick-up, hauled out a cable which he hooked around Bill's bumper, attached the other end, and slowly drove ahead. After side-slipping a few yards, Bill's truck was hauled back onto the road. It was now getting dark.

"Gosh, that was quick."

"I've a secret weapon in the back," said Gus with a grin. Bill peered in at the plywood box full of sand, which occupied half the truck bed. "You've got to have lots of weight on the back wheels. Where're you headed?"

"Vancouver."

"You won't make it tonight. Better follow me. The next motel is a long piece down the road. Anyway, come along to my place and have a bite to eat—glad of the company." Bill, a little more shaken up by the mishap than he wanted to admit and also mildly curious about his benefactor, agreed.

They pulled into Gus' spread in pitch darkness. In a few minutes Gus had lit the Coleman and set the fire crackling. After he had fed the dog, he started to prepare a meal of bacon and eggs.

Bill looked around him. There was only one room. Cobwebby rafters could be seen dimly beyond the peeled log beams. Bill looked hard at the elegant flooring which seemed out of place in such a setting. It was made of lengths of clear pine, short ones, about a foot long, alternating with slightly longer ones fitted end to end with well-made mortise and tenon joints. With a smile, Gus explained.

"I made the floor out of dynamite boxes. Salvaged them at the Whipsaw Creek mine, not far from here. Just knocked out the bottoms and opened out the sides and nailed them down."

An ancient cast-iron cookstove with heavy nickel-plate fittings twinkled against one wall. A bench with a couple of galvanized water pails sat next to a sink with a 2-foot wide spruce drain-board. A dipper and a grey towel hung nearby. A swede saw hung on the wall and a Lee-Enfield army rifle stood behind the door. Rough shelves held an old-fashioned radio of Gothic pattern and a few books. The Coleman lamp hung from a beam in the middle of the room over a plank table, two benches and a pair of chairs. Clothes hung on nails above a couple of steel cots and an old trunk occupied a corner.

After supper, sipping their tea, they got to know each other.

"A geologist, eh?" Gus asked. "Who do you work for? Used to do a bit of mining myself."

Bill named his company and outlined what he had been doing in the Cariboo.

"I've got a few claims myself." Gus said. "Four of them. Copper showing, up the hill behind the cabin. The guy I bought the land from drove a 50-foot adit. Didn't find much."

It was now getting late and it was decided that Bill would stay the night.

"It must be pretty quiet around here—no neighbours."

"We keep pretty busy, don't we, King?" Gus rubbed the dog's ears. "You'll see tomorrow there's lots to do. But it's not too quiet. I had a visitor last week. I was up the hill behind the cabin looking for windfalls for firewood. I saw this guy taking mud samples out of the creek, checking

his compass, taking notes. I watched him for a while. He never came near the cabin. Took samples from the creeks, below the old adit. Dug a few samples in the draws behind the claims. Pretty sneaky!"

"A dirt-bagger," said Bill.

"Dirt-bagger?"

"A geochemist from an exploration company collecting soil and mud samples. You didn't talk to him or see his truck?"

"No, I kept away from him and he kept away from me. I've a feeling he'll be back."

Bill shook his head. "Don't figure on it—these guys are all over the place and I'll bet you he isn't the first one on your property!"

The conversation got around to bears and it became clear that Gus hated them.

"A few years ago, I was down at the Coast looking for a new truck. Two of them broke into the cabin—ripped off the door. They cleaned off every shelf, dumped flour, tea, coffee everywhere, punctured every can of food and milk, and left through a window. Just last fall I was treed by a black bear. Probably would have been mauled or killed if my neighbour hadn't come along. Grizzlies can't climb trees unless the branches are strong enough to make a sort of ladder, but black bears go up a bare tree trunk like a squirrel."

Bill, the enthusiastic explainer, said: "Probably grizzlies are too heavy to feel at home in trees. As an animal gets bigger, its weight increases more quickly than its strength and it becomes less agile. There are no 200-pound gymnasts or figure skaters." He was about to explain the theory of scale models but Gus, only rarely having a captive audience, was not to be diverted.

"A prospector I knew in the Yukon was back-packing supplies into his camp about 15 miles from the end of the road. Grizzly killed him. The Mounties figured that the grizzly ambushed him, jumped him from behind, broke his neck before he had time to cock his rifle. A week later, all they found was a bare skeleton, except for his feet which were protected by his boots. Now that grizzly was a meat-eating killer. I can't understand organizations who want to protect grizzlies. What good are they? Nothing feeds on grizzlies or depends on them, so what harm would be done if they were wiped out? But I guess there's nothing wrong with having them in places where there aren't any people."

Gus said that he shot bears whenever he encountered them near his cabin—provided the game warden was far away.

Bill was forced to agree with much of what Gus had been saying. Black bears were a nuisance but usually could be scared off unless they were protecting cubs. But grizzlies were different. They were unpredictable. He and his geological friends respected and feared grizzlies, and with good reason. Several had suffered unprovoked attacks and a few had been mutilated. He had been told by an old-timer that grizzlies had become more aggressive in recent years because a few helicopter pilots thought it great sport to chase and harass them when they came across them in open country above timberline—the monster rearing up, swiping in 15-foot arcs as the teasing chopper pulled up just out of reach. Like King Kong and the fighter planes.

Bill and Gus discussed the problem of protecting oneself from bear attack. Carrying a rifle was impractical in rough country or thick bush. Moreover, placing a bullet in the right spot in a charging grizzly in the few seconds

usually available was a job for an expert shot, since a wounded grizzly was doubly dangerous. Bill had read that Moberley, an early explorer and hunter in the Canadian Rockies, had his own effective technique. When a grizzly had approached within a few tens of yards he would skim his broad-brimmed hat towards it. The startled bear would rear onto its hind legs, its attention diverted by this unusual bird, whereupon Moberley would coolly shoot it through the heart.

For himself, Bill said, in bear country he carried a pocket-sized launcher which shot a small fiery rocket a few hundred feet and could be directed at an attacking bear. Even so, Bill had mixed feelings about its effectiveness. He had heard about a couple of geologists, who, upon meeting a grizzly on a narrow trail, had lobbed a flare a little too high, the burning projectile landing behind the bear. They were trampled and bruised as the frantic bear escaped over them. Bill told of a friend who had a rule for travel in bear country: always choose a partner who can't run as fast as you can.

After breakfast next morning, the dishes washed, they walked up Gus' back road, across the creek, disturbing the red-winged blackbirds clinging to the rushes. A woodpecker machine-gunned in short bursts at the top of a towering cottonwood. They climbed the hill towards the old adit. A grouse exploded like a land-mine under King's nose. From the adit dump they had a grand view of the lake and the surrounding hills. Bill looked down at Gus' cabin and at the flat below the lake.

"What the devil are those?" Bill asked.

At first glance, the flat resembled a heavily shelled battle-field or bombed area. It was pocked by giant craters 5 to 10 yards across. He soon noticed that none of the craters was superimposed on another, thus differing from lunar impact craters or war-time shell-holes. Fifty-foot pines grew in some of the depressions. He turned to Gus, who grinned, pleased that he had to explain such a simple thing to his highly-educated friend.

"Keekwilee houses. Indian houses. They scooped saucers, maybe 3 or 4 feet deep in the ground. A centre post held up roof logs that reached out to the edge of the pit. Like a flattish teepee. The roof covered with sod and earth. They got in and out through a smoke hole in the middle—had a ladder or a notched pole. In some places you can find villages of fifty keekwilee holes along the Fraser River and up Bridge River. Houses all gone."

"How old are they?" asked Bill.

"They were still using them in the late 1800s—there used to be a photograph of one in the lobby of the old hotel in Lillooet. But I've heard that the experts claim that some of the big villages were abandoned hundreds of years ago. If you keep your eye peeled walking around them you can find stone arrow-heads, that sort of stuff. Some have been bull-dozed by people looking for Indian stuff they can sell. Damn that dog. King, get out of there!"

Gus threw a pine cone at the dog who side-stepped just enough to let the missile whiz by. King had been about to supplement his breakfast from a great pile of what looked like brown pigeon eggs. Between fifty and one hundred spilled over the bunch grass. Bill had often wondered by what miracle of peristalsis the moose manufactured these perfectly formed and sized ovoids.

They sat on the dump in front of the adit and Bill broke a few pieces of rock, looking for copper minerals. He found the odd flake of chalcopyrite, the copper-iron sul-

fide and one of the main ore minerals of copper, but the rock was of negligible value and he saw nothing that would encourage him to believe that he was close to a large ore deposit.

He filled his carbide lamp and picked his way through and over the fallen timbers into the adit. A pack-rat had built a nest of grass and twigs on a supporting beam just in out of the weather. Bill screwed up his nose at the acrid stink. A rock ledge was covered with pack-rat dung which over the years by some mysterious natural alchemy had collapsed into a black, shiny, tar-like mass, in form vaguely like a bunch of coalescing grapes. He knew that such accumulations were common in abandoned adits and root cellars in the dry southern interior parts of British Columbia and had puzzled many a prospector. Bill smiled as he recollected that samples of this material were routinely sent for testing to the geology department at the university in Vancouver in the belief that they were asphalt or tar—seeps from unrecognized oil fields. One perplexed but careful prospector had accompanied his 10-pound sample with a list of the few physical properties of the substance that he had been able to determine: "Hardness, about 2; density, near 0.8; colour, black; streak, brown; texture, botryoidal." His final observation seemed to have been written in a rather shaky hand: "When dissolved in water and boiled, it makes a mildly intoxicating drink."

Although Bill found a little pyrite in the adit, a few rusty streaks, and some green copper stain, he saw little to encourage a miner. He marvelled at the persistence of such prospectors. Whoever had driven the adit must have been a determined optimist to continue to labour with so little encouragement. Drill, blast, wait for the fumes to clear, pry, wrestle the wheel-barrow out to the dump, day after day. He would interrupt his mining and go logging or fishing for a few months at a time, earning money for dynamite and grub, thinking—no, knowing—that a giant copper deposit lay concealed a few feet further into the hillside. British Columbia has hundreds of such adits driven by such hopefuls and, indeed, in a few cases such work has led to the development of mines. But Bill knew that most often, if an ore deposit was eventually proved, it was developed years or decades after the first work was done.

Bill reflected that most mining camps had a history of early failure and final success. A typical story runs something like this: A prospector stakes some interesting mineralization. His claims are optioned by a mining company which cautiously spends some money on trenching and sampling. It fails to find enough ore to support a mine and the venture is abandoned, the claims reverting to the prospector. After twenty years of inactivity, the claims are picked up by a new outfit, perhaps encouraged by discoveries nearby, and another cycle of exploration begins, perhaps with a different approach or in a previously untested part of the property. Again, failure to find enough ore and the claims abandoned. Ten years later, metal prices have risen. A prospector scouting the claims becomes lost in the underbrush and falls into an overgrown exploration trench that hasn't been looked at for decades. He takes a sample which runs half a percent of copper, with a trace of gold. His backers, operating on a shoe-string, take this information to a promoter who puts out a misleading prospectus, raises some money and reluctantly spends some of it on trenching, sampling and drilling. Much to his surprise, he finds himself the principal owner of a valuable ore-body. By this time, the original prospector is recycling tea bags in a skidrow hotel room.

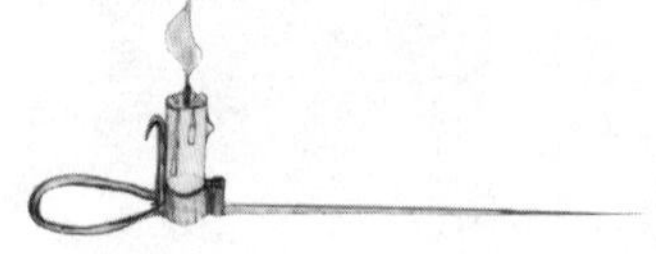

◊ ◊ ◊

Next morning Bill packed his gear and said thanks and goodbye to his new friend. As he drove south towards Princeton, his mind saturated with thoughts of quartz veins criss-crossed by seams of yellow gold, he thought of the Conquistadors and of the tons of gold shipped to Spain. Of course, not all of it made it back. Many gold-laden galleons were lost in hurricanes in the Caribbean. Others, loaded with Inca gold, foundered on the Pacific side. As the hundred millionth pine tree flashed by, he asked himself: what would be the fate of such a gold-laden ship? His imagination took over.

A Spanish galleon takes on 20 tons of gold at Callao, Peru. Originally these ingots were placer gold which had been fabricated by the Incas into ornaments and sacred statuettes. The ship sets sail for the Isthmus. Caught in an August storm, the ship's wormy planking opens up and she sinks in 3,000 fathoms onto the western flank of the South American oceanic trench. Quickly, in as little as two thousand years, she rots, and the gold ingots sink into the bottom ooze and mud.

The oceanic tectonic plate, made up of volcanic oceanic crust, creeps eastward at the rate of 5 centimetres per year, 5 metres per century, 50 kilometres per million years (about the rate of growth of one's finger-nails) and dives under the edge of the South American continental plate. In 4 million years (the blink of a geological eye) the shipment of gold has slipped under South America and is at a depth of 100 kilometres where the temperature (about 850 degrees Celsius) is such that the gold, mud, ooze, and the underlying volcanic rock, melt, forming a few tens of

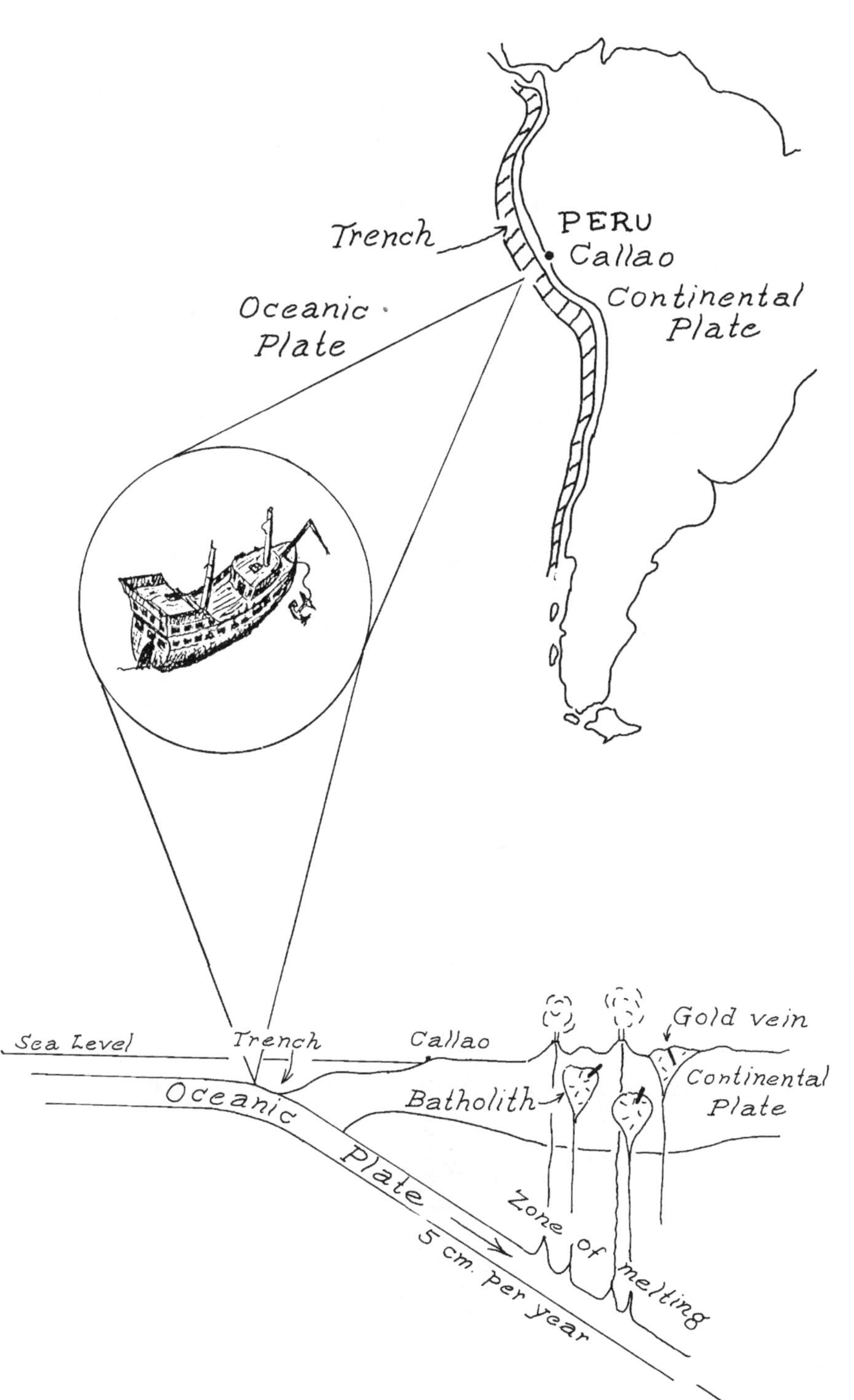
Trench
PERU
Callao
Oceanic
Plate
Continental
Plate
Sea Level
Trench
Callao
Gold vein
Oceanic
Batholith
Continental
Plate
Plate
Zone of melting
5 cm. per year

cubic kilometres of magma. This magmatic melt oozes upward to cool and crystallize as large granitic bodies known as batholiths. Here and there some of this molten rock leaks out onto the surface forming volcanoes in a landscape not unlike the present day volcanic terrain of central Mexico.

The molten Inca gold lags behind the magma and dissolves in watery silica-rich solutions which work upwards into fractures in the overlying still hot granitic rock and form quartz veins laced with films of gold. All this taking place a few kilometres below the land surface. After another 10 million years (blink), weathering and erosion have removed these few kilometres of rock. The gold veins are exposed at the surface where the dank, warm tropical climate hurries the disintegration of the quartz veins and releases the indestructible gold into the soil. This finds its way into a stream where a small-eared, web-footed aquatic pack-rat, of a species unknown in the twentieth century, selects a golden nugget to add to its cache of pretty stones. This in the year 14,000,004 A.D.

Did any of this, Bill wondered as he approached Princeton, have implications for his Cariboo gold veins?

Probably not. Maybe.

◊ ◊ ◊

Monday morning. Bill arrived at the office early, bustled past Julie with no more than a nod, shut his office door and got to work on his report.

A bit miffed, Julie said to Chris: "He hardly said good morning. Did he say anything to you?"

"Not much. I asked him how it went. He looked mysterious and excited but didn't tell me anything. Maybe he's found something. He'll be handing his report to Jay. Jay'll check it over and evaluate it for Isaac."

Bill's brief report was completed by Wednesday.

◊ ◊ ◊

Wednesday night. Ben Richards lay on his bed in Cache Creek. Ten o'clock and still not dark. The sweat rolled off his body—the room was still hot as hell. He heard indistinct voices from the room below and memories crowded into his mind of that disastrous night when everything started to fall apart.

Nine-year-old Ben lay in his cot in his attic room, the full moon framed in the window that looked down into the corral. The vague threatening forms of discarded furniture, old trunks, boxes and battered suitcases lurked where roof met floor. A horse snuffled and moved its hooves. He sat up and listened.

His mother's piercing voice: "What mortgage?"

Ben's father muttered something.

"Mortgaged our farm? Our farm?"

More muttering. He distinguished the word 'lawyer'.

"Needed money for the lawyer—fees, expenses, appeals—and now the bank is foreclosing on our farm?"

Ben was able make out the words 'Cougar Lake'.

"Cougar Lake. Cougar Lake! That's the last straw."

A long silence.

"We're finished—I work like a slave to keep this two-bit

farm going and you piddle it away on worthless mining claims and lawyers. I've had enough. I'm leaving.'

More mumbling. He made out the name 'Ben'.

"To hell with that. He's your boy, you look after him." A door slammed.

CHAPTER 10

BILL IN LOVE

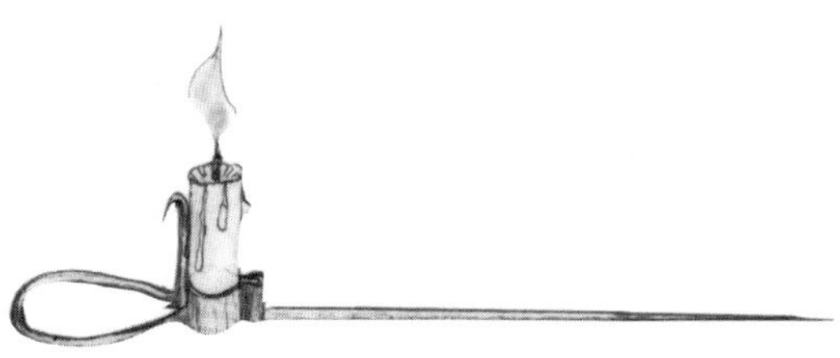

Now more or less at loose ends, Bill decided to try his luck with Julie. At university, paying his way with summer earnings, he had had little money to spend on girls. Or time. He had had to work hard at his courses. Not that he didn't think about girls—as he fought his way through problems in calculus or statistics his mind would wander, and every integral sign became a narrow waist and swelling hip, every bell curve a rounded breast.

After observing Julie's movements for a couple of days Bill contrived to come by her desk in the late afternoon just after quitting time when the rest of the office people had left for the day.

"Hi Julie. Still here?" His stupid question was received with a smile.

"Had a few things to finish up. Glad to be back in town?"

"Sure am. But it was interesting up there. Have you been to Barkerville?"

"My room-mate and I were there a couple of years ago—fascinating town." Bill's face fell and she added quickly: "Liz and I had a great time—trying to pan gold, canoeing."

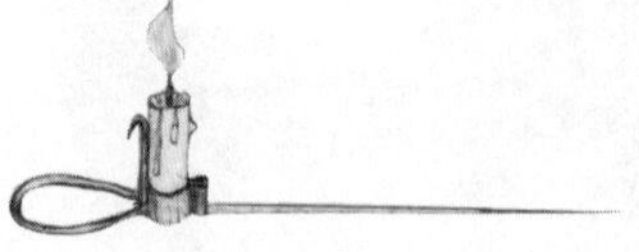

Relieved, he asked, "I'd like to hear about it. Say, why don't we have dinner some time? We could compare notes."

"Well, yes, thanks. Sounds like fun."

"How about tonight?"

She appeared to think for a decent interval, as if making sure that she had room on her social calendar and, finding to her surprise that this was a free evening, replied, "Yes, sounds great."

"I'll pick you up at seven-thirty."

◊ ◊ ◊

Bill was a little shaken when she came to her door. She was wearing a simple, rather clinging dress with a cross-over top that emphasized her breasts and fit smoothly over her hips. The dress, high heels and a bit of eye shadow had transformed her, in Bill's startled eyes, into an exotic long-legged creature right off the cover of one of the glossy magazines that crowded the checkout stands at the supermarket. Bill was wondering simultaneously whether he was the luckiest fellow in the world or whether he was a bit out of his league. Julie, however, put him at ease, perhaps sensing that he hadn't had much experience with women.

They drove to one of the many Greek restaurants in the West Broadway district. This establishment was much like a dozen others: blue and white checked tablecloths, walls decorated with shepherd's crooks, hammered brass and bright woolen rectangular bags from Crete. A ceiling fan flickered silently over their heads. Plaintive ballads sung by lovesick Greeks filled the spicy air. For years to come, whenever he entered a Greek restaurant, the aroma of mixed spices would carry him back to his first date with Julie.

Bill was still a little unstrung by the appearance of his companion. His agitation was justified as he noticed heads turning at nearby tables as he shifted her chair. Damn, I should have worn a jacket. Idiot! The menu was unfamiliar to him but with help from the waiter they ordered. Bill had a beer and Julie a glass of white wine. Their conversation was awkward at first but by the time dinner was on the table they were talking easily.

"Have you done any camping?" he asked.

"A little. Liz and I canoed around the Bowron Lakes." I wish I'd worn something a little less formal. Damn.

"That's more than a little. I've never seen them. I'd like to do that some day." God, I'd love to take her camping.

Julie described the Bowron Lakes area, a provincial recreational park lying east of Barkerville in the Cariboo. Separated by short portages, the lakes formed a rectangle whose perimeter was about 60 miles. Flanked by mountain peaks, the area was uninhabited and completely unspoiled.

"Birds would fly over the canoe and perch on my hat," Julie said. "Moose paid no attention to us."

"What did you do for food?" Bill asked.

"Well, we certainly didn't eat like this," pointing her fork at her well-filled plate, "we mostly used dehydrated food—we had to keep the weight down—there are several portages. It takes ten or so days to go around the chain of lakes, unless you hurry. I hear that it is becoming so popular that reservations have to be made weeks ahead with the parks people." That tie doesn't suit his colouring—green would be better.

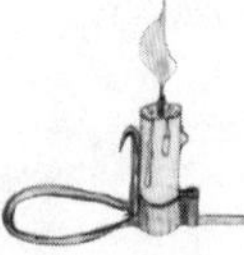

In a scant half hour Bill had fallen head over heels. Be sensible, he warned himself. Does she have a boyfriend? She hasn't mentioned one. No engagement ring. She was free tonight but maybe she's booked solid for the rest of the week. Or maybe she doesn't like men. She hesitated when I asked her. God, what beautiful eyes. How old is she?

"Gosh. How old were you when you made that trip? Weren't your parents worried about you?"

"Oh, we were both eighteen," Julie said. "And we didn't run into any problems. A bear tried to get at our food but we had hung our packs from a tree branch."

"When did you go around the lakes?"

"Oh this was a few years back." Julie smiled. The sly rascal—he's trying to find out how old I am. Well, too bad. I wish he'd quit grinning. Wonder if he's ever been out to dinner with a girl before. What nice strong hands, long fingers, keeps his nails short. And clean. I wonder if he likes red nail polish? She clenched her hands and then defiantly flattened them.

"I'd like to canoe the lakes some day," Bill said. "But I've never travelled in a canoe." Damn. Well, she's probably around twenty. She likes camping. The vague outline of a camping trip began to form in his mind.

They went to a nearby movie. Bill's mind was not on the film. He was inventing fantastic scenarios revolving around Julie. He dropped her off at her door and after a few minutes of small talk, they kissed. Bill drove home a very happy man.

For the next week he was very unsettled. On the one hand, he was in love. Julie was constantly in his thoughts; he saw her daily, and she seemed to like him. On the other hand, two days after he had submitted his proposal for exploration in the Cariboo, he was edgy and irritable, anxiously waiting for some reaction and imagining all sorts of disastrous outcomes.

His principal worry was that some other geologist had had the same idea about the white and yellow gold, had tested it, and found that it was nonsense. Even more worrying was the possibility that some other company had stumbled onto the notion and even now was staking the ground and assembling equipment for a program of trenching and drilling. But even if they hadn't figured it out for themselves, perhaps Jay had blabbed while holding forth at one of the fashionable bars which he no doubt frequented. Or maybe he had quietly and deliberately tipped off the geologist of a rival company and would be rewarded with the offer of a better job, stock options and bonuses. Bill didn't trust him—anyone who affected a pigtail and wore highly polished black shoes could not be depended on. Nonsense. More likely Jay had read the report and had tossed it into the waste basket as unsubstantiated hypothetical nonsense. No, he couldn't do that—Isaac would want to know what Bill had been up to. More likely, Jay had passed the report on to Isaac and he, the reactionary old conservative, not wanting to commit money to a wild idea, had put it aside. He's probably wondering whether he has made a mistake hiring me, Bill thought. Jeez, I may be looking for a job next week.

And so his thoughts went round and round. Bill was suffering the pangs and doubts of every inventor, discoverer and innovator. A new idea once arrived at, understood and digested, becomes familiar and trivial and the inventor imagines that what he can see so clearly is obvious to everybody. He feels that he must protect his discovery, which is sitting there for everyone to see, by patent or

copyright by noon today or he will have lost everything. Such thoughts as these were partly offset by his visions of being in charge of an exploration program in the Cariboo during which he uncovers half a dozen rich veins, becomes famous and wealthy, and carries Julie off to Greece. Sunny beaches, Julie in a bathing suit, candle-lit dinners. Waiting for a decision, Bill couldn't concentrate on anything and couldn't accomplish anything. During this time he took Julie to lunch and dinner several times, but he was not good company—he was preoccupied, worried, on edge. Julie understood his problem, thought he was over-reacting, and tried to reassure him.

◊ ◊ ◊

At the next staff meeting, Chris was making his usual covert appraisal of those around the table and soon sensed that Bill and Julie were exchanging glances that were something more than casual greetings. Aha, he thought, an office romance?

Chris' eyes swivelled left and lit on Jay Bateman's massive gold cuff-links. So Jay's going to make a proposal. Must have something to do with Bill's work in the Cariboo. Hope he remembers to mention Bill—Jay's a little slow to pass credit around. Why is he like that? Chris' mind wandered off on another genealogical speculation. Upper-class arrogance. Rich man's son—spoiled rotten. Old English stock. Part of the Toronto Establishment. Tons of money. Upper Canada College. University of Toronto. Fraternity. Snob network.

As usual, Chris had it all wrong. Jay's father, Ramon Batista, a driller at the Cliffside gold mine in northern Ontario, had been dismembered and buried in a rock-burst, 6,000 feet below the snowy landscape. Jay's mother had survived on a widow's pension. Early on, Jay had set out on his only avenue of escape: he excelled at school, foregoing hockey, abandoning friends and winning a scholarship to university. He changed his name from Jesus Batista to Jay Bateman. He worked single-mindedly on his studies, clawed his way to prize after prize, and on graduation accepted a job with the conservative and prestigious Magnalode. A fast learner, he had quickly assumed the manner and trappings of the power brokers.

Julie put down her notebook and pen and glanced around the room. I wish I could tell what Chris is thinking. He's so damned relaxed. No ambition? I wish someone would tell him not to wear black shoes with brown trousers. Now Jay: he's got real color sense. And nice clothes. Really stuck on himself. Probably has an inferiority complex. Never really relaxed. Creepy. He stands too close when he talks. He's never invited me out again. Did he expect me to fall into bed on the first date? She looked to the left at Carl. He never gives me the usual appraising once-over. Sexless as a fish. What does he do for kicks, except tidy his office. Like to see his home. Hobbies? His wife seems normal enough, a little restrained? Here comes Isaac. I wish he'd wear a tie and look the boss. Looks more like a farmer than the boss in charge of a million dollar budget. I wish Bill wouldn't stare at me all the time. What nice blue eyes. It's nice to be noticed but he overdoes it. What would it be like to be married to him? He could be lots of fun. I'll bet he's thought about it. What kind of kids would we have—his red hair and freckles and me being dark?

Bill was feeling relieved that Isaac had smiled at him as he passed him in the hall. But what exactly does the old

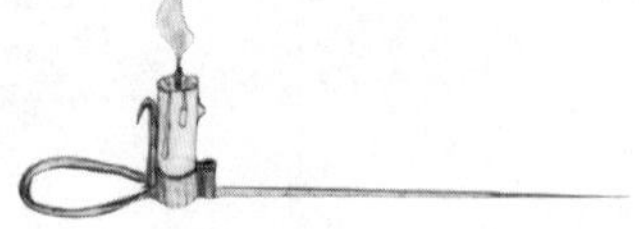

bugger think of my idea?

Isaac settled himself beside Julie, dropping a couple of files on the table and glanced around, counting heads. Bill studied him for clues.

Isaac flicked a glance at Jay, thinking: This is mostly Bill's proposal. But you'd never know it, listening to Jay. He's pushing it pretty hard—he doesn't often get excited. It'll take most of what's uncommitted in this year's budget. Maybe more. If it's a bust, Toronto won't like it. If it's a success, it'll give us a breather. A promotion? Back to Toronto where the big plays are? No thanks. Should I send Jay or Bill to the Cariboo? Isaac looked at Bill. He's nervous as a coyote. He's done a good job. Why is he staring at Julie? Something going on there. Oh to be young.

Jay was aware that he had played down Bill's part when he revised Bill's exploration program. Glancing at Bill, thinking: he gave me a pretty vague proposal—I've refined it, made it into a practical proposition, and sold it (I think) to Isaac. Bill's got no reason to complain.

Chris, off in cloud-land, shifted his buttocks. These goddam hard chairs—talk about bevelled buns, facetted glutes, polygonal nates. He looked across at Isaac. Jew? Greek? Lebanese? His name's no help—he's no more a McLean than I'm a Mandela. Armenian or Turk? Chris's mind slid sideways: perhaps like Ambler's character: a fig packer from Smyrna. Ha. A rag picker from Ragusa. A coke sacker from Cardiff. A gold beater from Gondwana. A woodpecker from— Isaac cleared his throat.

"Jay has an interesting proposal to make," Isaac announced, and he nodded to him to go ahead. Bill's heart beat faster. Julie winked at him. Jay passed around photocopies of his proposal for exploration in the Cariboo.

"Gold has hit bottom and all the experts say it's on the

way up again. Basically, I agree. As you know, Bill has been up at Wells, checking recent activity in the area and attempting to put together some sort of play, possibly for this summer. He's come up with an interesting idea which with a good deal of refining and modification I have developed into a viable proposal for a modest exploration program. He has got some fairly shaky evidence pointing to an area not far from the producing mines, an area that hasn't been properly looked at for fifty years or more."

Bill felt pleased but a little uneasy.

"Mind you," Jay continued, "the prospect that has caught our eye is shown on Johnson and Uglow's 1923 Geological Survey map and sooner or later somebody would have gotten curious about it."

Bill's smile faded.

"However, as outlined in this summary," Jay said, waving his photocopy, "we have some evidence suggesting that it would be worthwhile doing some trenching to see what's there. The area is completely covered by drift and there's not an outcrop within a mile. According to the government maps the showing is in the right formation and the claims have long since reverted to the Crown so we can pick up the property by staking. So it'll only cost us peanuts. I've put together a proposal for trenching and sampling, and, if we get any encouragement, the area will be easy to drill. I've gone over the reports and Bill brought down a few grab samples from the dump—these average almost two tenths of an ounce per ton. Not bad. I recommend that we get up there and get the show on the road. I think we've got the jump on the competition but we should move fast."

Jay expanded on the proposal. At first he gave Bill credit for his work, but as Jay warmed to his subject, Bill's part

became less and less prominent. Jay was a persuasive talker. In the end, to Bill's dismay, it was made to appear that Jay had taken a rather nebulous, tentative suggestion of Bill's and had made it into a practical and promising exploration program.

Carl spoke up: "Sounds like a good bet to me. But shouldn't the first move be a geochemical survey of the area? This might provide some targets. It would involve some surveying and soil sampling."

A hairy parabola became a straight line as Jay dismissed this suggestion: "If you stop and think for a minute"—his tone of voice implied that Carl didn't think, or couldn't—"this would be the best way to call attention to the area and our interest in it. This particular area hasn't been looked at for years. The district's full of placer miners and prospectors, not to mention scouts from other companies. They'll be watching like hawks. Let's be smart on this one"—another dig at Carl—"and move fast."

"Have you considered the effect of glaciation in this area?" Chris asked mildly. "I mean, supposing the placer gold has been moved bodily by the ice, and redistributed later by streams. I mean couldn't this really foul up the theory?"

Jay dismissed this objection, not troubling to hide his contempt.

"Our best confirmation is that it works," Jay said. "The bottom line is that we found a vein, with gold." Bill squirmed at the 'we'. "The right kind of gold, just where it ought to be. Let's show some decision here. Every play is a gamble—this seems to be a better than average one, could be world class. If we don't go after it, someone else will. We aren't the only ones who can figure this out!" He was now nodding vigorously as he spoke, driving home the force of his argument. "And if we're going to do anything this summer, we've got to get a move on. We can collapse the time frame a little if Isaac phones Toronto this morning and we stake right away."

Isaac didn't like being told what to do, but he put aside his irritation. "It looks like a good bet and I agree we can't sit on it," he said. "I'll recommend it to Toronto and I think they'll go for it. We can check out the critical area, and it'll cost less than $100,000 to get some answers. Jay — your Bridge River crew will have to get along without you for a few weeks. You'll go up to the Cariboo as soon as confirmation comes from Toronto. Bill, you know the area, you'll go along and give Jay all the help you can. We'll start by trenching but we could be drilling in a few weeks. Next meeting in a couple of weeks."

Back at his desk, Bill was upset that Jay would be in charge. After thinking it over, however, he realized that Jay had much more experience than he in the handling of men and setting up drill programs and it was probably a sensible arrangement. But he was angry that Jay had taken nearly all the credit for the proposal.

At his apartment that night, Bill lay in the tub. He felt good. No. Euphoric. He was unhappy that Jay had hogged most of the credit for the Cariboo project, but Isaac had praised his work and the proposal was going to be acted upon. And he was going out with a wonderful girl. He gazed over the pale landscape in which his belly button lay concealed. Out of sight, out of mind. But it occurred to him about once a year that he should check his navel. He didn't like doing it—it seemed a dangerously vulnerable orifice and he feared that if he stuck his finger in it, it

might break through to god-knows-what organ or compartment and on withdrawal be followed by an extrusion of slippery, bloody bits of who-knows-what. But today seemed to be a lucky day and since it ought to be done, he would do it. He tensed his abdominal muscles and probed gingerly with his little finger. Aha—a clump of sodden fluff the size of a bean, no doubt made up of contributions from underwear, pajamas and shirts. Under the fluffy ball some dark gritty material. He cautiously reamed it out and examined it closely. A bit of twig, a probable seed, some nondescript debris. Should do this more often. Probably from that last trip where I was fighting through that shoulder-high brush on the hill above that placer showing. The fluff on top of the vegetable bits must have accumulated since that last expedition. As he worked out the sequence of the various layers, he considered a project, perhaps suitable for an academic thesis. The student, armed with a tiny spoon, tweezers, capsules and notebook, would ask: "Pardon me, sir (or madam), I'm making a study of the stratigraphy of belly button deposits. Could you spare me ten minutes?" His mind wandered to Julie. He climbed out. Don't want to be late.

◊ ◊ ◊

That evening Bill and Julie went to dinner at a small restaurant overlooking a marina in False Creek in downtown Vancouver. They sat in a corner seat, at the window, watching the setting sun. A fresh breeze rattled wire halyards against hundreds of aluminum masts—the tapping of ten thousand tinkers. A heron side-slipped through a cat's cradle of stays, spreaders and boom-lifts, stalled, and stepped down from the air. It slow-marched to the end of the dock and froze, beak just above the water.

After dinner Julie invited Bill around to see her apartment and to meet Liz, her room-mate.

Liz, a part-time university student, worked at a nearby pharmacy. She was very different from Julie. Her pale elfin face was framed in loose black curls. She wore enormous horn-rimmed glasses, tiny silver earrings and a silver chain. Slight figure. She looked dainty and vulnerable. Her arms and legs were thin and elegant. Practical Bill wondered at her fragile ankles which looked no more robust than his thumb. She seemed to be delicate and defenseless and exuded an air of innocence, even naivety. Her sweet soft voice reinforced an impression of unworldliness. She aroused in Bill a feeling that she needed protecting from the harshness of the world.

Knowing that Julie liked Bill, and thinking to please her, Liz went out of her way to be pleasant to him and soon they were talking like old friends. She asked about his work and he told her that he was soon going to the Cariboo to look at a new gold prospect.

After days of self-doubt and uncertainty, Bill was feeling intense relief. His mind kept coming back to the fact that his project had been approved. He was drunk with relief as his spirits rebounded. So the compulsive and enthusiastic explainer, anxious that everyone should understand how and why things work, described at length how he had zeroed in on the potential gold mine. Liz listened, not understanding much of his bubbling explanation and appearing more interested than she really was, trying to be agreeable to Julie's new boyfriend. Bill, on the other hand, exerted himself to be attentive to Liz, hoping to gain approval from Julie. After all, she was Julie's best

friend. The talk became more general. It turned out that Liz knew some of the professors Bill had had at the university.

"Did you take first year English from Ambrose?" he asked.

"I did. Never skipped a lecture. He used to stand behind his desk swinging his watch on its chain. The watch would pass within an inch of the desk—the class waited for it to hit and fly into a million pieces. It never hit, but we always hoped."

"He did that with us too," said Bill. "I think it was a trick to keep us awake."

Julie ventured: "Why would he have to keep you awake? I mean, weren't you interested?"

Bill turned to her. "It's hard to explain. You'd have to have been there. We had long reading lists—most of the work was done in our own time. He really didn't teach us a heck of a lot." He swivelled back to Liz. "Did you ever read all those books?"

Bill and Liz were enjoying themselves, each trying to top the other's anecdote. Julie, who had not been to university, unable to make much of a contribution to the conversation, tried to be agreeable and interested but she began to feel left out.

"Did he ever tell you about the time he was on Vesuvius? Dante was his specialty. He told us, straight-faced, 'Two of the world's greatest scholars in the field of medieval studies were sitting on the rim of Vesuvius, looking over Naples on the one hand and Pompeii on the other, and I turned to Radcliffe and said etc. etc.' But he really wasn't stuck on himself—I think he just liked to talk and couldn't resist a good line."

Neither he nor Liz realized that Julie was being neglected, and as Bill innocently made some extra effort to be nice to Julie's friend, dredging up recollections of some of the famous students of their day, Julie became quieter and quieter. Bill ploughed blindly on. For the first time in his life, he found himself the centre of attention of two lovely females and his usual good judgement went out the window. When he left for home, he was dismayed when Julie rather frostily bid him goodnight. No goodnight kiss and tight embrace. What have I done? he wondered.

Two hours later, Bill was still wide awake, running over the evening's events, wondering what had gone wrong. Had Julie found a new boyfriend? Who? Not Jay! Bill shivered at the thought. He looked at his watch—3:00 AM. He closed his eyes. Wide awake. He concentrated on a technique that he had found useful on other sleepless nights. Kill off thoughts as soon as they appear. The idea was to think of nothing, to have a completely empty brain. To make his mind a blank. As soon as a thought entered his head, he obliterated it—pulling blinds down over windows, closing doors and turning pictures to the wall. Images and visions would creep around the window blind, ooze under the door or stream through the keyhole only to be immediately smothered and replaced by blackness, by nothing. His method seemed to be working—he started to doze. Now his guard relaxed, and he saw Julie in the office or in the restaurant. Immediately he was wide awake. A round lost. Try again. Thoughts germinated, swelled, were nipped in the bud. Scenes from the past were wiped from the screen. Don't think about what you're trying to do. Blank mind; wipe it clean, like washing the Beetle—must get a new car—muffle it, choke it! After several cycles of thought suppression, his system triumphed and he slept.

Next day at the office, Julie, having spent much of the

night considering Bill's unfaithfulness, was thoroughly angry and would hardly speak to him. Bill was perplexed and spent the day in futile speculation. What could he have done to provoke such a reaction?

Two days later, Jay and Bill left for the Cariboo. They took with them a crew who would stake a block of claims centred on the old shaft and covering a large part of the Snowshoe formation lying inside Bill's magic circle.

When Bill left Vancouver, there had been no reconciliation with Julie and he was puzzled, hurt and depressed.

Sunday afternoon. Getting close to the longest day of the year. Chris dozed in his deck chair. He had spent the morning thinning the apples and stamping flat several mole hills which had appeared overnight.

How to get rid of the little beggars? Perhaps his methods were wrong—brute force and intimidation had failed. Perhaps a more subtle approach was needed. As Chris dozed in his canvas chair, a scheme formed in his mind. He would find a nest of moles and abduct two or three mole kittens, then construct a pen with walls of wire mesh extending far into the ground. He would bring the babies up, feed them earthworms, play with them, gain their confidence, even love, and train them to scatter the spoil from their tunnels evenly over the grass, rather than pushing up those offending hills. Like captives in Stalag IX disposing of the sand from their escape tunnels. This mole-supplied top dressing would rejuvenate the lawn. Having trained these youngsters, he would release them into the underground as moles in the hope that they would indoctrinate their cousins in the new methods of tunnel-waste disposal.

Chris woke with a start, his neck in a crick, aware that he had had a pleasant dream. Unable to recall the subject or the reason for his satisfaction, he knew only that it had had something to do with the garden. As he adjusted to a slightly more comfortable position, he thought of the Spanish saying: *How nice it is to have nothing to do, and afterwards to rest.*

◊ ◊ ◊

Ben Richards sat in the pub in Cache Creek scanning the Kamloops Herald. The paper steadied as he found the item:

ASHCROFT, July 20. R.C.M.P. are investigating the apparent hit-and-run death of Jack Sutherland of Ashcroft. His body was found yesterday on the branch road connecting Ashcroft and the Trans-Canada. He suffered massive head injuries. Death was instantaneous.

The well liked Sutherland, age 70, was the mining recorder in Ashcroft for thirty years. He supervised much of the frantic staking of the major copper properties in Highland Valley in the sixties and settled many an acrimonious dispute. He is survived by two daughters, Edna, who lives in . . .

Kamloops Herald July 20

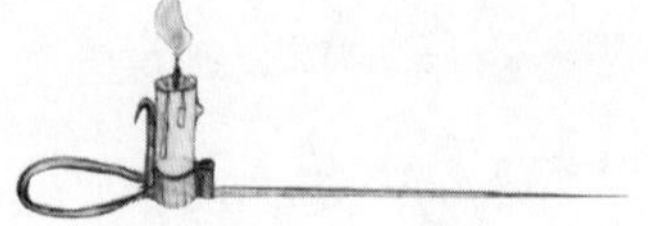

Ben nodded. They found him fast enough. But why nothing about Bancroft's wife? She's missing. Aren't they looking for her? Stupid bastards!

Chapter 11

Boris and Mousy of Howe Street

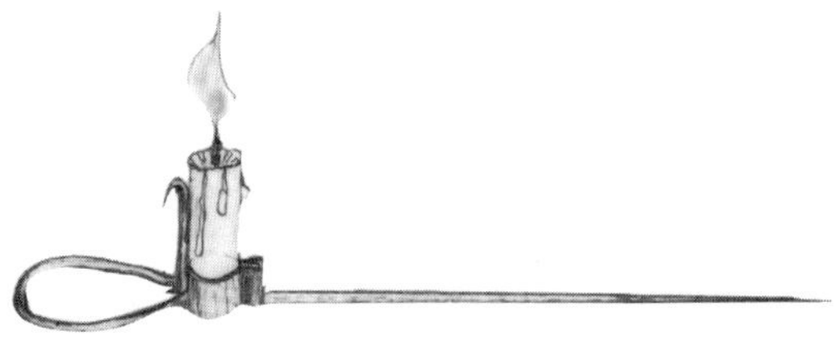

"Hi Liz."

Liz was in the Graduate Student Centre cafeteria, stirring her morning coffee. She moved her briefcase from the table and Steve sat down.

Steve Collins—short neat brown hair, alert blue eyes, cheek-bone jogged by steel-rimmed lenses, open-necked plaid shirt, jeans, comfortable moccasin-type shoes—was a graduate student in geology. He usually spent the summer months working for a mining company but this year was staying in town, in the university's geological laboratories, carrying on research for his master's degree. Like many of the graduate students in geology, he enjoyed a good life and seemed to be in no great hurry to get his degree. Well-paying jobs with exploration companies lasted through the summer vacation. During the winter, most graduate students held assistantships which required attendance for only a few hours a week, many in junior-level teaching laboratories, and these didn't interfere with weekend skiing. And there were other sources of income. Steve and his mates exchanged information about new mineral finds—news picked up while working at their summer jobs. Often they would have vital drilling results

long before they were divulged to the general public. Making use of such information, they played the stock market. A few were so successful that they were almost ready to retire on their profits before they had won their degrees.

After they had exchanged the usual small talk, Steve asked: "And how's that glamorous room-mate of yours? Has she got a steady boyfriend? What's cooking down at Kingfisher?"

Liz hesitated for a moment. "I gather they're excited about a new gold find in the Cariboo. But I don't know anything about it."

"Whereabouts?"

"I don't know. Somewhere not too far from the old mines."

Steve changed the subject, talking of mutual friends, his impending sailing holiday in the Gulf Islands and describing progress in his research project. He then gradually steered the conversation back to Kingfisher. He managed to wheedle from Liz a good deal of what Bill had told her.

Steve made his way to the nearest telephone and called Behemoth Enterprises. He had worked for the company during the previous summer, preparing a report on a small asbestos showing in the McDame area. He and Boris Gundelfinger, Behemoth's president, had hit it off from the beginning and had become good friends.

"Boris. I may have some hot information for you—I'll be down to the office in half an hour."

Steve parked his rusty Jeep on Howe Street where most of the mining property promoters had their offices. As he stepped off the elevator into deep wall-to-wall carpet, he was confronted by the name Behemoth

Enterprises in 6-inch high gold letters. Recorded music filled the air. He touched the heavy gold bar on the thick glass door and it opened magically. The walls were panelled in pale oak over which were ranged large framed photographs of mines and mining tycoons famous in British Columbia. A tall blonde beauty sat behind a carved oak counter, her hair chaotic and tangled as if she had just emerged from the shower. Heavy makeup. Her dark eye-shadow suggested to Steve that she had been on the losing side in a fist fight. Her half-inch-long crimson talons made him wonder how she managed the typewriter.

"Hi Stevie, I've missed you," she crooned. "When are we going to make that trip to Hawaii?" Steve was never sure whether he was supposed to take Patti's invitations seriously.

"Hi Patti. Boris is expecting me."

Feigning deep disappointment, she wiped an imaginary tear and nodded him through to an inner office. Boris rose from behind his desk and extended a giant hand.

"Hello, Steve. Long time no see. Si'down. Coffee?" He pressed a switch and spoke into the intercom. "Patti sweetheart. Get us some coffee." Turning back to Steve, Boris asked, "Well, what's up?"

Bright blue eyes startlingly set off by thick black lashes under dark bushy eyebrows. Thick wavy greying hair. Strong white teeth beneath an imperial nose. Boris was a big man, six foot four, carrying a generous belly which he made no attempt to hide and which seemed to radiate prosperity. He wore an expensive suit, heavy gold wristwatch and a signet ring set with a large diamond.

Boris had learned his trade in Toronto, starting as a clerk in a stockbroker's office. He was hard-working and smart

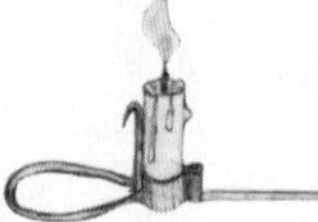

and was soon a floor trader at the stock exchange. When he saw that most of the trading was through promoters and those promoters were making bags of money, he moved into promotion. After the Fandango scandal he moved west.

In Vancouver Boris was very successful. His activities were not limited to mining properties—he promoted a wide variety of projects and ideas. One of his promotions was Photosculpture International. Its assets consisted of a process for converting holograms into three dimensional replicas. Just as a two-dimensional image could be fixed on photographic film, so a three-dimensional hologram could be reproduced as an exact replica in three dimensions by spraying the hologram with an appropriate fixative. Since the company's breakthrough formulas had not yet been completely protected by patents, the process had not been demonstrated publicly.

Another of Boris' companies, Realworld Mirrors, would supply the giftie that Robbie Burns had yearned for. This was a reflecting device made of two mirrors fastened together at exactly ninety degrees, allowing one to see a true, unreversed image of oneself. To be able to see oneself as others see one is important to violinists and other instrumentalists and to dancers and actors. Also, with a set of Realworlds, the most inept driver would be able to back a trailer into a driveway or down a boat-launching ramp.

Boris' newest company was Albedoban. Its product was a dull-lustred scalp paint for men whose hair was thinning. It was claimed that Albedoban could delay the appearance of a bald spot by up to ten years. Other companies he owned were involved in oil wells, giant computers, magnetic carburettors which would allow a

Cadillac to go 200 miles on a gallon of gasoline, and land developments in the deserts of New Mexico.

Ignoring the coffee, an excited Steve blurted his news: "I think I may be on the track of a new play in the Cariboo. Kingfisher has been nosing around up there and my information is that they are onto a hot gold prospect. I think I'm the first outsider to know about it."

"Oho. That'll be Jay Bateman—he's one sharp cookie. Tell me more."

"Well, it's not exactly Bateman's play although he's in charge. They have a new fellow—Bill something." Steve hesitated. "Look, Boris, I'm working on my thesis research this summer and I'm nearly broke. Can I make some money out of this if my information turns out to be valuable?"

Boris smiled. "We can easily work something out. Look, if we were to do anything, you would be in on the ground floor, stockwise, and with luck, you'd score big when the stock went up. As finder, you would be entitled to a special deal. We'll work it out—you'll do well if anything comes of it. Trust me"

Steve hesitated only for a moment and then grinned at Boris. "Good enough. Now here's the situation." He outlined what he had heard from Liz. Boris had some knowledge of the Cariboo area. They spread the relevant maps on Boris' ping-pong-table-sized teak desk.

"She says the showing is at an old shaft about 5 miles from the operating gold mine. And it's only a mile or so from an operating placer."

"Okay. And it's probably in the Snowshoe formation, so it's got to be in this belt of rock here."

"Right," said Steve. "It looks as if it's got to be in this area here." He stabbed the map with a finger. "Look, that

symbol marks a prospect shaft. Right distance, right formation. That could be it."

Boris' eyes gleamed. "Okay. Now here's what we'll do. The chances are Kingfisher is on the way up there to stake. We've got to get up there and stake around them. Once we have a large block of claims surrounding them, we're sitting pretty. We can ride along behind them. If they drill, our claims will rise in value. It's a natural. Can you get a couple of fellows, maybe students, and go up there right away? Find out where Bateman is staking and surround their ground as closely as you can with blocks of claims. Don't worry about showings or workings or geology—get moose pasture—as long as it's close to the Kingfisher claims. Stake over him if necessary to avoid gaps. If you stake over Kingfisher ground we'll lose the overlap but the rest will be ours." As Boris sidled over to a filing cabinet, his belly lagged, caught up, swung past and returned to wobbly equilibrium. He took an envelope out of the cabinet, counted out a pile of bills, and handed them to Steve.

"Here's some cash for your expenses for now. We'll pay you and your helpers well for the staking trip. You'll stake as my agent. Keep your eye peeled for anything we can use as a sample. Float. Anything."

Float referred to loose boulders, blocks or chips of rock or vein material lying on the surface or in the soil. It may have separated from the bedrock near the point of discovery or, on the other hand, from bedrock 20 miles distant, having been transported by glacier or stream. Float was certainly not necessarily representative of the bedrock material immediately underlying the soil and drift in a heavily glaciated area like the Cariboo.

Early next morning, Steve and two students set out for

Wells. Steve knew Jay Bateman by sight, having seen him at several mining conventions. That evening, Steve and his helpers were having a beer at the Golden Cache hotel when Jay, Bill and their staking crew entered, muddy, tired and thirsty. They headed for the dining room. After they were settled, Steve got up and casually strolled outside. A truck, engine creaking as it cooled, axes and saws visible through the window, was parked in front of the hotel. Back inside, Steve kept an eye on Jay through dinner and at last he saw Jay and Bill go upstairs. His helpers soon followed—they'd had a hard day.

Next day, Steve and his two fellow students were up while it was still dark, had breakfast, and watched the Kingfisher truck from their parked vehicle half a block down the street. Jay and his crew emerged, complete with packs, and drove off to the east on the main highway. Their tail-lights were easy to follow and after half an hour Steve saw the lights stop, move left, start slowly up a hill and disappear. Steve parked at the intersection and smoked a cigarette. He then inched cautiously up the hill as quietly as he could, finally reaching a small clearing where they found Jay's truck. Steve checked his location on the geological map. The only showing in the neighborhood was the old prospect shaft, less than a mile away.

"That must be it," he said to his crew. "They'll be staking a block around the shaft. We'll start here and put in a block of claims to cover this side. If we hear any chopping or shouting, we'll try to figure out where they are and stay clear of them.

"Roy, ease the car down the hill and park it out of sight at the first side road. We'll establish the first location line starting over there, just the other side of that pine. You'll find us easily."

Fifty years ago, 1,500-foot claims were staked individually rather than in groups or blocks as Steve would be doing. As claims were staked in thick bush across cliffs and swamps, distances were measured by counting paces, directions by hand-held compass. Errors of location and direction of the blazed lines were very common. The square claims as laid out by the stakers didn't fit together like floor tiles, and narrow triangular spaces would often be left unstaked between the claims. These could be staked as fractional claims and if staked by outsiders could be a great nuisance to the company holding the earlier, full-sized claims. To avoid this possibility, surveyors working for the company would carefully check the claim boundaries soon after they were staked to find any fractions, and to stake them before others became aware of their existence.

Story has it that during the staking of the famous Nickel Plate gold mine in southern British Columbia, surveyors, relaxing in the evening in the beer parlour, talked too loudly about a fraction they had discovered on the steep mountainside. When they resumed their surveying next day, they discovered that a fractional claim had been staked by an outsider. It turned out that the main orebodies, here having the shapes of flattened pipes, and in general lying about parallel to the earth's surface, plunged vertically for several hundred feet just under this fractional claim. Since the rule is that claim boundaries extend vertically towards the centre of the earth, a sizeable proportion of the ore in the mountain belonged to the owners of this annoying tiny fraction and was lost to the principal company.

◊ ◊ ◊

Two days later, Boris walked into his partner's office. Mark Mulvaney, chartered accountant, was known to his friends as Mousy.The name fit. His small bright eyes were set close to a long, bumpy, turned-up nose.The base of his nose was short and his upper lip was a long slope back to a mouth full of narrow, widely separated teeth; this slope was repeated in his receding chin. He was small and lightly built. When he sat at his desk, sharp eyes twinkling at some clever misrepresentation in a company prospectus, he looked like a mouse about to enjoy a bit of cheese. He stayed in the background and handled the financial and legal side of their ventures while Boris dealt with the public.

"Mousy, I think we've got another good one." They reviewed Steve's information and the steps taken so far.

"Last night Steve phoned to say that we have blocks of claims that pretty well surround Kingfisher's ground on the north and west. He's still staking. He's picked up some interesting float. We can start planning the new promotion."

Mousy nodded."We'll go ahead as usual.We'll use one of the shells. Croesus Holdings will fit the bill nicely."

A shell company is just what the name suggests, an empty shell, a company owning nothing of value.The shares in such a shell can be sold and the shell company can acquire assets, such as claims, patents, or shares in other companies. The usefulness of such a shell is that it can be activated almost over night. In contrast, listing a new company on the stock exchange can take a year or more. Also, being listed already, a reactivated shell company does not have to undergo close scrutiny from the authorities. It is not obliged to prepare a

prospectus listing the assets, plans and reasons for its existence. There are scores of shell companies—every promoter has them or can get his hands on one for a price. Money is transferred to their treasuries and the stock offered on the open market with a minimum of outside interference or supervision.

"Croesus Holdings is ready to go," said Mousy. "I've been picking up the stock for the last eighteen months. I thought we'd need it for the Stikine play but that's been put off until next year. Croesus will acquire Steve's new Cariboo claims. It was capitalized at ten million shares and I've managed to corner most of the issued shares—mostly for less than ten cents a share. I didn't file the last quarterly financial statement so a cease-trade order is in effect. The stock that's still out there can't be traded. We'll have that order lifted when we're ready to roll."

"We've got to move fast so we can get a free ride on Kingfisher's coat-tails," warned Boris.

"Right. Now to cover running expenses. I'll apply for an Exemption Order that will allow us to issue 100,000 treasury shares. We'll sell these to Hans Bauer in Dusseldorf. Our German friends love gold-mining stock. This'll net us about $50,000." Mousy grinned.

◊ ◊ ◊

In the Cariboo, Jay and Bill got down to the exciting business of trying to find out what lay concealed under the hundreds of acres of forest and bush that they had staked. A bull-dozer pushed a crude road up to the old shaft where Bill had panned the crushed quartz. An office tent, a cook tent, four small sleeping tents and an outhouse were in place before the day was out. Next morning a thumping diesel generator provided power for light and refrigeration. Cook-stove, cots, folding chairs, tables—all the comforts of home. Suddenly a little community appeared among the pines. By the second day the whiskey-jacks were begging scraps at the cook-tent door.

Bill strolled up the new road, hammering chunks of white quartz float and examining the freshly broken surfaces with his hand-lens. He didn't find any gold. He consoled himself with the fact that in many successful gold mines, the gold in the hard white quartz is microscopic, and the miners never see a speck of the valuable metal. Are these blocks of quartz ore? What exactly is ore anyway? He remembered the substance of one of the Prof's lectures:

Ore is defined as mineral matter that can be mined at a profit. Many factors must be taken into account when deciding whether a mineral deposit is ore. Some of the obvious ones: the richness of the deposit in the valuable metal, the market price of the metal, and the cost of mining and extracting the metal from the mineralized material. Since it may take years to build and equip a mine and metal prices vary, what is ore today may be waste two months hence. Under average conditions, vein material that contains one troy ounce of gold to a ton of waste can be mined at a profit and is ore. Of course if there were only one ton of this material and it were to exist 200 feet from the surface, in solid rock, it would not be ore because the cost of sinking a shaft and extracting it would be much greater than the value of the single ounce of gold. In very large deposits, where mining can be carried

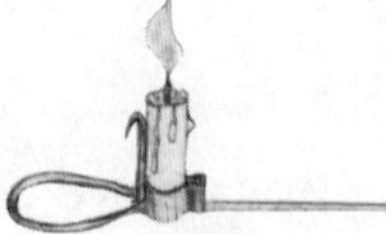

on in large open pits and where mining costs are low, material containing a small fraction of an ounce of gold per ton of rock can be mined at a profit. A vein running 50 ounces of silver per ton would be ore in California but waste in Greenland because of the high cost of operating in the Arctic.

Will our veins be rich enough and thick enough to be mined at a profit? Bill wondered, as he watched a back-hoe cut a couple of deep trenches which would allow him to establish the direction of the vein that had been found in the shaft fifty years before.

They then began systematic trenching on lines that crossed the projected extension of the vein, exposing it and showing that it had a length of at least a few hundred feet. Large samples were cut from the vein and sent off for assay. During the trenching, three other veins lying about parallel to the first were found and sampled.

Using his crushing and panning technique, Bill was able to determine that the gold of the new veins was the yellow, high purity variety and that his hypothesis that these veins could have supplied much of the gold of the near-by placer was holding up. This satisfaction was partly offset by an ever-present heart-ache and sense of loss—he had had no word from Julie.

The first few weeks passed quickly. Jay reported to Isaac that somebody had staked blocks of claims completely surrounding Kingfisher's but Isaac was not surprised.

Things were going well—a little better than they had any right to expect. The weather had been dry, the mosquitoes had all but disappeared, and the back-hoe had not been breaking down. Jay and Bill had uncovered five veins and three of them had yielded encouraging assays. Their excellent cook was not only not threatening to quit; he was turning out pies and cakes as if his job depended on Bill's approval. Progress reports were phoned daily from Wells to the Vancouver office so that Isaac was kept on top of events and could anticipate the next phases of development.

The gossip at the Golden Cache was that they were onto a good thing.

Smelling success, Jay began to go out of his way to make it clear that he was the boss, that the project was his, and that any credit for developing a new mine would belong to him. Fearing that the neophyte Bill might garner some of the credit for the new mine that Jay could see in his imagination, he began in subtle ways to denigrate Bill with the other employees and with the many visitors who arrived as news of the encouraging results leaked out. Jay's actions, at first hardly noticeable, became more obvious to Bill the better the prospects for developing a mine appeared.

For Bill it was an interesting time. He had never had the opportunity to be in on the development of a property from the very beginning. He was learning about coordinating various parts of the operation and about dealing with the problems of employees. Best of all were the visits by engineers and geologists from rival exploration companies. Most of these would spend a few hours walking over the claims, climbing into the trenches to hammer specimens from the quartz veins. They volunteered useful information and ideas based on their observations in other mining camps. Bill made many new professional contacts and several new friends.

At the same time he resented the fact that Jay didn't give him credit for his role in starting the project. After all,

Bill was the one who had deduced the source of the yellow placer gold. Jay, whose smooth and confident manner was very intimidating to the inexperienced and tentative Bill, made it quite clear to the visitors that he was the brains behind the project.

The veins showed reasonable continuity on the surface and the assays were encouraging. The mining inspector would soon be urging them to backfill their trenches and the pressure was on to move to the next phase. A decision had to be made as to whether to take the next step, to drill. Or should they stop and consider? Drilling would tell them how far the veins extended below the surface, their thickness, what values in gold they contained, and whether other members of this particular family of veins existed in the bedrock far below. Should they drill? It would cost real money.

After conferring briefly with Toronto, Isaac gave the go-ahead signal. A bull-dozer tore crude roads through the woods and made small clearings where the drill would be set up. The drillers appeared a few days later.

The diamond drill used in mineral exploration is, in simplest terms, a pipe, on the end of which is fitted a detachable cylindrical drill-bit, like a thick napkin ring studded with small industrial diamonds. The drill bit is pressed against the rock and revolved. Water is pumped down the inside of the pipe to cool the bit and wash away the cuttings and returns to the surface along the outside of the pipe. A cylindrical rock core, commonly an inch or so in diameter, the size of the inside of the napkin-ring drill bit, is formed as the drill advances. At first, this core remains attached to the bedrock, but as drilling progresses, it breaks free and is retained in the drill-pipe as pieces a few inches to a couple of feet long. When the pieces of drill core have filled the lowest section of pipe, the drill is withdrawn, and the loose pieces of core removed and placed in order in a core box. As the hole deepens, new lengths of pipe are screwed onto the original pipe, and at intervals, the dulled diamond-studded cutting bit is replaced.

The standard core-box, 5 feet long, 1 foot wide and 2 inches deep, is divided length-wise into compartments to accommodate the pieces of core. Each box will hold about 30 feet. As the pieces of core are removed from the drill, they are placed in order in the box along with markers showing distances from the surface. When the hole is complete, the core-boxes contain a continuous sample of the rock penetrated by the drill.

Drills seldom bore in a straight line. Although a drill may start vertically, the drill may gradually turn through a considerable angle in a distance of a few hundred feet. There are many stories of wandering drills. In Australia, an exploration company drilling from the surface, was extending a vertical 2,500-foot-long hole. Suddenly, without warning, the drilling water ceased returning to the surface and the drill advanced without resistance for a couple of feet. After a few minutes, the drill jammed. They retrieved a badly chewed-up and burned drill bit. Later, when the crew returned to their truck, they found it standing in a large puddle. The drill had travelled in a gradual curve, returned to the surface under their truck, and penetrated the truck body before overheating and jamming.

It is, of course, vital to know where the drill has gone and thus, where the core has come from. In one method of surveying a hole, a tiny gimballed magnetic compass with a clockwork-delayed locking mechanism is lowered down the hole and records the orientation of the drill hole at various depths.

If, on drilling, ore is intersected, the length of the intersection is of great interest—obviously a 2-inch intersection is of less significance than a 20-foot one. Unscrupulous operators have been known to deliberately drill along rather than across a vein in order to be able to report vein intersections tens of feet in length.

◊ ◊ ◊

Back in Vancouver, it was a Saturday afternoon. Chris had some laurel clippings to dispose of. The easiest way to get rid of them was to dump them across the street, but the authorities had posted signs forbidding the dumping of garden refuse. Nevertheless, like most of his neighbours, Chris usually sneaked the biodegradable but uncompostable cuttings into the woods when the coast was clear. Following his usual practice, he furtively advanced across the street with his almond-smelling load. He looked to the right. A swaying pendulum in the distance resolved itself into a virtuoso roller skater. To the left, a gray squirrel wove its way across the black-top. Chris advanced about 50 feet along one of the many rough paths which extended a short distance into the trees. As he was about to drop his cuttings, he noticed a pile of alder leaves. It was not the usual trash from someone's garden, but looked as if it had been roughly scraped together from last autumn's accumulation. Chris kicked at it—a resistance. Suddenly cautious, he moved his foot around tentatively and hooked something—a shoe, an ankle, and then a sickening stench. He hurried back across the street and phoned the police.

◊ ◊ ◊

In a matter of hours, yellow plastic ribbons marked off an area of half an acre. A team of uniformed Mounties and detectives in plain clothes scoured the woods. Cameras flashed and bits of trash were bagged. The local householders thronged the sidewalk and chatted quietly. Neighbors who hadn't spoken in years exchanged their accumulated news. Old friendships were renewed, neighbors recounted the exploits of children and reported the names and sexes of new grandchildren. New neighbors introduced themselves. Finally, the covered body was placed on a stretcher and taken away in an ambulance. As Chris crossed the street and went into his house, he glumly concluded that, in the interest of neighborhood morale, the area should have a murder at least every six months. Almost as good as a funeral, he thought, for renewing friendships.

A little later, Chris' doorbell chimed. A Sgt. Fortier introduced himself and asked Chris to come to the station to give a formal account of his finding the body.

Later, at the station, while Sgt. Fortier shuffled papers and files, Chris sized him up. Alert snapping black eyes, large nose, black whiskers shaved close but lurking darkly beneath his slightly yellowish skin. Springy black curls. Fortier was large. He looked tall even when sitting. His torso strained the stitches of his khaki shirt. Probably born in Montreal, Chris thought, but little accent. Comfortably bilingual. You've got to be if you want to be promoted in a federal job. Probably sent out to Vancouver for seasoning and will end up as a senior officer in Ottawa. Paper on the desk was organized in neat piles,

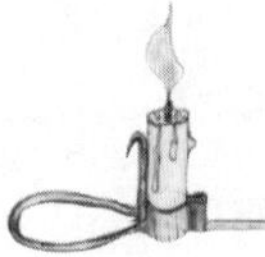

mostly in labelled filing folders. Is there that much crime around here? Chris wondered. He tried not to make comparisons with his own desk—he hadn't seen wood in months.

"You do not mind if we tape our conversation?"

Chris could see no reason to say no. Constable Victor Handforth, sitting to one side, was introduced. He would take notes. Twenty-five? Big, blonde, tough-looking.

"What were you doing over there in the trees?" Fortier asked.

Chris explained how he had been dumping a small load, really only a handful, of garden cuttings.

"The dead woman, did you know her?"

"I don't know. I haven't seen her face—I don't think I want to. What was her name?"

"We have not identified her as yet."

"Do you have any idea how long she had been there?" Chris asked.

"I cannot say for sure. Since a week or ten days maybe. Have you seen anybody?"

"Well, a week ago Thursday night, a few minutes after 1:00 AM, there was a pick-up parked in front of the house on the far side of the street by the woods and I saw a fellow get in and take off. I remember because I let the dog out after my wife and I watched the late movie."

"Good. Please give me a description of the man."

"Well, I didn't get much of a look. He was outside the direct light from the street lamp. And he was wearing a hat. Average size and build. Maybe on the short side."

"Can you describe the vehicle?"

Chris wasn't very helpful there, either. He thought it was a muddy pick-up truck, probably dark-coloured. But he didn't keep up with the dozens of makes and models—they all looked nearly the same to him.

"Black, red, green, blue, grey?"

"Can't say. Pretty dark."

The mounties thanked him for his help and told him that they would probably be in touch.

Next day Fortier received the official report from headquarters. The victim was Betty Forbes, age 31, of 4827 Greenall Road, Vancouver. The identification had been confirmed by her landlord. She was a graduate student at the University of British Columbia. She had an assistantship which paid $1,500 per term.

Her right leg and pelvis were shattered and a broken rib had punctured a lung. Contusions to left side of face. She had not lost any blood. The immediate cause of death was strangulation.

It seemed probable that she had been hit by a car. Then, when she was near death, strangled. She was then probably stored or hidden in a foetal position, constricted, on her side when rigor mortis had set in. The body when found was still contorted and twisted. The person who had hidden the body had probably been unable to straighten the limbs. The body was probably hidden, therefore, between 3 and 30 hours after death. A receipt for a medical prescription was found in her coat pocket.

A small fragment of plastic was found in the folds of her coat. This appeared to be a piece of the grill, head-light mounting or some ornamental part from the front of a car.

The victim had lived about four blocks from where her body was found.

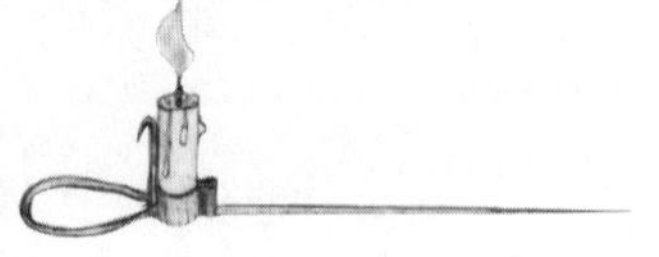

◊ ◊ ◊

Sgt. Fortier asked the landlord, who was watching from the hall, "Did Miss Forbes go out often in the evening?

"Pretty often. I didn't keep track of her particularly. A lot of the time I think she went back to the university, to the library. And she'd often go out for a walk in the evening."

"What can you tell us about her? Did she have a family in Vancouver?"

"She came from Kamloops. Mother in an old-folks home—Alzheimers. Father dead. No brothers or sisters."

"Did she have a boy friend?"

"Never saw one. She never mentioned one. I think she was a loner—never had any visitors."

Back in the patrol car: "If it is premeditated murder there must be a motive. Unless it is a simple hit-and-run and he panicked and finished her off. But it is still murder.

"Well, Victor, our best bet is to find the car. It is probably a pick-up. It is not great research work to find that out. Go to headquarters and examine that morsel of plastic they found with the body. If it looks promising get them to photograph it, close-up, from several angles."

"O.K. Maybe the best way to find out what model car the piece of plastic came from is to cruise the parking lots at the university. Look at a few thousand radiator grills. They park about ten thousand cars a day and that's as good a sample as we are going to get. If it doesn't work, I'll try the used car lots."

"It is unfortunate that Bancroft could not tell us the colour of the car."

◊ ◊ ◊

Chris hadn't volunteered the fact that he was one of the one-in-ten males who suffers from a degree of colour blindness. He had discovered his rather mild red-green deficiency at the ripe age of eighteen when he had chanced upon a set of diagnostic cards, each spotted circle looking like a bad case of measles. He then understood why he found it impossible to distinguish blues from most purples and some browns from greens and why he had trouble identifying certain minerals whose colours were definitive. The pale green of malachite was an off-white to him. Small bits of the rosy pink and red of cinnabar were grey.

On the other hand, he discovered that he was particularly good at picking out certain colours. He could spot the bright yellow of some molybdenum and uranium minerals much more quickly than could most of his friends. He could starve to death standing in a field of wild strawberries but could spot a banana at a thousand yards. Useful in Costa Rica but not a great advantage in British Columbia. As his wife remarked, he was not colour blind—his colour-detecting apparatus was simply more sensitive to yellow than to red. And he wasn't going to be able to help Fortier with the colour of that pick-up.

CHAPTER 12

CARL AND GUS

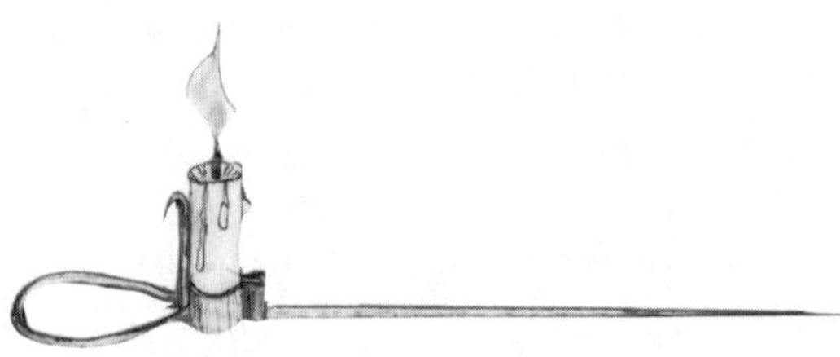

As Chris sat at the computer he looked enviously across the office at Julie who was arranging geochemical analyses in tables on her monitor with relaxed expertise.

Chris had not been brought up on computers—they had appeared in the office long after he had been a student. He was afraid of them. Always in the back of his mind was the fear that an ill-judged key stroke would wipe out all of the programs, destroy the files, or innoculate the machine with a fatal virus. Or obliterate the last two hours' efforts. He had studied the manuals and was convinced that their jargon was deliberately contrived to withhold their secrets from people like himself. He sighed as Julie finished her task and disappeared into Carl's office—he had been born thirty years too soon.

His most shattering experience with the computer had occurred one evening when, alone in the office, sitting at the keyboard, he was trying to master a program that would display the true widths and assays of a series of diamond drill samples. As he despairingly followed the incomprehensible instruction manual, his little finger, never very reliable, pressed two keys simultaneously, somewhere near the right-hand side of the keyboard. The machine gave a little cry and the diagram on the monitor faded as the ceiling light and desk lamp died. The fan inside the computer slowed and stopped. No light, no sound. Not only had he destroyed the computer but he had blown the circuit-breaker for the office. He felt his way to the outside door and twisted the knob with a clammy hand. The hall lights were out, only the red emergency light glowed near the elevators. He had blown every circuit on the fourteenth floor. He made his way to the window and looked out—the adjacent building was in complete darkness. Below, he could see that the traffic lights were dead and cars were locked in automotive chaos—he had destroyed a sub-station and eliminated power for the whole district! A blinding flash was followed closely by a crash of thunder and he realized that somewhere lightning had struck a transformer and that, after all, his little finger had not darkened one-quarter of the city. It took him several days to restock his little store of confidence in his ability to use the computer.

Soon after Julie left, Chris heard excited talk from Carl's office. Glad of an excuse to get away from his computer screen, he decided to see what was up.

He leaned over Carl's shoulder to inspect the large maps showing the results of scores of stream sample and soil analyses.

"Hmm, look at those copper values," Chris said. "Well above the average for that part of the world. They stick out like a sore thumb. And a little molybdenum too. Those values are impressive. Look at that one—nine hundred parts per million! How was it missed? I mean to say, all these years! That area's been stream-sampled and dirt-bagged a hundred times. Well, maybe not a hundred, but dozens. Several times. But why wasn't the anomaly picked up? How could it have been missed? . . . And it's so big . . .

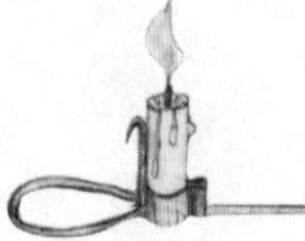

Well, not too big, it seems to peter out a bit north and south, but those creeks where you took the sediment samples drain a fairly big piece of ground."

Carl explained, twin maps reflecting from his sunglasses: "Well, if you look hard at the high values, you see there are not too many of them along the trail up to the lake, and I'll bet that's where the earlier dirt-baggers took their samples. But the stream sediments are loaded with pyrite. And copper's strong in places along the upper trail and along this draw. But we've only got a few soil samples. We were trying to work on the sly—these claims are still held and we don't want to get the owner excited. If you look in detail, there are lots of nils, so it's spotty—but look at the extent of it! And look at these values along this draw." He looked up from the map.

"I think we're on to a big one here. The chemical signature is that of a porphyry copper deposit, with much more copper than molybdenum. A funny thing, though, is that the copper and molybdenum seem to be independent of each other. A lot of the moly anomalies don't show any copper—we don't have the whole story yet. I'm going to have a word with Isaac in a few minutes. I think we've got to move on this one." Carl was clearly excited.

Chris asked, "Any showings around? I mean old shafts or trenches. Generally there's some sign that somebody's poked around."

"There's an adit, partly caved," Carl replied. "I've checked the Department of Mines reports and there's a reference to it. It was sampled in 1945. Reported low copper values."

Chris looked at a geological map published by the federal government. "The geology looks reasonable—a complex of Jurassic-Cretaceous intrusions cutting Paleozoic sediments. Nobody's done any real work on the area for a long time—not a bad spot for a porphyry copper deposit."

They assembled in the board room that afternoon. Carl arrived carrying a bundle of maps, file folders and publications.

Isaac started the meeting: "The Cariboo gold venture is going well. Jay's found several new veins and some of them are close to being rich enough to mine. Maybe this is our year. One of Carl's dirt-baggers has made an interesting discovery—a copper anomaly not too far from Highland Valley and maybe we're on the track of another Cougar Lake deposit. Carl, tell us about it."

"One of our summer people, a university student stream-sampling Piebyter Creek and its side-streams north of Princeton, picked up a strong anomaly. Copper and a smell of molybdenum. No exploration action at all in the neighbourhood and there hasn't been any for a long time. We may be the first to spot it. There is an old adit and brief mention of copper in a Department of Mines report. We went back in, took a few more soil samples and confirmed that there's definitely something there. I think it's worth gambling some time and money on. It's our bad luck that an old farmer owns four claims right in the middle of things and his cabin is close to the anomaly. He has been hanging on to them for years and I'm afraid we are going to have to deal with him. I haven't approached him and I don't know the best way to handle him. We can't very well do any more sampling without asking his permission. As soon as we show any interest in his claims he'll up his price."

"Are the claims in good standing?" asked Isaac.

"Hard to be sure," Carl replied. "I think he's been restak-

ing every year and we might get away with staking right over him and proving that he holds the claims illegally."

Isaac frowned. "We don't want a messy law suit. We could lose and anyway we would get all the locals against us. We don't want that."

Carl nodded. "It seems to me that there are only two ways to play this. We can ignore the old geezer's claims, stake the country all around him, and if it turns out we have something good, we buy his claims. This could be expensive and we might end up bidding for his claims against some other company. To be sure of getting the whole thing, we've got to option his claims. If we play it cool, don't let him know we are really interested, I'll bet we can get them cheap."

Isaac asked, "What's cheap? Give me a ball-point figure."

Carl said, "My information is that this guy is an old bum, lives like a hermit in an old cabin, has a beat-up truck. He probably doesn't see a twenty-dollar bill from one year to the next." He outlined a schedule of payments which he thought would be irresistible to the owner of the claims but would allow easy escape for the company should the property turn out to be worthless.

Isaac made a quick calculation.

"For a year's option on a good prospect—$34,000. A mere bag of shells. Why, we paid $50,000 for a look at that uranium loser near Nelson."

Chris spoke up. "Would it be wise to stake around him before we have an option? If he catches on to what we are doing, he'll probably raise his price. On the other hand, if we hold off, word could leak out and we could lose the whole thing."

Carl replied: "The country's quiet right now. All of the

base-metal companies are up in the Yukon, looking for lead-zinc. I think if we sneak in quietly from the north, not using the old geezer's road, he'll never know we've been staking in there. In the meantime, someone should get up there and wangle an option on his claims."

"You'll have to be careful," Isaac warned, "Some of these guys aren't as dumb as they look." He paused for a moment. "We'll have two new projects on the go if this one is approved. With Jay and Bill in the Cariboo, and Chris scheduled for sampling at Cougar Lake, we're going to be short-handed. It looks as if this new one is going to be your baby, Carl."

It was decided that Carl should talk to the owner. A little later the meeting broke up.

◊ ◊ ◊

Gus was cutting wood for the kitchen stove. As he split each round of pine into four, he wondered why the grain in almost every log formed a gradual spiral, twisting around the log like a very gradual thread on a machine screw. He had convinced himself, over the years, that the spiral grain generally formed a right-hand, rather than a left-hand thread. Did the tree turn as it grew? He wondered whether the trees in Australia had a grain forming a left-hand thread. As he split another round, he heard a motor, and a truck emerged from the trees. He flipped the axe into the chopping block and wiped his brow with a hairy forearm.

A stranger stepped down, looked slowly around the

clearing and turned towards Gus.

"Hello there."

"Hi. You lost?"

"No. I'm looking for Gus Hammerstrom."

"You've found him. What can I do for you?"

"I'm Carl Costello. I'm a geochemist—work for Kingfisher Explorations. Office down in Vancouver. We're checking out properties in this area and I noticed down at the mining recorder's that you own four claims and some kind of a copper showing."

"Sure do."

They shook hands. Unable to see Carl's eyes through the green lenses, Gus felt vaguely uncomfortable. He waved to a rustic armchair on the porch. "Sit down. I was just going to have a cup of tea." He brought out a pot of tea and a plate of cold baking-powder biscuits. Carl, who had been pacing up and down, finally sat.

"Have a biscuit. Made 'em myself. I hear there's talk of opening up the old Copper Mountain mine. Anything in it?"

"Price of copper's rising. Could happen. Now I understand you've got some kind of a copper showing. An old adit."

"They say it's a copper deposit," said Gus. "The adit's pretty well caved. At the portal anyway. Speaking of mines—when I first came to this part of the world, in the fifties, there were several mines going. Copper Mountain, Hedley gold mine, Bridge River and Cariboo—gold. And each mine hired hundreds of men—big bunk-houses, families, schools, company towns. But now you go to one of the big mines, say over in Highland Valley—they look practically deserted. A couple of drills working, a shovel, a few trucks moving, but hardly any people!"

Trying not to show his impatience, Carl answered:

"The biggest expense in running a mine is people. So the smart operators use machinery instead of men. A bulldozer doesn't demand overtime pay, accident insurance, medical coverage, or pension. They'll spend tens of thousands of dollars on machinery that'll do the work of one man. Now, your showing up the hill—have you had any assays?"

"No. No point. Never saw any high-grade on the dump. Now that's why I always vote for the Socialists—they'll buy back the mines, or just take 'em, spread the profits around and put people back to work. Right?"

"Well, it's not quite as simple as that," Carl countered. "Anyhow, there is some copper in the adit?"

"Well, yes," replied Gus, crumbs falling liberally down his shirt. "But I'm told it's pretty spotty. Sure you won't have another? Pass your cup. Now if Copper Mountain was to start up again, it would sure give the country a boost."

"I've been reading about that old adit. The government report says they found a little copper in it."

"So I've heard. I haven't been in it for years but I guess they wouldn't have done all that work if there wasn't something there. Must have cost a lot of money."

"My company would like to have a look at it, to see whether it could possibly be of economic interest."

"Help yourself. No problem. Go on up and have a look. I'll come along if you like."

"Well, actually, our company policy is that we like to have some sort of a hold on anything we look at. And while there's probably nothing there, before we spend

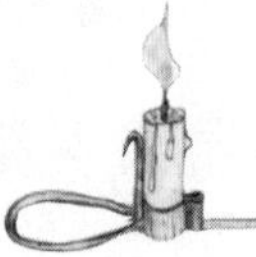

money on sampling or assays, we like to have an agreement that would allow us to buy the property if it were to turn out to be worth really doing some work on. Pretty unlikely, but you know what these company lawyers are like. What we really need is an option."

Gus appeared to be puzzled. Spraying biscuit crumbs, he protested. "You don't need an option. Why, Sam Joliffe, you know him—Todhunter Explorations—came by about a month ago. Spent most of his time roaming around those outcrops up behind the adit—don't think he ever went in it. He didn't say anything about paperwork."

With the news that somebody else was interested in the area, Carl decided that he must act.

"Look, the head office likes us to follow certain procedures when we examine a property and we've got to keep Toronto happy. Suppose we offer you some cash for an option. This will allow us to do some work without worrying about other companies. Before the year is out we will either buy your claims outright, or if we don't find anything, all of the claims will go back to you. It's a good deal—you can't lose. I happen to have an option agreement out in the truck and we could settle this thing right now."

"How much money are we talking about? I could use a bit of cash—the old truck has just about had it."

"Suppose we make an option payment of $10,000. And also we pay $2,000 a month. If, at the end of a year, we want to buy your claims, we pay you $200,000 for clear title. If we decide at any time to abandon the project, we stop the monthly payments and all of the claims, including any that we have staked, revert to you. We fill in the trenches and leave things pretty much as we found them."

Gus thought for a minute. "That sounds good to me. I suppose I should have a lawyer look at the papers before I sign?"

"You don't need a lawyer. But it's up to you. I'll leave a copy of the option agreement with you and I'll come back before the end of the week. I'll bring a cheque." So it was agreed, and Carl drove back to Vancouver feeling that he had made a good deal and probably just in time. He couldn't quite place Todhunter Explorations but he thought it was probably one of the many fly-by-night exploration companies that were always nosing around for a property on which they could float shares.

◊ ◊ ◊

Two days later, Gus noticed that King was restless, sniffing and growling and looking up the valley. Gus knew that if Carl had any sense he would have a crew staking a large area around his original four claims before some other company, hearing some gossip and putting two and two together, started staking claims in the area. Not wanting to complicate things, Gus stayed close to the cabin.

Gus was right. Carl had brought in a staking crew to surround Gus' claims. They came in from the north, avoiding his access road and working quietly. Carl had also made a quick examination of the adit. He walked down the old trail and as he came around a bend caught sight of the cabin. With his binoculars he was able to study the old guy in his long johns standing at the chopping block, hammering a wedge into a knotty round, the desynchronized axe sounding on the upswing. Stupid old bastard, thought Carl—sitting for twenty years on a billion dollar copper deposit.

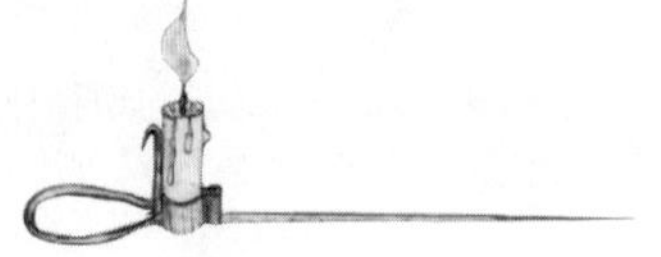

◊ ◊ ◊

Carl and his helper turned up before the week was out. "You've had a look at the agreement? Any problems?"

"No, it looks O.K. to me. Well, I guess I'd better sign it. Did you bring the cheque?"

Gus could see that Carl was anxious and impatient. He didn't like Carl's cold business-like manner or the way that he had been sneaking around behind his back, sampling and staking. After a prolonged search of shelves and drawers, Gus retrieved a pair of mail-order reading glasses and, lips moving, checked the agreement. Finally he sighed and nodded. Rejecting Carl's offer of a ballpoint, he spent five minutes finding his favorite pen. Then the bottle of ink eluded him. Carl frowned. Gus ignored him and sat down at the kitchen table. He adjusted his chair, found the space allotted to his signature, and ran a tentative signature in the air to make sure that he wouldn't run over into the typed text. He wasn't satisfied with the effort, adjusted his chair, shifted the paper a little, and, to Carl's chagrin, ran another signature one quarter of an inch above the paper. Gus gave Carl a weak smile, and, clutching the pen in his massive paw, seemed to gather up his courage. This time he put pen to paper. The pen was dry. Gus dipped the pen, made another airy pass over the document and then signed. With the agreement dated and witnessed, Carl wasted no more time. After an abrupt goodbye, he started back to Vancouver, feeling that he had put one over the silly old bugger.

◊ ◊ ◊

Gus drove into town next day and, to the surprise of the bank teller, deposited a cheque for $12,000. He stopped at the liquor store and bought a dozen bottles of Scottish ale.

CHAPTER 13

HOWE STREET HANKY-PANKY

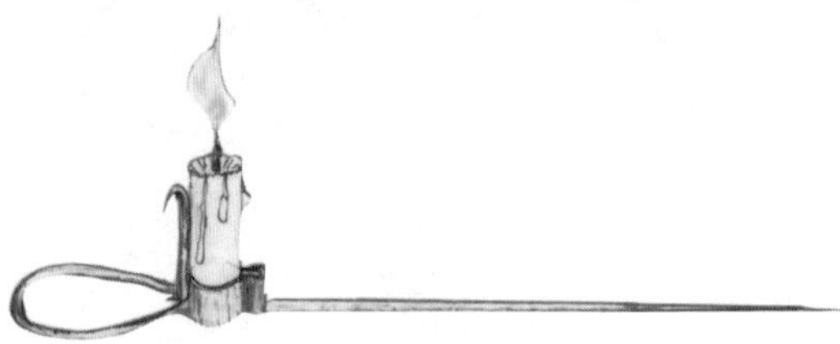

Boris was in Mousy's office.

"It's time to start pushing the Croesus stock. I've been in touch with Arnie in Toronto, Yves in Montreal, Sol in New York, and I've got three phoners here. We'll start slowly, sell a few blocks of shares here and there. It's a natural now that Kingfisher's drilling has started."

The phoners consulted their lists of stock market gamblers and made their calls, assuring the speculators that this was their chance to get in on the ground floor in a promising gold property in the Cariboo. Only 5 miles, they said, from the fabulous Cariboo Gold Quartz mine and the great Island Mountain deposit. These produced for years—millions of ounces. The price of gold was on the rise, they said. Kingfisher was starting to drill less than 2 miles south of the Croesus property.

Although at first the public reacted slowly to the sales pitch, many shares were being traded. Boris, Mousy, Arnie, Yves and Sol were now buying small blocks of Croesus stock from each other. The transactions were made through reliable friends and relatives so that the names of the promoters did not appear. The newspapers reported activity in this unknown gold-mining company and the financial pages showed that about 300,000 shares were being traded daily. On some days, 95 percent of the trading reported in the papers was by this illegal, incestuous buying and selling. The stock crept up to ninety cents as the speculators sensed that the stock was on the move.

In a few days, by dint of phone announcements, spreading of rumours about Kingfisher, and low level but continuous trading between the promoters, the stock had reached $1.45 and seemed to have stalled. Investors seemed to be waiting for some firm information. Mousy was pacing the deep carpet of Boris' office.

"You're right," he said to Boris. "We need some stimulating news. Exciting drill results. Or assays. What's going on at Kingfisher?"

"Apparently they're drilling, but we don't know whether they are hitting anything. But Steve's comc up with an idea. It'll cost us a bit but I think it's a good gamble." Boris explained the situation and Steve's suggestion. Mousy was dubious at first, but finally gave his approval.

◊ ◊ ◊

The first assays from the diamond drill cores were reported to Isaac and Jay within two weeks of the start of drilling. They were encouraging—up to 0.5 ounces of gold per ton. The first two holes had been shallow ones, sited to test the continuity of the veins exposed at the surface. They then moved the drilling rig onto the next claim to the northwest to test the thickest and most promising vein at a new location and at a greater depth.

At the new site, the drill had penetrated a couple of hundred feet. Jay and Bill had been checking the core

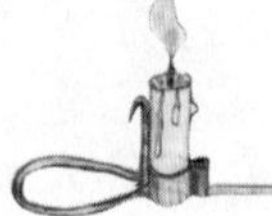

box—nothing so far but dull grey, faintly laminated sandstone.

"Same old Snowshoe formation," said Jay. "But we can't expect anything else for another 300 feet or so. I wonder whose that is?" They both looked up at the sudden flippety-flop of a low-flying helicopter.

"They go east every morning and back in the afternoon, regular as clockwork," Bill said. "Maybe forestry. But I heard that there's an exploration camp over by the Bowron River. Maybe it's them."

In the helicopter, claim map on his lap, ten power binoculars clamped to his eyes, Steve spoke into his tape recorder. "I'd judge they are on the No. 5 claim, about 1,000 feet northwest of the camp. This is their third hole. They are drilling southwestward, down at about forty-five degrees. The core-box is on the south side of the rig. The current core-box is about half full. The core is all dark grey—probably Snowshoe sandstone. No white quartz as far as I can see. No intersection yet."

The helicopter continued on course for a few minutes. Then, well out of sight of the camp, it made a long, low turn over the empty wooded landscape and returned to a clearing near the highway. Steve climbed out and waved goodbye to the pilot, who took off immediately on another project. Steve drove to the nearest pay phone and reported his findings to Boris. The procedure was repeated in late afternoon, the route now reversed and the machine flying over from the east.

Two days later, as the chopper went over, Steve could see that the latest core was white. He phoned Boris before noon and reported that they had hit a vein. That afternoon, on the basis of what he saw on the return flight, he phoned again.

"Hi Boris—Steve. They've got a good intersection."

"Great. Can you give me any figures?"

"It's not easy to be sure. But it looks as if five compartments in the core-box are full of white quartz—that would make it at least 25 feet. Probably a true thickness of something like 20 feet. A pretty healthy vein."

"Good work, Steve. Keep an eye on things."

Boris rubbed his hands together as he relayed the information to Mousy.

"O.K.," answered Mousy. "We'll never have a better chance. I'll get Yves to leak to the Howe Street Nugget that Kingfisher has hit a big vein. We've got to do this immediately, before they have the core assayed. Just in case they're duds. Assays will take several days. When Yves has done his job, we'll get the phones busy."

Next day, at Kingfisher, Julie's phone was ringing constantly with enquiries about their new strike. Reporters and speculators besieged the office, trying to get information. Julie consulted Isaac. Isaac was puzzled—the drill results had gotten to him just as the phone rang. It was a reporter for the Vancouver Sun.

"Have you had a vein intersection in the current drilling?" she asked.

"Well, yes," Isaac admitted.

"How thick is the vein? We hear 50 feet."

"I think that's an exaggeration," said Isaac.

"How many ounces of gold per ton?"

"Nobody knows. It hasn't been assayed yet."

"It's rumoured that there's visible gold," the reporter persisted.

"I haven't seen the core."

"Is it true that the vein is headed for Croesus ground?"

"Well, yes. It must be, because Croesus has completely boxed us in. But they're a long way away."

◊ ◊ ◊

Meanwhile, Mousy had his phoners calling old customers telling them that there was still time to get in on the bonanza, reinforcing rumours from Montreal describing Kingfisher's exciting drill intersections.

Boris fanned the flames by complaining to a reporter: "Why is Kingfisher being so secretive? Why are they hiding the news about the new vein intersection? Why don't they release the assays?"

While Boris was asking these questions, Mousy, Yves, Arnie and Sol had their agents buying and selling to each other to maintain the appearance of great activity and demand.

The next day the stock leapt to $3. Mousy and his friends gradually reduced the trading among themselves because there was now a strong participation from the public—695,000 shares were traded.

Next morning, a rumour circulated that the new vein showed visible gold, assayed at three-quarters of an ounce per ton, and was headed towards Croesus ground only a few claim lengths away. By 9:00 A.M., the stock had hit $4 and 1,500,000 shares had been traded. Now Boris began to unload his ten- and fifteen-cent shares, being careful not to offer so many shares that the share price would level off. His aim was to allow the market to rise slowly and steadily, satisfying the frantic buyers and allowing only a moderate rate of increase in the price of the stock.

In a week, Croesus was hovering around $6.

Reporters for the financial pages of the daily newspapers were pestering Boris for some hard information.

"To this point in time," he answered, "geologists haven't completed a detailed survey of our claims." He didn't explain that the company had no geologists and there was little a geologist could do in the area—bedrock was completely concealed under glacial drift.

"We do have one sample from our property. It looks pretty good. Assays will be out shortly. We expect to finalize a drilling contract in the near future, but we won't drill until we have a clear picture of what's going on. We're not going to spend the company's money until we have some targets." Next day, he fed the reporters another morsel.

"We have one assay from a quartz sample from the Croesus No. 26 claim—it runs 0.3 ounces of gold per ton. This is not, of course, necessarily representative of the veins on Croesus property."

He did not point out that this sample was a piece of float. He also did not explain that such an assay result was almost meaningless. There was no indication of the thickness or extent of the vein from which the float had come. It could have been torn by the glaciers from a one inch-thick vein extending for only a foot or two.

◊ ◊ ◊

Isaac was disappointed with the gold assays from the drilling on No. 5 claim. The assays from the deep cores were not as good as those from the surface exposures. Moreover, in the deeper hole the vein showed changes in

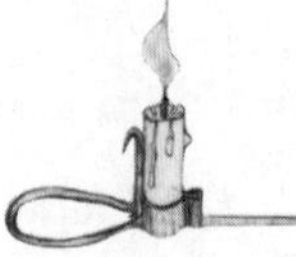

its mineralogy and texture, becoming richer in iron carbonate and poorer in pyrite, and losing the closely spaced cracks that characterized the richer samples. He consulted Chris, who shook his head.

"It looks as though the vein could be bottoming out. Or at best we are seeing a lean zone. I don't like the way the vein seems to be changing with depth—a bad sign. Mind you, the next four holes are deep ones and will tell a lot more."

◊ ◊ ◊

In the Cariboo, Ted Brook, of Transaurum Ventures, was visiting the Kingfisher operation. Jay was dominating the conversation.

"A lot depends on the next assays; I'll have them in a week. My next move will probably be to cut some new trenches to cross the northern extensions of my No. 2 vein. Which reminds me—Bill, check with Ralph, make sure the cat and the back-hoe are ready to move up there. And then bring those maps up to date." Jay turned back to Ted.

"As I was saying, when I've got a little more surface length on these veins, and if they continue to kick, I'll test them with some deep holes."

Jay was making it clear that Bill was a very junior member of the team. More and more, Bill was ignored at or excluded from meetings with visitors. His opinions on geological matters were not only not asked for, but when offered were rudely or sarcastically rejected. Bill was beginning to feel like the office boy.

But worse was to come a few days later. People who

work in buildings, in rooms with thick walls and doors, take some time to adjust to the fact that canvas is not an effective sound absorber. One day, as Bill passed the office tent, he couldn't help hearing Jay's confident voice.

"Oh, Bill? He's quite useful. U.B.C. grad. No experience. Doesn't have a lot on the ball. But he'll learn. Now, to answer your question: how did I tumble to this area? It wasn't difficult. If you look at the colour of this gold, you'll notice it's much yellower than the gold from the mine across the valley. Now if you look at the placer gold from the Golden Rainbow placer operation, down the river a bit, you will find that they produce two kinds of gold. ..."

Jay was entertaining the chief geologist for Mega-Development Gold Corporation with the story of the brilliant series of deductions that had led to the successful pinpointing of this area. The only trouble was that Jay was making it sound as though he had made the brilliant deductions. And not only was he stealing credit that should belong to Bill, he was going out of his way to make Bill appear to be a mediocre and ineffective member of the team.

Bill had had enough. When their visitor had gone, he charged into the office tent.

"Jay, you're a first-class shit. You treat me like a—a—servant. You take credit for my ideas and you bad-mouth me behind my back. I'm quitting." He rushed out of the tent, tangling a boot in the fly-bar netting as he went, not stopping to free it, and nearly pulling the tent down before it ripped free.

Red-faced and shaking, Bill went to his tent, packed his gear, revved up his Beetle and headed for Vancouver.

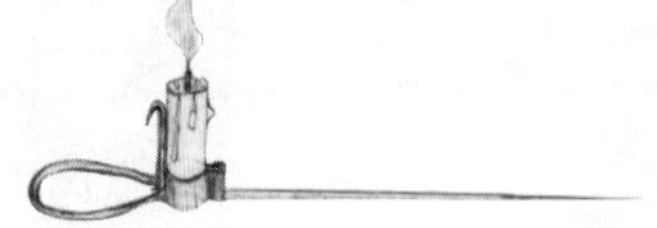

Jay was relieved to see him go but at the same time a little uneasy.

◊ ◊ ◊

Isaac was on the phone. "Why did Bill quit?" he asked Jay. "Everything going well?"

"I think maybe he was getting bored—wanted to get back to the big city. Maybe girlfriend trouble. Now, about the drilling. We need a couple of long holes to test these veins at depth."

Isaac replied unhappily: "At $15 a foot we can't afford many long holes. I'll think about it and get back to you tonight."

Isaac discussed the situation with Chris.

"Jay is optimistic and is asking for another 3,000 feet of drilling but if things don't pick up, we're going to have to take our losses and close it down. I have the horrible feeling that Jay's got the bit in his teeth and is flogging a dead horse. Assays from the last deep intersection average 0.06 ounces. And no pyrite. A bad sign because, in this part of the Cariboo, pyrite is always found with the gold. It looks bad. Jay's not being too smart, I think."

Chris nodded. "I don't like this Bill business either. Why did he quit?"

"Maybe he wasn't up to the job. Maybe we shouldn't have hired him."

"I think you're wrong, Isaac. I think we were lucky to get him. Well, pretty lucky. Clever, finding those veins, using the different kinds of gold. He may not be a whirling piss-pot but he's a damn sight better than most of the youngsters we've hired."

Isaac conceded,"I guess you're right. He's a good head. I wondered about him sometimes, though—in office meetings I got the feeling that he was sitting there day-dreaming. But I'm sorry he quit. Jay can be pretty hard to live with. Actually he's an arrogant bastard. Probably Bill just couldn't stand him any longer."

"He and Julie had something going for a while but I think they had a scrap. She's been down in the dumps lately."

"Well, Chris, I think I had better get up there and see what's going on. You can hold the fort here for a couple of days."

Chris agreed. Jay's enthusiasm and persistence in the face of negative geological evidence and bad news from the assayers reminded him of his own actions when, years ago in the Chilcotin country, he was on his first moose hunt. He and his partner had separated in order to cover more ground. Striding along over 4 inches of new snow, he emerged onto a natural meadow and there before him the snow was criss-crossed by moose tracks. He judged that he had stumbled upon the traces of at least four animals. He quietly slid a shell into the chamber, cocked the action, and set the safety. He picked a prominent and fresh set of tracks and set out to follow them. It soon appeared that his particular moose was an unusually agile one because it could slip between saplings less than a foot apart but he put this observation aside as he hurried after his prey. In one place the moose had negotiated a passage between a rock bluff and a 2-foot-thick pine that he himself had trouble getting through and this observation led to some unease. A few minutes later, it struck him that this moose was very light on its hooves because some of the tracks didn't penetrate the snow down to the ground. He stopped, his

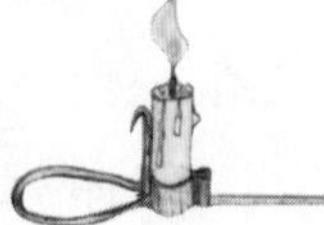

cheeks flushing hotly, and looked around, hoping that his partner was far away. He had been following rabbit tracks, each body print of the bounding rabbit making a reasonable facsimile of a single hoof print. He should have realized this much earlier but he had been so excited and so intent on sighting his quarry that commonsense had deserted him.

Chris realized that Jay was in the same situation—so determined to find a mine that he was not thinking logically.

◊ ◊ ◊

Meanwhile, in Montreal, Yves spread a rumour that Kingfisher and Croesus were negotiating a deal. There was no substance to this gossip but it would have been a logical move for Kingfisher had they encountered a rich vein that seemed to be headed for Croesus ground. The stock climbed to $7.50 in two days. By this time Boris and Mousy had sold all of their shares.

Steve walked into the Behemoth office. As usual, Patti batted her eyes at him.

"Make a killing on Croesus?" She flashed a new gold bracelet at him. "I got out at $6, but I didn't have much." Steve had sold his few shares at $5. Having bought his shares at ten cents, a special deal, he had made more than enough to allow him to replace his old car.

"I did O.K. Next time better. Let me in on the next one, eh?"

Boris was out but Mousy welcomed Steve with twinkling eyes and a two-handed handshake.

"Steverino! How's it going? You got out? Good." Nose

twitching. "I think we've peaked but don't spread the word around. The stock's at $7.75. We are anticipating a downward correction."

Steve looked puzzled and then understood. "I guess a lot of people are going to lose their shirts when it nose-dives." Mousy smiled.

"Not too many. May lose a sleeve or two. But it won't nose-dive. We'll control the fall. Leak the odd bit of good news. If necessary, we'll buy back a few shares of the stock as it falls to make sure there's always a buyer—no panic selling, no crash. It'll fall slowly over the next few weeks and months. We can't allow the stock to go down too fast—we don't want to attract the attention of the authorities—makes us look bad. In the short run, it'll cost us a bit of money but overall we'll do quite well. In the end, we'll have some of the stock. If Kingfisher ever comes up with some good news, which seems unlikely, we can run the stock up again. Anyhow, the suckers have a lot better chance of making a few bucks with us than they have by buying lottery tickets." Mousy warmed to his subject and continued.

"There are going to be a few soreheads around who buy at the peak and hold on—some will whine that they've been swindled. But most of these idiots will have had lots of chance to get out—they're just plain greedy. Or stupid. But most of them end up feeling foolish and most don't advertise their stupidity. So they keep quiet. On the other hand, the winners make a lot of noise, boasting about how smart they have been and this doesn't hurt us a bit."

"You seem very pessimistic," Steve said. "Kingfisher could still get some good drill intersections and Croesus might still have a gold mine. Nobody knows what's under

that glacial drift."

Mousy looked off into the distance. "My information is that Kingfisher's deep veins are not ore, and that they're petering out at depth. I'm told they may close it down." He thought for a moment and then continued. "Anyway, we're much better off without a mine."

Steve couldn't believe his ears. "What do you mean? I thought that was the whole point of the exercise."

Mousy smiled and patted Steve on the shoulder.

"Much better not to have a mine. We'd have to raise a lot of money and this would be a real pain. It's not easy, once the first excitement is over. And there's not much in it for us. And we'd have to start messing around with geological reports, mining engineers, feasibility studies, deals with other companies and all the rest of it. And lawyers. My God, the lawyers."

Mousy's smile disappeared. "And worst of all, the environmentalists. And the government bureaucrats who are scared to death of them. These bureaucrats can delay a perfectly straightforward mine development for years, even forever, for fear of offending some do-gooder from California. And during all these negotiations, more lawyers, applications for permits and licenses, the dollars are going down the drain." Mousy gave Steve a final pat on the back.

"No, our business is promotion and we can be thankful that we're not stuck with a potential mine."

◊ ◊ ◊

Ten days after the drill intersection had been seen from Steve's helicopter, and with the drill now working on hole No. 5, Kingfisher announced some new assay results. Hole No. 3 showed 0.07 ounces of gold and 2 ounces of silver over a width of 17 feet; hole No. 4 was of even lower grade.

Veins of such material could not be mined at a profit, Isaac knew. Such a result was not fatal but it was discouraging—the hoped-for bonanza had not materialized. He would have to shut down the Cariboo operation.

As the information became known, first to insiders and later to the general public, investors started to sell their Croesus shares. The price of the stock fell, but after allowing a small drop, Boris and his friends bought just enough stock to control the decline and prevent panic selling. They released an assay from another piece of float and reassured the public that the stock still had a chance. These occasional cushioning moves allowed the stock to fall slowly and, in the end, after a gradual decline, the stock stabilized at eighty-five cents.

◊ ◊ ◊

Jay was not pleased at Isaac's arrival at the Cariboo property. He considered him hopelessly unimaginative and old-fashioned. Jay spread out the maps and cross-sections and enthusiastically pushed his ideas on further drilling, involving deep holes over a large area. Isaac could see that most of the veins were thinner at depth and concluded that they were seeing the bottom of this particular group of veins. Jay seemed shocked by Isaac's lack of optimism.

Isaac put it bluntly. "The drilling shows that at deeper levels the mineralization is petering out. You're probably

drilling the roots of the vein system. This set of veins has been nearly all removed by erosion and we've got to cut our losses."

"What about extensions down to the south," Jay complained. "We haven't done much trenching in that sector. I would have done some work down there but Bill was all on fire to concentrate on the ground to the northwest. Never did think much of his wild theories—these young guys are strong on theory and weak on practice."

Isaac growled, "You were pretty enthusiastic about them a while ago. Anyhow, we've spent all the money we're going to in this neck of the woods. We're closing down the operation right away."

After a few more objections, Jay reluctantly agreed.

◊ ◊ ◊

Isaac set out on the long drive to Vancouver. How can Jay be so smart and so dumb at the same time? he wondered. Why did Bill quit? Missed! Why do gophers run across the road when they see a car coming? Get gas and something to eat at Clinton. June is the best month.

As he approached a turnoff a few miles north of Cache Creek, he looked at his watch. He slowed and turned right. Twelve miles of twisty gravel road past small Indian farms, to Hat Creek junction. Then right again, through the Marble Canyon. A narrow, fantastically blue, impossibly blue lake hemmed in by white, grey and iron-stained limestone mountains on whose crests mysterious stone towers plough the clouds. At the ancient Indian village at Pavilion, the road cut across the snout of a giant landslide. It then descended towards the Fraser and wound south to Fountain, its ancient gold diggings now hardly recognizable. A few miles more and he looked down on the mouth of Bridge River. He parked and watched a native fisher. Motionless, legs astride, balanced on a crag above a quiet eddy in the turbulent Fraser, he suddenly twists, lunges and draws his twenty-foot dip-net from the water, a coho writhing in the meshes. He untangles the salmon, bends its head back until the spine snaps, and tosses it onto the mossy rocks behind him.

Half an hour later, Isaac looked across the river at Lillooet. He continued south, crawling carefully along the twisty disintegrating shelf opposite Texas Creek, then speeding past irrigated alfalfa fields, bright green squares contrasting abruptly with the grey-brown semi-desert. He turned at a side road, lifted a sagging gate, and drove around and between several chrome-rich ancient cars, some on blocks, others on flattened tires; none would ever move again. Chickens scattered, a nondescript dog appeared, barked. The door of the log house opened.

Short. Broad. Straight black hair. Quilted cheeks. Her front teeth solid gold. A cigarette locked between lumpy fingers. When she blinked, her lower and upper lids closed over black eyes, lizard-like.

He smiled and spoke haltingly in the Interior Salish dialect: "Greetings, sister of my mother. How are you today?"

Not a Jew or a Greek or a Turk. Chris had missed the boat again.

◊ ◊ ◊

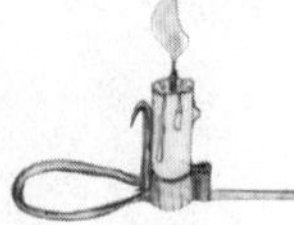

That afternoon Ben Richards sat in his wooden chair, Vancouver newspapers scattered around him on the linoleum. A tap dripped in the rusty sink. A horse fly attacked the dirty window.

He looked up from his paper as the cheerful news announcer moved on to a new item:

"The body of a woman found in bush in 4900 block Greenall Road has been identified as that of Betty Forbes, age thirty-one, a graduate student at U.B.C. Forbes is possibly the victim of a hit-and-run. Her body appears to have been in the bush about a week. Police are continuing their investigations."

"God damn it to hell," Ben muttered. "But I'll get him yet; I'll get him."

Chapter 14

Bill and Julie go Camping

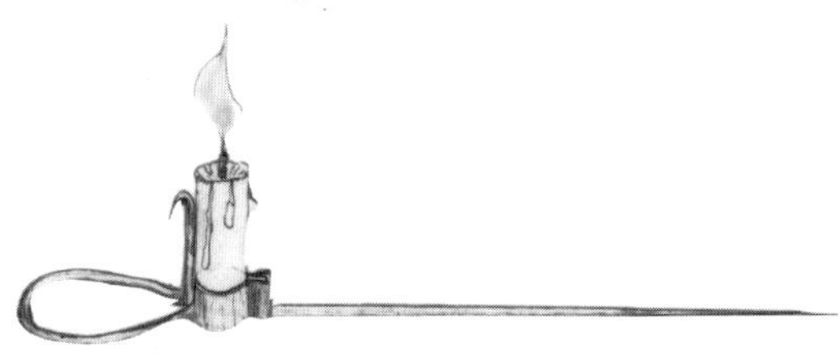

It was a Tuesday morning. Bill had been back in his West End apartment for a week, his mind feverishly busy. He desperately wanted to see Julie but he didn't look forward to facing Isaac whom he felt he had left in the lurch by quitting.

He had slept badly. Having nodded off at 3:00 AM he was half awakened at 5:00. The hissing and yowling of a pair of cats had aroused a Doberman whose frenzied barking echoed through the neighbourhood. Bill had pulled the covers over his head as the Gordon setter living three doors to the west and the shaggy terrier a block to the south informed the neighbourhood that they were on guard and would, given the chance, tear the Doberman to shreds. More distant dogs took up the cry.

The fading sounds had inspired a fitful dream: the barking spread in all directions, a two-dimensional chain reaction, sweeping across the city, into the suburbs, north, east, and south across the continent, leaping oceans, mountain ranges, and deserts, and finally expanding like a net over the entire globe.

Bill woke up exhausted. After a listless breakfast, he made a decision, gathered up his courage, and called around at

the Kingfisher office. He told himself that his purpose was to pick up his pay cheque but he really wanted to see Julie. As he came in, Julie saw him out of the corner of her eye and looked down at a report that suddenly needed all of her attention. He tried to be casual.

"Hi Julie."

"Oh. Hi Bill. What are you doing these days?"

"Not much. A bit of holidaying. Looking around. Keeping an eye open for a job." Julie seemed friendly and Bill was relieved.

"What's new with you?" he asked.

"Nothing much. This is always a slack time of year. Typing boring reports on mining properties."

"Is Isaac in? I guess I should see him."

"He's alone at the moment—I'll give him a buzz. Go on in." Bill knocked on the open door.

Isaac straightened up from the map table. He motioned Bill to sit down, closed the door, and subsided behind his desk. He looked speculatively at Bill and waited for him to speak.

"I haven't got my last pay-cheque."

"Right. It's here somewhere." Isaac fished an envelope out of his desk drawer. "Well, Bill, I'm sorry you quit. You left us a little short-handed. What was the trouble?"

Bill was in a quandary. He didn't want to get a reputation as a whiner but he felt that he had been abused and had had every right to quit.

"I just couldn't stomach Jay any longer," he said. "He treated me like dirt. He has a low opinion of me and made no secret of it. We had lots of visitors, you know—I heard him ...Well, never mind. But he's a son of a bitch. He hogged all of the credit for my original idea and the more veins we found, the worse he got. I think he was trying to push me into quitting. I suppose he'll be the man-of-the year when the mine gets going." Bill stopped, wondering if he was making a complete ass of himself.

Isaac was silent for a minute. "That sounds like our Jay. He's got a terrible ego. You're not the first one to walk out on him. But he's a good geologist and he's done some good work for us. I wish you had stuck it out. Well, that's say la vee. We've closed down the operation."

"You did? I though it was going great guns. We had all those new veins. What happened?"

"The deep drilling was very disappointing. It was a good try and nobody's fault. Jay's gone back up to the Bridge River area." Isaac got up from his chair.

"Dammit, I'd like to have you back. But sooner or later you'd have to work with Jay and that wouldn't do. I'll give you a good reference. Things are quiet in town right now—they always are in July—but you might find something. I'd try one of the new copper shows. They're always short of geologists."

A relieved Bill shook the offered hand and returned to the outer office feeling a little more buoyant than when he had come in. He stopped at Julie's desk and took the plunge.

"Look, why don't we have lunch?"

"Well, O.K. Actually I can get away right now."

They sat facing each other across the table, neither knowing what to say. Bill was dying to know what had gone wrong with their relationship and Julie was afraid he would ask. By some unspoken agreement they acted as if their estrangement had never taken place.

"You heard that the Cariboo gold project has closed

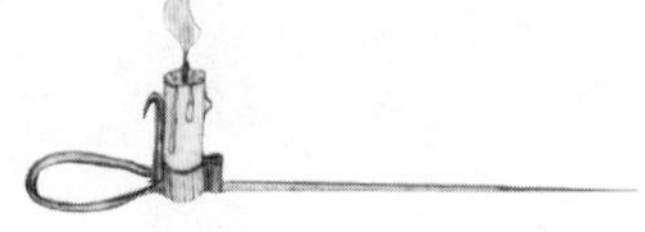

down?" Julie asked.

Bill nodded. "Isaac just told me. It was looking pretty good when I left. I was surprised."

"Apparently the assays were disappointing and Isaac went up to Wells and closed it down."

"I hope he broke Jay's heart."

"Jay tried to give the impression that you were partly to blame but I don't think he fooled anyone. Anyway, he's off on another project. Chris is getting ready to go up to Highland Valley—big sampling job. We haven't found anyone to take your place."

Bill explained why he had quit and Julie said that she and Chris had not been surprised that there had been some friction between them. She agreed to go out to dinner with him that night. They were now back on excellent terms.

They went to one of the many Italian restaurants and had the specialty of the house, a tasty pasta with a shrimp sauce, complemented by a biting red wine. Not that they noticed. They were completely engrossed in each other and the attentive waiter might just as well have saved his smiles and flourishes and fed them canned cat-food. Outside the door to Julie's apartment, Bill pulled her to him and kissed her hungrily. Unfortunately for them, Liz was home that night and although she soon discreetly withdrew to her own bedroom, they felt a little constrained.

After weeks of uncertainty, frustration and misery, relief had made Bill reckless. "Look, why don't we go away for a few days? Can you get some time off?"

She considered only for a moment. "I'm sure I can. Things are slow at the office and I've got a lot of holiday time saved up. Where'll we go?"

After a few moments, Bill recovered from his surprise and delight at her quick agreement, and a plan of action took shape. "Here's what you need," he said, "some warm clothes, hiking boots, small back-pack, camera and personal stuff—towel, soap and so on. I'll bring everything else."

"Okay, but where are we going?" she asked.

"Can't tell you exactly. Consider it a mystery trip. Have to talk to a fellow and do a little arranging. We'll probably go in the next day or two."

Bill had a friend who was pilot and part owner of a small helicopter company and he wangled the promise of a free ride on an empty chopper going out on a forestry job. He bought a large scale topographic map at the government office and marked his destination. The weather was settled and he could depend on a week of perfect summer days.

Two days later, Bill and Julie drove to Lytton, 200 miles northeast of Vancouver. He parked the Beetle near the helicopter pad, which was simply a dusty clearing in the pines beside the road. The helicopter sat in the open, its blades drooping in the sun. A pick-up wheeled into the field. A small, blond fellow walked over to them.

"Hi Russ, this is Julie."

"Hello!" admiring once-over. "Ever flown before?"

"No. I'm looking forward to it. But Bill won't tell me where we're going."

"Shame on you, Bill. I don't know either." Russ' tone became serious. "Wherever we're going, you have to follow a couple of rules. First, if we land on a hillside, dismount and leave on the downhill side and, second, stay away from the tail rotor at the rear end of the machine."

They stuffed their gear into the cargo compartment and strapped themselves in. Bill and Russ conferred over the maps. The small craft shook as the rotor gathered speed. After studying the gauges, Russ made mysterious adjustments to certain knobs and levers, the blades began to bite, and they lifted above the now dust-obscured clearing. Julie found it a little unnerving to be able to look down between her feet at the tree-tops, but with Bill's reassuring hand holding hers, she soon succumbed to the exhilaration and magic of helicopter flight. They climbed steeply, crossed the Fraser and turned west into the Coast Mountains, entering a major river valley. In about ten minutes, they turned south, the pilot following Bill's hand signals. Their destination was a tiny lake about a quarter mile across. This lay at timberline in a bowl at the head of a valley whose U-shaped cross-section was typical of those that had at one time been filled and shaped by scouring glaciers. The machine settled on a clear spot. Heads low, Bill and Julie scrambled out onto the heather. Bill extracted their bags from the cargo locker.

"See you in three days," he shouted at Russ. "If the weather closes in, come when you can—we've got lots of grub."

Russ winked at him and gave him a thumbs up. They watched the nose-down chopper take off. The roar of the rotors diminished quickly and the machine was out of sight and hearing before they had picked up their gear.

"Well, what do you think of the place?" asked Bill.

Patches of snow survived in clefts and shaded draws in the naked cliffs which formed a backdrop for the lake. The mountains were treeless but near the lake a few stands of small, very narrow spruce trees perfumed the air. Slightly lower, beside the creek which issued from the lake, heather gave way to grasses and wildflowers in white, yellow, blue and red which covered the gentle slopes. The only sound was the whistle of a marmot from the far side of the tarn and the hum of bees working in the heather.

Julie had never been in such a place and found it breath-taking.

"Why is such a beautiful place deserted?" she asked. "It looks as if no one has been here before. Where is the trail out to the highway?"

"There are hundreds of places like this," Bill explained. "The maps don't show any trail—that's why it's deserted. It's less than 10 miles from the highway, but it's 5,000 feet higher and not many people are going to fight their way up here through the brush. And anyway, most people don't know it's here."

Bill chose a level spot close to the creek for the tent. Here they were a little protected from the wind but still in the sun and close to water. In a few minutes Bill had it erected, a nylon hemisphere held up by lightweight metal arches. He tossed the foam mattresses and sleeping bags inside and suggested they walk around a bit. Julie couldn't resist picking specimens of the various wild flowers. Before long, they came to some excavations about ten feet across and 2 or 3 feet deep.

"Exploration pits?" Julie asked indignantly. "What were the prospectors looking for? And it never occurred to them to fill in their holes and clean up their mess? At least they didn't leave a lot of garbage lying around!"

"No," laughed Bill. "These were dug by grizzlies. They were digging out marmots. Geez, look at the size of that boulder they moved—it must weigh a ton!"

Julie was now uneasy, "Is it safe to be up here? Bob

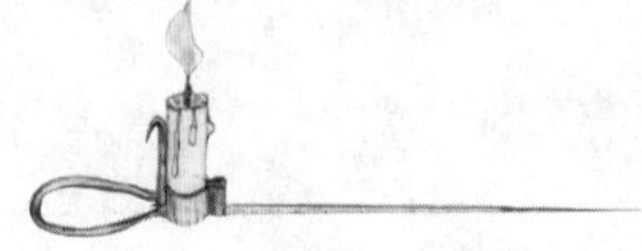

Fowler—he worked for Electrum Resources—Bridge River—was mauled last year."

"Perfectly safe. These are at least ten years old—see how they're grown in. And we've not seen any recent sign. They're long gone."

They climbed a little higher. Shreds and tangles of white wool hooked on stiff bleached dead branches marked a goat trail where it passed through stands of wind-blown half-dead and stunted spruce trees.

Suddenly a loud thrum, like forty guitars sounding a single chord. Julie screamed, staggered off balance and clutched at Bill.

"What was that?"

Bill steadied her, holding on a little longer than was absolutely necessary.

"A hummingbird."

"Why would it attack me?"

"He wasn't attacking," Bill explained. "He took your red plaid shirt for a flower."

Still higher, the only vegetation was heather and they noticed a curious phenomenon: as they looked ahead at a rocky knob, they couldn't tell how far away it was. With no trees for scale, they found it impossible to say whether it was 100 yards away and about 50 feet high, or a mile away and 800 feet high.

Back at camp, Bill picked a spot for a fireplace at some distance from the tent. He didn't want flying sparks burning holes in it. A few boulders on edge formed a low back wall to support the fire and a couple of flat ones in front served as a low platform for plates and pots. He broke off an armful of dead limbs in a nearby grove of spruce. Covered with dry sparse moss, they made excellent kindling. As the fire took hold, he collected a pile of bleached dead sticks and small logs. He hung a large pot of water over the fire on a horizontal stick supported in a couple of crotched uprights. Bill had brought packaged pre-cooked meals sealed in heavy foil. In half an hour, chicken and rice were steaming on their tin plates. Bill fetched a cold bottle of wine from the creek. Making do with enamel mugs and mismatched knives and forks, they had a feast.

The shadows of the spruce trees became grotesquely long, the sun reddened the slopes and in a few moments slipped behind the cliffs. An enormous moon, double its usual size, its maria and craters sharply etched in the clear cold air, appeared over the ridge. After they put on sweaters, Bill threw some big chunks on the fire and they sat and watched the flames. He leaned against her, putting an arm around her shoulders and kissed her ear. She turned her face to him.

They felt and stumbled their way to the tent. While she held the flashlight, Bill found to his profound relief that he could zip the two sleeping bags together. They undressed in darkness and, amid outbreaks of nervous giggling, crawled into the sleeping bag.

Bill had visualized this moment a hundred times and had plotted every move. Alas for his plans—it was over before he reached step one. He clasped Julie tightly, head buried in her shoulder, unmanned and broken. Julie, instinctively summoning up some female wisdom, stroked his head and in whispers told him to relax and wait. Next time, modest success. They separated and tentatively explored each others bodies. He, fascinated by the magic buttons that rose at the touch of his lips; she, marvelling as she ran her hands down his lean flanks and compact buttocks. Half an hour later, their passion was

rekindled. This time their love-making was prolonged and satisfying to both, and Bill heaved a sigh of relief and happiness.

As they relaxed, lying side by side, Julie's head on his shoulder and his right arm holding her close, Bill told her how he had become infatuated with her on his first day at work, how he had made plan after plan to invite her out but was awed and deterred by her beauty and worldliness. She in her turn told how she had been aware of his interest and had been disappointed that he hadn't been quicker to act.

A stick cracked like a shot in the nearby patch of woods. They froze, and listened, hardly breathing. Another crack, and they could hear a large animal—a bear, Julie thought, probably a grizzly—moving slowly through the trees towards the tent. Bill didn't have a gun and the axe was somewhere out by the fire. He groped in the dark for his jack-knife—he might be able to divert the beast's attention while Julie made an escape. He cursed himself for not bringing a rifle. He thought of those giant excavations by the lake and remembered some of Gus' stories of marauding grizzlies. They listened as the animal approached the tent, pawing and sniffing. The tent shuddered as it brushed against a supporting strut. They lay perfectly still and were able to breathe normally again only when the sounds gradually diminished and finally stopped. The brute had lumbered off down the valley into the thick timber. In spite of Bill's assurances that the beast had departed for good, Julie was still nervous. After a while they fell asleep.

Next morning, Bill poked a cautious head through the door slit, saw that all was clear, and crawled out of the tent. He almost stepped into a large, fresh cow pat and then he realized what had happened in the night. He crawled back into the tent and explained things to Julie.

The local ranchers, most of them Indians, had small farms on the benches that clung to the valley side along the west bank of the Fraser River. In June of each year a rancher would drive a few dozen cattle up a trail into the mountains, and as he returned, block the trail at a narrow place along the cliffs with a make-shift fence. The cattle, trapped above, would spend the summer pasturing in the lush wild meadows of the high country. In the fall their owner would remove the barrier on the trail and as the nights grew cold, the cattle would find their way down to the farm. Apparently something had disturbed one of these animals and it had blundered into their camp.

Julie had been imagining all sorts of dire scenarios in which she had been eaten alive by grizzlies and she was wondering how she was going to survive for two more days. She was so relieved at Bill's explanation that he was able to cajole her back into the sleepingbag. They emerged an hour or so later, tired, relaxed and content with the world.

Bill led Julie along the lake to a narrow cove where the sparkling water was only a few feet deep. They peeled off their pajamas. Snow melted only a few feet away and the water was paralysingly cold. Julie swam quickly across to the heather bank some 30 feet away. Bill dove, his momentum carrying him across to the far side where he scrambled out onto the heather and into the sunshine, puffing, snorting, and shivering. When they returned to camp, Bill produced a gigantic breakfast of bacon and eggs. Thus began the first day of their mountain idyll, which they would never forget.

Over the next few days, they continued to explore. On

one expedition they headed down valley, following the creek which disappeared and reappeared in the heather. Bill carried his rock hammer and cracked the occasional boulder while Julie added to her collection of wildflowers.

"Julie. Have a look at this."

"That *is* a pretty rock—shiny, almost apple-green—is it greenstone?" She had heard the name used by the geologists in the office.

"No, it's serpentine. See, it's soft and slippery-looking. There must be a serpentine body around here somewhere." Bill looked up and scanned the bluffs on each side of the valley. "And there it is. See the orangy-brown cliffs up there? That's where it's coming from. There'll be patches of green serpentine in them. And look here. Now here's something." He handed her a chunk of dark green rock. "Now that's different, hard and tough. I'll bet we can find some more—the creek washes the boulders clean. Here's another piece."

"What is it?"

"Jade," he said.

"Real jade?"

"Sure. There's lots of it around here and on the river bars in the Fraser—or there was before the rock-hounds started collecting it. It's tough and it'll hold an edge. The Indians used to make tools from it. I read the other day that they used to set the value of a good jade axe at three slaves. The slaves were captives from other tribes. This is where it comes from, or places like this. It's found along the edges of these serpentine bodies. There are several small abandoned jade mines not far from here, all of them money-losers, I suspect. The glaciers scoured these valleys and scattered the loose blocks and boulders far and wide.

A lot of them ended up in the Fraser. They've found 10-ton jade boulders in the Bridge River and its side-creeks."

"But look," Julie objected. "This stuff is right here, lying around underfoot. Why doesn't someone gather it up and sell it?"

"It wouldn't pay," Bill explained. "Rough jade's only worth a couple of dollars a pound. How do you get it out to the highway? Helicopters cost hundreds of dollars an hour. Building a road is out of the question. And it's got to be mined, culled, transported and sawn into blocks. Also, mining is tricky. Too strong an explosive charge and you shatter the jade. Most of the value of jade is in the carving. Some of the pieces I've seen must have taken Chinese artists years to carve." They satisfied themselves with collecting a few choice specimens as souvenirs and started the long walk back to camp.

They were startled by a shrill whistle and looked across the valley to see a marmot scramble from its lookout rock and dive into its hole. An eagle floated past, and 300 yards down the valley they heard another whistle as the next sentry sounded the alarm and went to earth. A succession of diminishing whistles marked the flight path of the eagle as it disappeared.

Thus they spent the next two days, hiking and exploring, learning about each other, even bickering a little. The only intrusion from the outer world was an occasional invisible, silent jet liner, its course marked by a white lance advancing across the sky. The weather was kind to them and the helicopter picked them up on schedule.

Back in Lytton, as they climbed into the Beetle, Bill said: "Let's drop in on a friend of mine—a rancher who lives near Merritt. It's only a couple of hours out of our way. You'll enjoy meeting him. He's a real character, a tough

old bachelor."

"Okay, but I have to be home tonight."

Bill wanted to show Julie off and felt that the more the world knew that they were lovers, the more secure their precious relationship would be.

◊ ◊ ◊

Gus straightened up from the tractor engine as he heard Bill's noisy Volkswagen. He wiped his hands on a piece of sacking, grinned at Bill, and raised his eyebrows as Julie climbed out.

"Julie, this is Gus."

"Well, where has Bill been hiding you? Come in. Are you staying the night?"

"No. Julie has to be back at work tomorrow. We're just saying hello."

"Stay for a cup of tea, anyway."

Soon they were sitting at the rough table and Gus poured the tea. In honour of Julie, he had rummaged through the back of the cupboard and found three elegant china cups and saucers which didn't quite fit with the can of evaporated milk and the bent spoons. He filled and handed the cups and picked up his own. The cup seemed very fragile in his banana-sized fingers with their ridged, cracked and pitch-stained nails. He lifted his cup to drink and Bill could not believe his eyes. What normally might be referred to as Gus' pinky (but clearly inappropriately since Gus' fifth digit resembled a gnarled root or weathered piece of driftwood) extended at right angles from the cup in his massive grip. Bill concluded that at some time Gus had been told or had observed that it was genteel, when holding a teacup, to extend the little finger.

"Well, what's new Gus?" he asked. Gus set down his cup and leaned forward.

"You remember the last time you were here I told you about the dirt-bagger sneaking around on my property? Well, a guy from a mining company dropped in on me about a week ago. He says he found something interesting in the soil up by the old adit. Anyhow, they're paying me to let them to do some work on my claims. Pay pretty well too."

"What company is it?"

"Kingfisher Explorations."

"Why, that's my old company! Julie still works there. Who were you dealing with?"

"Guy named Costello."

Julie had been listening, astonished. She had been present at the Kingfisher meeting at which Gus' showings had been discussed.

Gus continued: "They're going to start work in a day or two."

Bill was a little disconcerted because he had not offered Gus much encouragement when he had walked over the property a month earlier, but Gus seemed to have forgotten Bill's lack of enthusiasm. They drank their tea, and after a short inspection of the cabin and a walk around the out-buildings, Bill and Julie took their leave. As they reached the highway, Bill asked: "What did you think of him?"

"I hope Kingfisher gave him a decent deal. He's a nice old guy. I hope Carl didn't trick him into signing away his claims for less than they're worth." She shook her head.

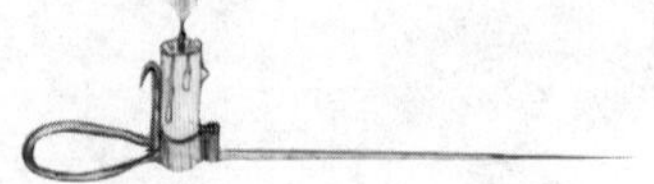

"Must get awfully lonesome up here. I don't think he meets many women."

Bill was pleased. He had seen that Gus liked Julie.

Chapter 15

Gus and Carl

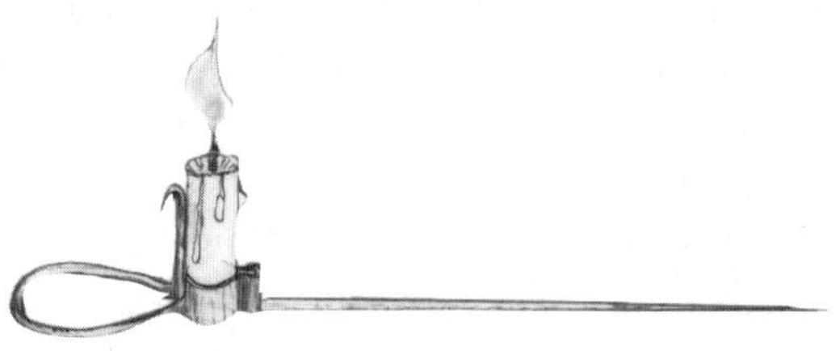

Gus looked up from the saw he was sharpening as a muddy car led a bull-dozer and a back-hoe into the clearing. Carl stepped down and introduced a couple of his helpers, gave them brief instructions and waved them off up the hill towards the adit.

Gus grumbled, "I hope you guys aren't too late. Somebody's been staking claims up above the lake."

Carl reassured him. "It's probably O.K. We staked a few claims up there the other day—I think we beat the competition." Gus looked surprised.

"Ron and his crew will live in a motel in Merritt. Here's what we're going to do: sample the adit—I assume the adit was driven on the best surface showing. Then we'll cut some long trenches up behind the adit, aligned across the creeks and draws, and we'll sample the bedrock. Those deep draws north of the adit probably lie along faults—maybe mineralized. We'll trench across some of them. Then, who knows. Maybe in a month we'll have the drills in here."

"Jeez, you're going to make an awful mess."

"Don't worry—we'll backfill the trenches when we're through sampling."

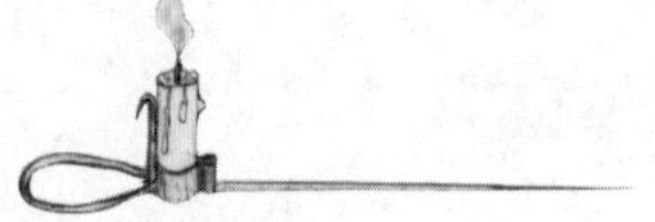

Gus asked, "Do I get a look at the assays?"

"Not right away. But if we decide to walk away from the property, we'll leave you a complete set of the assay maps. Might be useful some day."

For the next few days Gus watched with satisfaction as the bull-dozer cleared roads into some of the forested parts of his property. Even if they didn't find any ore, the new roads would give access to timber that he would cut for firewood. He might even log some areas that before had been inaccessible. He kept busy bustling around the trenches and watching Carl supervise the taking of samples from the newly exposed bedrock in the bottoms of the trenches. The samples were broken from the bedrock with pick and sledge-hammer, placed in heavy plastic bags, labelled, and trucked to Vancouver for assay.

◊ ◊ ◊

A few weeks later, Gus and Carl met near the adit. Carl looked worried, perplexed.

"Well, how are things going?" Gus asked.

"No assays yet." Carl was lying. He had just received three pages of them, sixty in all, but he wasn't going to show them to this annoying hayseed until he had had time to study them. But he had had time to run his eye down the figures and they were discouraging.

"Well, how does it look?" Gus persisted. "Are you finding lots of mineral?"

"Not much to see yet. But we've just started. We won't know anything definite for a couple of weeks."

To Gus, Carl didn't look like a man who had just uncovered a valuable copper deposit, and in fact, Carl was puzzled and discouraged. He had concentrated his work in the areas near the headwaters of the side-creeks, upstream from the copper-rich stream samples. The newly exposed bedrock, not deeply weathered, was not well mineralized—it was hardly mineralized at all. He had found a little copper stain in a few places but no concentrations of sulfides of copper or molybdenum which the stream and soil sample results had given him every right to expect. A quick reading of the new assays of samples taken from the rock in the trenches had confirmed his earlier observations. Most samples yielded nils or only traces of the metals they were seeking. A few, taken in places where rusty shear zones cut the diorite, showed a few hundredths of one percent of copper but no molybdenum. In general, the mineralization was not as strong as in the adit. Carl couldn't understand it. He restudied the maps on which he had plotted the geochemical results and assays and walked over the ground, map in hand. It couldn't be a mistake in location—everything fit—the road, the creek, the adit, the lake. Could the metal content of the soil have been brought by the glaciers?

Carl walked a short distance along the hillside above the lake, breaking boulders and pieces of float. The rocks were fresh—no sign of green or blue copper stain.

Copper ore minerals, such as chalcocite (copper sulfide) or chalcopyrite (copper-iron sulfide), are chemically unstable where exposed to oxidizing and hydrating conditions near the moist ground surface. They slowly decompose and react to form various new hydrated minerals, just as shiny steel turns to brown rust. The most common of these secondary copper minerals is malachite, a mineral which coats the rocks like pale green paint. Azurite, less common, is a vivid blue. Prospectors and geologists are

thoroughly familiar with these and on finding them, generally on rusty, weathered rock surfaces, will smash into the underlying fresh rock where the original metallic-lustred copper sulfide will be preserved.

Carl couldn't understand the absence of copper sulfides or malachite in the bedrock upstream from the strong copper geochemical anomalies shown by the stream samples. Something didn't make sense.

◊ ◊ ◊

Four weeks after starting the program, Carl had enough assays to show that they had another dud. There seemed to be no correlation at all between the geochemical anomalies from the creeks and soils and the assay results from the trenches. He thought of collecting some more soil samples but a nagging suspicion was growing in his mind that something was wrong. He had informed Isaac that it wasn't panning out and Isaac had agreed that, unless there was a dramatic improvement, they should close down the operation. He made up his mind as he finished inspecting the upper workings and he told the foreman to start filling in the trenches. Soon after, he found Gus chopping wood at the cabin.

"How are the assays?" Gus asked.

"Bad, I'm afraid. We're getting practically nothing. I don't know where the pyrite in the creek's coming from. The bedrock is practically unmineralized." Gus listened sympathetically but, to Carl, he seemed strangely unmoved. Relaxed. The old bugger couldn't have known all the time that the assays would show nothing, could he?

"I've been talking to head office. We're closing down and getting out. I've told the back-hoe fellow to fill the trenches and we'll clean up and get the equipment out. I'm afraid we're not going to find a mine around here."

He watched Gus for a reaction—disappointment that there would be no mine, that he would not be wealthy. Again he was surprised at Gus' stoicism. What was going on? What had the old bastard been up to? Baffled and frustrated, Carl was reluctant to give up and walk away from this mystery. He strolled over to his car, which was parked beside Gus' pick-up truck. Perhaps subconciously delaying his departure, he glanced into the back of the truck.

"What's in the box?" Carl asked, pointing to the bin in the pick-up. He took a pinch of the material where it encrusted the lid.

"Sand I carry for extra traction in the winter."

Carl took off his sunglasses and rolled the sand between his fingers. It was fine-grained and gritty, and when he put his hand-lens on it he could see that it was mostly pyrite.

"Where did you get it?"

"Down at Princeton. There's a sort of quarry in old mine tailings just south of town. It's free and there's any amount of it."

With this last bit of information, the critical piece in the jigsaw fell into place and the puzzle was solved.

Carl weighed possible courses of action. He could accuse Gus, and the company could take him to court, recover the option money, perhaps even damages. But Gus would end up a hero and he, Carl, would become a laughing stock. He could see the headlines: DID FARMER BAMBOOZLE GIANT MINING CORPORATION? Better to put it down to experience and keep his mouth shut. The company could afford to lose a few bucks. They'd thrown

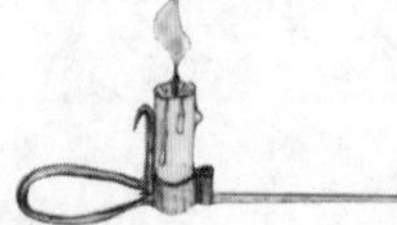

money away on worse prospects than this. Nobody else knew. Chris might ask a few questions, but Carl could snow him with mysterious metal ratios and arcane chemical terminology.

Carl scowled at Gus and, without another word, climbed into his car.

◊ ◊ ◊

Back in Vancouver, the Kingfisher phone rang. Julie answered.

"Kingfisher Explorations."

"Yes. I'm calling from Ashcroft. Name is Jones. I've got a copper property in Highland Valley and I'd like to show it to one of your engineers. What I'm wondering is, will any of your people be in Logan Lake this summer? Maybe we could meet?"

"Mr. Bancroft will be going up to the Cougar Lake deposit but he'll be very busy and won't be looking at properties."

"Well, maybe I could have a word with him—tell him about my showing. When will he be at Logan Lake?"

"He'll be there around August 15, but I'm sure he'll be tied up. He's involved in a big sampling program—a very tight schedule."

"Thanks. Maybe I'll be able to contact him at night, after work."

Julie frowned as she put down the phone. Something about the voice disturbed her, though she couldn't say what.

Chapter 16

Witchers and Mounties

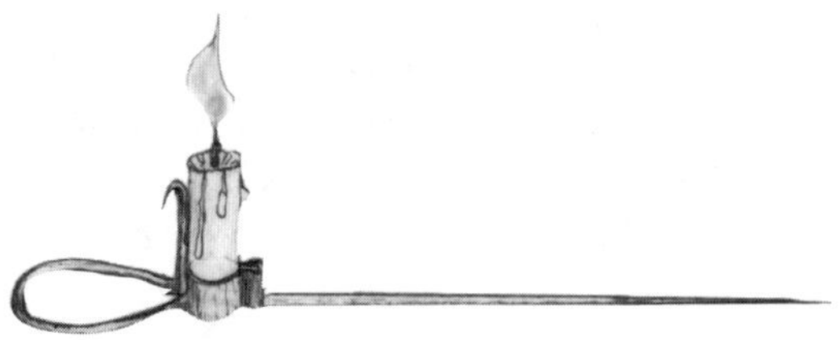

Now without a job, Bill had been nervously watching his small bank account diminish. Although he would have given his eye teeth to stay in town near Julie, he had to find work. He decided to take Isaac's advice and try his luck at one of several new copper mines being developed near Kamloops. He had never worked at a copper mine and perhaps here was an opportunity to broaden his experience. He had lost his enthusiasm for gold mines.

On his way north he left the main highway and turned towards Agassiz, looking forward to a visit with the Prof. But the Prof didn't seem especially glad to see him and even Newton's greeting lacked its usual ferocity.

"Hello, Bill, off to the wilds again?"

Bill sensed that something was wrong. "I'm going up to Highland Valley—hear the copper mines are looking for geologists. I quit Kingfisher. I just dropped by to say hello—can't stay."

The Prof stood aside and pulled him in. "Have a cup of coffee anyway."

As Bill stirred his cup at the kitchen table he could see that he had caught the Prof on a bad day. He didn't seem interested in hearing the details of Bill's Cariboo adven-

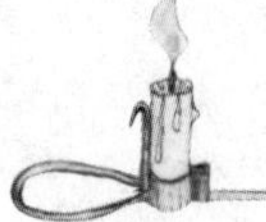

tures or of his difficulties with Jay. A little puzzled, Bill left the subject and the conversation languished. He shouldn't have come. He tried again.

"So, how are things going? Garden looks good. Big crop of veggies?"

The Prof grunted. "Alright, I guess. Aphids on the beans." He said no more. Hoping to provoke a reaction, Bill described his encounter with the gold-witcher at the placer mine in the Cariboo. The Prof's eyes brightened as he rose like a trout to the lure.

"I don't know how people who drive cars and use electric light and radio and television can believe in this nonsense. I read the other day of a dowser in California who finds water for a farmer in Kansas by swinging a pendulum over a map of the man's farm. Another, at his desk in New York, sites a well in New Mexico by holding a forked twig over an aerial photograph! I once met a woman who suspended a ball of knitting wool with a steel needle stuck through it to find gold. The needle would point like a compass to the best location and she would swing the ball like a pendulum and count the swings, and the count gave her the depth to the mother lode!"

Bill couldn't resist a chance to bait his friend. "Well, you know, a lot of people claim that they have found water by following a dowser's advice."

The Prof's eyebrows contracted, the antennae now pointing somewhat forward like the horns of a bull about to charge. "You know perfectly well, Bill, that in most areas the water table lies about parallel to the ground surface. The gravel below the water table is saturated with water. If the ground is permeable, and most of it is, it is much more difficult to avoid water than to find it!"

"Have you ever seen a dowser in action?" Bill asked.

"Oh yes. Many wells in the Fraser valley are sited by dowsers. Most of them use a forked branch from a willow or peach tree. Generally the twig seems to twist or convulse in the dowser's hands as he passes over an underground flow of water. Many claim to be able to tell the depth to water and even the rate of flow to be expected in a well. For depth, some use a straight willow shoot and count the number of times the tip bobs when held over the critical spot, the number of bobs giving the depth in feet to the water source. They use the same technique in France but there each bob indicates a metre of depth."

"But it must work," Bill prodded. "They find water. If they didn't they'd be out of business."

"It doesn't work! Water witchers have submitted to rigorous tests and in these they get no better results than one would get by tossing a coin. These tests have been described in a book by . . ." He grimaced in frustration. "My memory's going—I was looking at the book at the library only last week. Damn, it's right on the tip of my tongue. Well, anyway, probably the most convincing kind of test is this: the dowser, blind-folded, is led across a field and uses his forked stick to identify a spot he believes to be above an underground water course. He is then led by a different route across the same spot to see whether he can find it a second time. If the test is rigorously supervised, with no possibility of peeking under the blindfold or otherwise knowing where he is, he always fails to find it.

"In one experiment, described in that book by so-and-so, some thirty dowsers, one at a time, were tested in a large field in New England—Maine, I think. Each selected the best spot for sinking a well, estimated the depth to water and the strength of the flow. Test wells were then

drilled at each selected spot. Each diviner failed completely in his estimate of depth and flow rate. But they do have successes. They use common sense—it's generally better to drill on the valley floor than on the top of the hill. But their forked sticks don't—"

At this moment the house began to shake, the frying pan tap-danced across the stove top, and concentric ripples formed in the coffee cups. The deafening blast of a train whistle told Bill that it was not an earthquake. Shaken, he picked up the conversation. The Prof already looked much happier.

"Why do people pay any attention to them?" Bill asked.

"Well, for one thing, most people who do it at all, drill a well once in a lifetime, so they try to use every aid they can enlist. And for many people the unshakable confidence of a water witcher is much more compelling than the tentative generalities and uncertainties provided, in many cases, by honest groundwater scientists. And, also, people hire witchers to ward off the remarks that invariably are heard at dry holes drilled without the advice of a witcher: 'What? You didn't get old Seth to witch your well? He never misses.' Also, I think many a driller is glad to have a dowser tell his client where to drill rather than having himself to advise the client in what can be a pretty risky and costly venture. The driller, you see, gets paid whether the hole is wet or dry, and he prefers to avoid responsibility for the dry ones."

"How do the dowsers explain their failures?"

"Any number of ways," the Prof snorted. "It's easy to say that the driller didn't go deep enough. Or that a nearby power line distorted the electric signals his forked stick was receiving from the underground river. Or that his helper was wearing an electric wristwatch or hearing aid.

Sunspots. A nearby radio station. After locating the well, weeks or months may pass before the well is drilled. The dowser can then say that a heavy bull-dozer crossed the field and collapsed an underground water conduit. Or the shock from nearby blasting caused the water to flow in a new direction."

"So they're all crooks, flimflammers?"

"Oh no. I think most of them are not. They believe in what they're doing—without, of course, understanding how they're doing it. As the dowser is walking around, willow wand clenched in his fists, his hands and arms tense and held in unnatural positions, he is subconsciously sizing up the topography, areas of bedrock, distribution and kind of vegetation. Probably he already has information on the nature of the soil and has considered any geological information available to him. He already has data from previous wells in the area. As he passes over the spot that he has subconsciously decided, on the basis of all of this information, to be the best place, his tense and tired wrist and arm muscles convulse involuntarily, and the forked stick, itself twisted or bent and under stress from his tight grip, writhes in his grasp. He honestly believes the force comes from the ground, but it is really his involuntary reaction to a synthesis of these accumulated observations. Psychologists have been studying this sort of involuntary response for decades." The Prof paused.

"Vogt and Hyman," he said.

Bill looked at him, puzzled.

"Those are the authors of the book on dowsing."

The conversation now began to lag, as if the Prof's denunciation of water-witching had exhausted him. Bill ventured a few remarks on subjects that would usually provoke discussion but the Prof remained glum and unre-

sponsive. As Bill climbed into his Beetle, he reflected that the Prof was becoming depressed, really down.

The Prof had reason. Today he had had a shock. But things had been going badly for months.

It had seemed that almost daily he was becoming subject to new aches and pains. A mild tremor in his left hand was getting worse; cups rattled on their saucers, and delicate work like threading a needle was becoming impossible. His hearing dulled and his eyesight became less acute. Nose hair and ear hair sprouted as never before. His mirror told him that his ears were now two sizes too large.

In his younger days he had hoped, no, believed that everyone had a special talent, generally latent and unrecognized. That there was some field in art or science or philosophy in which one could excel. It was simply a matter of finding the right medium or discipline. And then he would have the great satisfaction of being the best, or among the best. The best painter, weaver, flute player, glass blower, sonneteer, chess player, dog-trainer, wood-carver, tulip breeder. Best something. But lately he had abandoned such hopes.

Time seemed to pass more quickly—the weeks whipped by. In a wry mood he propounded a new law of physics: *the speed of time is proportional to the age of the observer.*

A persistent cough had finally taken him to the doctor. He sat in the waiting room, one of a half dozen unsmiling people isolated by their worries.

He was led into a windowless cubicle and deserted. After a long wait, a well starched sergeant-major poked her head around the door and instructed him to strip to his underwear. Then another long wait with nothing to read. Finally the doctor bustled in. "Let's check your blood pressure." Cold stethoscope. Thirty seconds silence. "Look at the upper right corner of the door". Lights out, blinding white glare. Other eye. Prolonged thumping of his torso. The requisite two coughs. Invasion by a greased finger. "Put on your clothes. We'd better have an X-ray."

This morning he had returned to the doctor's office to get the bad news: six months; declining strength; increasing pain. As a longtime smoker, he had half expected it.

He shuffled from the office, stony-faced, death sentence ricochetting around his brain-case. The lissome receptionist swivelled in her chair. Nyloned thighs flashed as her miniskirt twisted. The rattle in his skull was displaced by the rustle of perfumed sheets. His eyes brightened, a wave of warmth and well-being spread through his body. He took a dccp breath and strode smiling into the summer day.

Long before he had reached home, his black mood had reasserted itself. And then Bill had appeared at the front door.

◊ ◊ ◊

"Sarge, anything new on our Greenall Road body?"

"No. It is still a mystery. If she was deliberately run down and then finished off—a premeditated murder—then there must be a motive. But we have none. Now, Victor, you have been patrolling the parking lots. Have you had any success with that fragment of plastic that was found with the body?"

"Nothing. Found three rusted-out vans being used as student residences. Checked them out—hard-up kids, living like savages, minding their own business, drinking a little beer, using the showers at the gym, not hurting anybody. I left them alone."

Two days later, Handforth reported over the car radio that he'd identified the car model that carried the plastic fitting found in the coat of the murder victim. A 1979 Ford. They obtained a printout of all the Lower Mainland 1979 Fords from the Motor Vehicle Branch. Handforth started checking them, concentrating on the Point Grey area.

It came over the speaker-phone. "Car 2 reporting. Sgt. Fortier, I've found the car, the Ford with the broken parking-light rim."

"Rest there. Address? Shaughnessy? Give me the license number." Fortier phoned the motor vehicle office and made some notes. Twenty minutes later he pulled in behind a red Ford station wagon and joined Handforth on the sidewalk.

Shaughnessy Heights was developed before and after the First World War. Mansions, almost castles, half of them run-down, the rest maintained at great expense, sat on half-acre or one-acre lots. Many of them were built by timber and mining tycoons when first-growth giant firs and cedars clothed the hills and rich mineral deposits sat waiting for the miners. Or by daring bootleggers who ran whiskey-laden speed boats to the American west coast.

Where the car was parked, a 5-foot wall of dressed granite separated the grounds from the street. Through a wrought iron gate the officers could see mossy lawns treed with ancient maples, birches and cypresses grown overlarge and deformed. A gazebo, paint peeling, sat in a shaded corner. The house was huge. A broad granite staircase led to a shaded verandah extending around two sides of the house. The overhang was supported by thick tapering columns with formal capitals. Massive, elaborately carved beams ran out under the eaves. The house was dominated by a turret culminating in a swooping conical roof topped by an elaborate weathervane. They could see a building at the back of the property, two stories, modelled after a coach house.

Fortier compared the photographs of the fragment found in the murdered woman's clothes with the gap in the ornamental plastic surrounding the headlight.

"Perfect fit," said Fortier.

"Doesn't look right to me, Sarge. It fits O.K. but it doesn't make a lot of sense. If this car hit someone, broke bones, sent her flying, why would that piece of plastic get knocked off? It's pretty well protected by the bumper. And anyway, it doesn't come anywhere near Bancroft's description of the vehicle he saw. He said it was a pick-up."

Fortier grunted. "Perhaps. Let us speak with the owner."

As they approached the front door, something moved on the dimly lit verandah. A long cat spiralled to a flickering moth. A heavy brass knocker had been made obsolete by a push button. The door opened cautiously, restrained by a chain, and they heard a woman's voice, hesitant, uncertain.

"Yes?"

"R.C.M.P.," announced Fortier. "Mrs. Dickson? Could we have a word with you?"

After a pause, the chain was unhooked and a woman stood in the doorway. She restrained a large, friendly light-brown golden retriever. Fortier summed her up: short

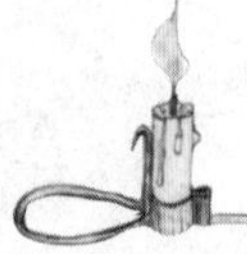

wavy blonde hair, medium height and weight, about thirty-five, expensive clothes, diamond rings and heavy gold bracelet. Her eyes flicked nervously from Fortier to Handforth. She seemed flustered and uncertain about whether to continue at the door or invite them in. She remained in the doorway.

"What seems to be the problem?" It took some effort to get the words out.

"There is, I think, no problem," Fortier replied. "That car—it is yours?"

"Yes."

"Such a car was involved in a minor accident a week ago. Does anyone but you drive it?"

She seemed to relax. "No. I've got the only keys. Ordinarily it's kept in the garage."

"Your husband, he has a car?"

"He has a Jaguar—he's at the office downtown now. He's a sales representative." She was now talking freely.

"Have you had the car for a long time?"

"Two or three years."

"May we look inside it?"

She was now cooperating, almost enthusiastically. "Of course. I'll get the keys."

Handforth opened the tail-gate and examined the interior of the Ford. It was covered with dog hair—the floor rug looked like brown felt.

"If our victim had ever been in this car, forensic would have picked this up," he said, as he tried to brush the hair off his pant leg. "It's not the murder car. Let's take another look at the parking light."

"It's a perfect fit," agreed Fortier. "But you're right—I

can't see how hitting someone would knock that piece off. And nothing else is dented or scratched."

Handforth was peering at the photos. "Look at these scratches. Could they be plier marks?"

"I think you are right. Merde! Someone is trying to throw us off the trail."

Fortier returned to the front door, returned the keys, and thanked the woman for being helpful. She was now all smiles. He refused her offer of coffee.

As they drove away, Handforth remarked,"She seemed awfully nervous at first, edgy. What had she been up to, d'ya think?" Fortier smiled.

"Victor, you know that most law-abiding citizens do not look a cop in the eye. They act as if they are hiding something. They become tense and perspire. They talk more than they need to. They look guilty. Most criminals, on the other hand, behave like innocent babies."

◊ ◊ ◊

She stood well back from the curtained windows and watched the police car drive off. After waiting ten minutes, she passed through to the kitchen and looked out at the lane. Satisfied, she opened a door and descended into a different world. The basement was one large windowless room. Ten-by-ten posts supported beams festooned with hundreds of feet of nutrient hose. Suspended racks held giant parabolic reflectors over glaring metal-halide lamps. Below, racks separated by narrow walkways supported a small forest in hundreds of plastic containers. She peered at dials displaying temperature, humidity and carbon dioxide concentration, then turned on an

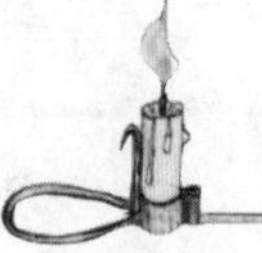

exhaust fan. She picked off a leaf, rolled the double-edged green saw blade between her fingers, sniffed and smiled a secret smile. Mona Lisa in the jungle.

◊◊◊

Later, back at headquarters, Fortier spoke to Handforth. "Forensic agrees that they are plier marks. He planted that plastic to throw us off the scent. But we shall get him."

CHAPTER 17

BILL AND GUS GO PROSPECTING

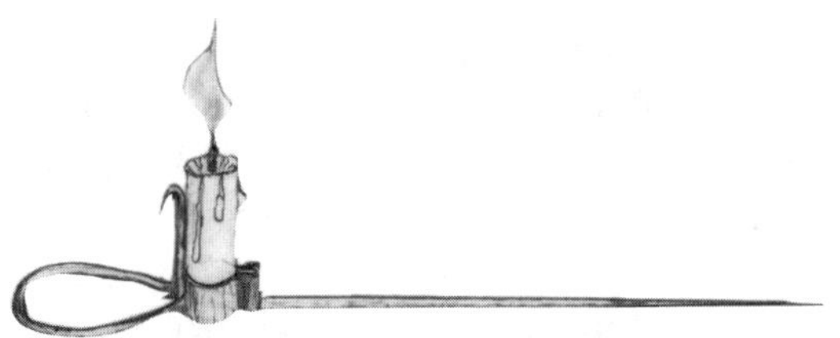

After visiting the Prof, Bill continued east through Hope and on to Princeton. Here he turned north and, an hour later, dropped in on Gus. He was persuaded to stay for the night. Unable to face beans and bacon, he talked Gus into driving into town for dinner.

They read the sticky menus in Gorgano's Grill and decided on pasta with meat sauce. As the steaming mounds were placed in front of them, Gus passed his napkin across his face and fumbled at his shirt pocket. He wound a forkful of spaghetti, dipped it in sauce, and spun it into his mouth. His mouth closed, continued closing, and closed some more. His upper lip disappeared and his chin grazed his nose. His eye closed and his brows climbed as he gummed and swallowed. He smiled blissfully.

Bill, startled, realized that Gus had slipped his teeth into his pocket.

"Gus, why did you take your choppers out?"

"Well, usually I leave 'em in. But when there's something 'specially tasty, I take 'em out. Things taste a lot better. The damned plates cover up the taste buds. Cuts down on the enjoyment."

Later Bill and Gus sat in the beer parlour of the Log Kabin Hotel, drinking Scottish ale. Bill pinched his cheek. Not yet numb but tingling a little—he was approaching his limit. As he raised his glass, he noticed Gus' attention had wandered. He was watching the barmaid, moving his head right to left to right like a hunting cobra, the better to resolve her third dimension as she retrieved some empty glasses. A moose looked down from his shield on the panelled wall. With his sad eyes, slightly twisted thin lower lip and chin-whiskers, he reminded Bill of Abraham Lincoln. Bill pressed a dime into the juke-box beside their table and Orris Brambley whined his latest hit:

Who put
The glow-worm in my gluhwein?
I'm much too young to die,
The looper in my lager?
Too soon to say goodbye.
The oyster in my ouzo?
O death, I hear your cry.

Who put
The weevil in my waffle?
A plot . . .

Bill took a swig and eased a silent belch. The eight and one-half percent alcohol solution must have dissolved his inhibitions or perhaps cleared his vision, for as he stared into the corner of the room, the fat white logs, intersecting in voluptuous curves, became a series, a stack of wanton crotches. With an effort, he returned to more immediate considerations.

So Kingfisher had dropped Gus' copper claims. Bill was relieved that his pessimism about the worth of the showings, which he hadn't bothered to conceal from Gus, had been confirmed by Kingfisher. He had been worried that he might have misled his friend. Now he was intrigued by Gus' detached and philosophical acceptance of the bad news about his property.

"Well, I guess I missed all the excitement," Bill said. "I didn't think those dirt-baggers would ever be back. And you made a deal with Carl Costello. Hope you made a little money out of it. Too bad they didn't find a mine. But there's always next time." The ale had loosened Gus' tongue.

"Oh there won't be a next time. I knew there was nothing there." Bill stared at Gus.

"Come on. How did you know that there was nothing there?"

Gus replied: "Whatever was there I put there. I've been salting the place, off and on, for years—hard work, too."

"You're kidding! No? How did you do it?"

Gus explained. "You know that box of sand that I keep in my pick-up truck? That sand is Copper Mountain mine tailings. There's still a fair amount of copper in them. Every time I go to Princeton I pick up a load. Whenever I go up the hill for firewood or a log or two, I spread the stuff around." Gus pushed back his chair. "Back in a minute," he said, as he headed for the washroom.

Gus' salting of a relatively large area with truck-loads of copper tailings was probably a unique scam, Bill thought, knowing that gold was the metal most commonly used in salting. Because of its high value, it took a very small amount of gold to produce spectacular assays.

Bill had heard many stories about salting a gold prospect. One method was to replace the lead shot of a shotgun shell with gold particles and fire the charge at the vein. Gold thus embedded in the cracks in the quartz

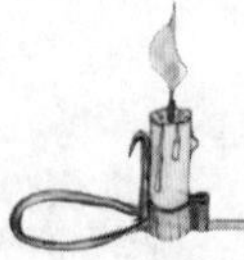

would contaminate a sample later chipped or cut from it. But there were many other ways. In one well-known swindle, a rascally owner drilled minute holes into the cutting edge of a moil, a heavy chisel used for cutting samples from rock or vein. He pounded gold into these, much as dentists used to pound gold fillings into teeth. He cheerfully loaned his moil to visiting mining engineers who used it to cut their samples. Bits of gold would be worn off the cutting edge and the samples would yield interesting assays. The smiling owner made many thousands of dollars by lending his moil and optioning his claims to mining companies. A more common ploy was to salt the samples after they had been cut. This could be accomplished by adding gold particles to the bagged sample or by injection of a gold chloride or gold cyanide solution by hypodermic needle through a sample bag. A common defence against this sort of skullduggery was to include among the sample bags a few containing rock known to be barren. High assays of these would be proof of salting.

Bill thought of the Prof's experience with salting. Early in his career, he had been sampling a gold vein, using a moil to chip an inch-deep trench across the hard, brittle, white quartz vein. His assistant, a local fellow, helped spread a clean tarpaulin to catch the cuttings which tended to fly in all directions. A spindled roll-your-own cigarette dropped ash as he used both hands to edge the cuttings into the middle of the tarp and coax them into the sample bag that the Prof held open. The procedure was repeated several times as different parts of the vein were sampled. Later, he crushed each sample and sent one half of each for assay. The results were erratic and several indicated an ounce or more of gold to the ton. Ore yielding such high assays should contain easily visible gold but he had not seen any in the vein. He panned the halves of the samples that he had retained and recovered a few gold particles. Under the microscope these were determined to be from a placer deposit. They were thin flat discs absolutely diagnostic of placer gold. His sample had been salted. But how? After reviewing the whole operation, the Prof concluded that his helper had probably rolled grains of placer gold into his cigarette, the gold falling with the ash into the sample cuttings. He had resolved never again to allow anyone near him when he was sampling.

Gus returned, steadied himself, and subsided into his chair.

Bill stared at him. "Come on," he demanded, "How could you salt so big an area? It's impossible."

"Not if you have lots of time and use a little of this psychology. You don't have to cover the whole area. Mostly I dumped it in the creeks that head near my claims and the adit. I used my little tractor and the trailer. A lot of it was washed downstream and into Piebyter creek. I spread some on the meadows above the adit but this was hard work. I didn't bother with the bushy or swampy places or where trees made it hard to get through, or where roots would make the digging tough for the dirt-baggers. I scattered it along straight draws and creeks that looked like good places for faults to go through—geologists are crazy about faults. I shovelled it straight off the back of the pick-up at spots along the road. I stayed away from areas with lots of outcrop."

"You crafty old bugger! You ought to be in jail. Did they ever suspect that there was something fishy?"

Gus laughed. "I think Costello caught on at the end but he didn't say much. After all, what have I done wrong? I didn't invite them to come sneaking around my property.

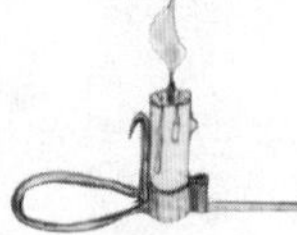

They dirt-bagged my claims and creeks without even asking me. I didn't offer to sell them my claims. I don't think they could prove anything if they wanted to.There's no law against adding some of these nutrients and trace elements to your pastures. But I think that's the end of it—I won't hear from them again. I made a bit of money, eh? And I've got my old claims back and about a hundred more they staked.And some new roads."

"Don't you feel a bit of a crook?" Bill asked. "You set a trap for them. I mean you're really stealing money from the company."

"Hell no. These big companies take little guys to the cleaners all the time. I once had a disagreement over some claims with Megamet Copper. I was hit with court orders, threats of injunctions, private investigators, lawyers' letters and God-knows-what-else. I finally just walked away and let the claims go. I've got no sympathy for the big companies—they can take care of themselves. Most of the time."

Gus paused, then added, "There's just one thing that bothers me. Where the devil did the moly come from? There's no moly at Copper Mountain." Gus was referring to molybdenite, the ore mineral of molybdenum.

"What moly?" asked Bill.

"Why, the moly that shows up on the geochemical maps!"

Bill was intrigued by this new bit of information. Molybdenite was common enough in copper deposits, but Gus was right—it was well known that there wasn't any molybdenite in the Copper Mountain deposit. Back at the cabin later that night, more than slightly tipsy, they checked Carl's maps. They showed anomalies up to four hundred parts per million of molybdenum occurring sporadically among the soil and stream samples.

"Well, I didn't put it there" Gus said defensively.

Bill pointed to the list of assays. "They didn't find any moly in the bedrock in the trenches or test pits."

"Not much copper, either," Gus added with satisfaction.

Bill, still wondering if Gus had managed inadvertently to salt his property with molybdenum, said, "If it's in the soil but not in the rock, it could have been dumped there by the glaciers."

"What glaciers?" asked Gus.

"The glaciers that completely covered this part of the world. They finally melted back about 10,000 years ago. The glaciers deepened and straightened old valleys, gouged new ones, and transported tremendous volumes of broken rock and sand and dumped it as glacial drift."

"What's all that got to do with the moly?" Gus asked.

"Well, moly and the rock it's in could have been ripped from the bedrock and dumped with the glacial drift on your claims. This would explain the moly anomalies."

"So all we have to do is follow the moly back to its source?"

"Well, it may not be as easy as it sounds," admitted Bill, "but it can be done. In Finland dogs are trained to sniff out boulders containing decomposing sulfide minerals in the glacial drift and the prospector-dog handlers trace the mineralized debris back to its source. And they did find a copper mine in this way. We'd better have a look around tomorrow."

Next morning, badly hung over, they rose late. They walked slowly up the hill, past the lake. Bill placed his boots carefully, avoiding sudden jars. Gus' eye resembled the great red storm on Jupiter. King looked back at them,

wondering at their sluggish pace.

Where was the moly coming from? They scanned the landscape. Bill knew that in this area the ice came from the north. He pointed towards a low pass beyond the lake.

"What's up there?"

"That geochemist told me that it's mostly granite," answered Gus. "One of the kids who helped with the staking said he saw some graphite."

Now Bill was not an old hand, but he had been around long enough to know that graphite and molybdenite could easily be mistaken one for the other. They not only resembled one another in hardness and colour, but they had a similar crystal form. Bells rang and Bill's mind began to race. They walked beside the creek towards the pass and after breaking half a dozen pieces of float and peering at them through his hand-lens, Bill found a few flakes of molybdenite in a chunk of granite.

Gus assured him that they were well within the large block of claims that Kingfisher had staked and that had now reverted to him.

They continued up the deeply gullied and brushy draw towards the pass.

"It'll be easier going if we cut around to the right," Gus suggested, "get out of this damned bush."

"I'm all for it," Bill said. "That's funny—it looks as if somebody dammed the creek there."

Gus kicked at a rusty axle attached to a rotten plank. "By God, it's an old boomer-gate."

Bill had never heard of boomer-gates. Gus explained how they worked.

The prospector would build a crude dam across a draw

or stream gully. A heavy wooden frame was set into the base of the dam at its centre and in it was mounted a wooden door or gate, swinging on a horizontal axle and weighted so it remained in the closed position. A couple of short buoyant logs were attached by chains to the bottom of the gate on the upstream side of the dam. In the spring, melt-water filled the reservoir. When the pond reached a certain level, the log floats triggered the gate. The impounded water rushed down the hillside, cutting a gully through the overburden and exposing the bedrock, which, it was hoped, contained some valuable mineralization. When the pond was nearly empty, a falling float triggered a pawl, and the weighted gate swung shut, and the pond behind the dam filled once more. The beauty of the boomer-gate was that it was automatic—it filled and spilled twenty-four hours a day as long as there was enough meltwater to fill the reservoir. While the pond was filling, the ditches below the dam would be redirected so that the next flood would cut trenches across a new, untested area.

Gus continued, "The old guys were looking for high-grade. In the '20s and '30s, nobody was looking for low-grade copper or moly. They wouldn't have paid much attention to stuff like this."

They continued hammering on chunks of float and finding scattered crystals of the aluminum-coloured molybdenite. It soon became clear that the diorite, which lay along the east side of the granite, was barren but that a relatively small granite body was the host rock for a molybdenite deposit.

Bill tried to contain his excitement. Suppressing visions of a giant open-pit mine, with monster trucks roaring up spiralling benches carrying molybdenum ore to a near-by mill, he assured Gus that the geological environment

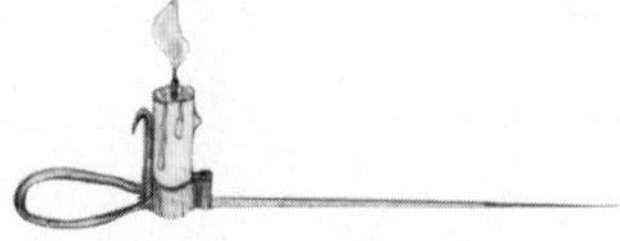

was about right for a disseminated molybdenite deposit. It was getting late and they headed for home.

That night, back at Gus' cabin, they considered what to do. But first, Gus had something on his mind.

"If there's any good to come from this, I want you and me to be equal partners."

Bill shook his head, but Gus persisted.

"We would never have walked up there if it hadn't been for you. Besides which, we're going to need a geologist and I'm not going to pay for one. In fact, we'll have to spend some money before we go much further and I'd like to spread the risk around. I say we're equal partners and that's settled."

Bill was persuaded.

"Should we try to option the claims to a mining company?" Gus asked. "Lots of outfits are looking for moly. Of course we don't have a heck of a lot to show them."

"Well, there are two ways to go," Bill said. "We could probably persuade a company—like, say, Foundation Metals—to option it and do some work—trenching, drilling, assaying and so on. If there's anything there, they'll get the lion's share—we'd end up with some cash and maybe shares, but we'd be on the outside, looking in. It would be out of our control. And the fact that Kingfisher has walked away from it won't make it any more attractive, 'though their geochem shows that there's lots of moly in the glacial drift.

"The other way would be to do some exploratory work ourselves. We could spend our own money on trenching or drilling. We could do a lot of the work ourselves. But it's a gamble—if there's nothing worthwhile there, we waste our time and lose our shirts. On the other hand, if we can demonstrate that there's a decent-sized moly deposit, we can make a much better deal with a company—we'd be in a much stronger bargaining position."

Gus replied: "Well, you're the geologist. What are the chances?"

Bill considered. "The moly seems to be restricted to the small granite plug which cuts through the older rocks. This is typical for this sort of deposit. In other words, the geology looks O.K. The geological environment is right. Mind you, we haven't seen anything we could call high-grade."

"Well, let's say we do it ourselves and leave the big companies out of it for now", said Gus. "What would we do? What would it cost us?"

"One option would be to trench it," Bill said, "to get a good look at a few sections right across the granite. The glacial drift is pretty thick—you saw the depth of those gullies below the old boomer gate. It wouldn't be easy to get down to bedrock in some places. And the rock in the trenches may be weathered—it might not be easy to get fresh samples."

Gus interjected, "But in places it's steep hillside—in lots of places. Easy to cut into the hillside and dump the muck over the side and down the hill."

Bill nodded. "The other way would be to drill it. A couple of holes poked into the granite would give us nice clean samples. But at $15 a foot, drilling can run into money. But drilling would give us some quick answers. I think the first thing to do is to make a detailed map of the granite and the immediately surrounding area. Then we'll have a much better idea of what we're up against."

And so it was decided. Bill spent the next few days making a geological map on a scale of 100 feet to the inch. In the meantime, Gus improved the logging road and trail

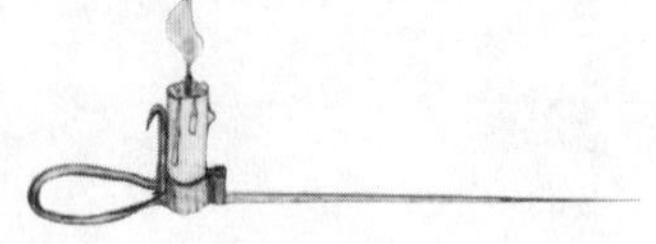

past the lake and towards the new showing.

◊ ◊ ◊

A week later they sat at the kitchen table under the hissing Coleman lamp, Bill's new map spread out.

"Well, Bill, what do you think?" Gus asked.

"It's not an easy decision to make. The mineralization seems to be widespread but we've still not found any real high-grade. Mind you, we've only got about 5 percent outcrop and we've no idea what might be hidden under the glacial drift. And most of the exposures are along the creek."

Gus growled, "I hate the idea of another company coming in, like Kingfisher, taking over the whole show, getting answers but not telling us anything until it suits them. I say let's do it ourselves."

"It'll cost a lot of money. I figure we should allow for a minimum of about a thousand feet of drilling—that's 15,000 bucks."

"O.K. with me. I'm flush, thanks to your friend Costello. I'll put up half. How are you fixed?"

Bill thought for a minute. "I've got some savings from last winter but I can't put up that much cash. I think Julie would put some money into it but she'll need some persuading. I guess we probably could swing it. But it's a gamble."

Next day Bill left for Vancouver. He would sound out Julie. He would also make enquiries at several drilling companies.

CHAPTER 18

CHRIS AND BEN

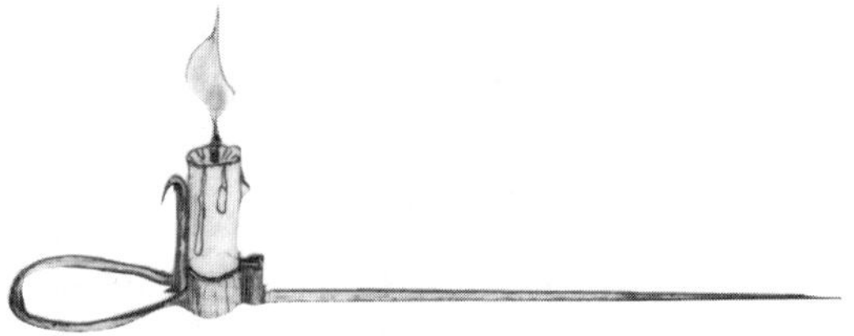

Did the earth move?

Of course it did—it never stops moving. The earth's crustal plates are in constant motion as they rub past each other or are dragged down to the depths at the oceanic trenches. Or are depressed as mud fills the sedimentary basins. Or rise as erosion destroys the landscape, removing a few millimetres of bedrock per century. Or sag or spring up as continental glaciers wax or wane. But it is unlikely that Chris' personal microseism puzzled the geophysicists as they studied their shaky recordings.

The delicious spasms faded and, as usual, he was overtaken by the mystery and absurdity of sex. He kissed the tip of Elaine's nose and buried his face in her hair, muttering into her ear: "Why? Why?" She giggled. Encouraged, he persisted: "What? What?" An indulgent titter, and finally, he raised his head and peered at her: "Who? Who?" Her reaction was a soft judo chop to the back of his neck.

He rolled over and fumbled at a switch. In a few minutes the teapot was burbling. Tea in bed was a luxury they enjoyed each morning. Cups, tea bags and milk had been ranged within easy reach at bedtime. He poured

two cups, flicked on the radio, and they listened to the news.

Chris felt good. Everything was going well. He loved and was loved. The kids had not, he believed, discovered drugs or sex and had been doing well at school. Everybody was healthy. He even seemed to be winning the battle with the moles. He had poured a couple of bottles of failed red wine down a hole and now, two weeks later, there had been no new hills. After a leisurely breakfast he assembled his work clothes, boots and hammer, packed a suitcase, and kissed Elaine goodbye. He made a late start—he would rather have stayed home.

An hour later the snow cap of Mount Baker appeared out of the mists to the southeast. A 10,000-foot peak, Mount Baker is one of dozens of intermittently active volcanoes which form a belt extending from a point northwest of Vancouver, through Washington and Oregon to California. At Hope, he turned north and followed the Fraser to Lytton, and then drove past Nicoamen where the first placer gold had been found.

Magnalode, Kingfisher's parent company, had a minority interest in the Cougar Lake copper deposit in the Highland Valley and, in partnership with several other companies, hoped to prove up a copper mine. A few of the larger deposits in the Valley were already being mined. They produced several million tons per year of copper ore, running about two-tenths of a percent copper, or four pounds of copper to the ton of ore. Since the price of copper was about $1 per pound, mining and processing had to total well under $4 per ton. The costs of mining a ton of ore could be kept at the necessary low levels by treating large tonnages from huge open-pits, using mechanical shovels and mammoth trucks and employing a relatively small number of miners.

Development of the Cougar Lake deposit had reached the stage where the owners had to make a decision: mine the deposit or put it on hold. Since it would take two or three years to prepare the pit and build the mill that would process the ore, much depended on accurate long-range forecasting of metal prices. A relatively slight fluctuation in the price of copper could close a mine, or, on the other hand, allow sizeable dividends. The Cougar Lake deposit was low grade and it was of critical importance to know exactly what the grade, the percentage of copper, was for the millions of tons that would be blasted from the projected open pit and fed into the mill. If the engineers were to overestimate the grade, they would waste $50 million on a mining and milling plant that might never make a profit.

Chris was to join the other engineers in designing a sampling program that would allow them to arrive at an accurate grade for the deposit. As he drove northwards towards Highland Valley, he relaxed and thought about the thrill and excitement of finding a mine. Over the years he had heard many yarns about the discovery of ore-bodies. Most often luck, rather than the rigorous application of geological principles, had led to success.

If one mine-finder had picked a different seat in the pub in Zeballos, on Vancouver Island, facing the shuffle-board game rather than the view through the windows, he wouldn't have idly asked one of his fellow drinkers: "What's that rusty-looking rock up there?" Luckily, they had a helicopter, the weather was clearing, and they had time to spare. They found that the rusty zone marked a large copper deposit.

On another occasion, a mining syndicate had raised

money for diamond drilling a silver deposit. This lay thirty miles up a rutted track in a wild river canyon leading from tide-water into the rugged Coast Mountains of British Columbia. A crew fought a flat-bed and drill up the partly flooded road, bouncing and lurching from boulder to stump, and got hopelessly bogged down 10 miles short of their objective. What to do? They conferred. Their leader spoke:

"We can't go on. Ernie says the road's washed out ahead so even if we can get across this swamp we're stuck. We can't go back and tell them we didn't drill—the money has to be spent." Then someone, obviously a man who would make his mark in the world, had a brilliant idea.

"Look. One part of this God-for-saken, dripping, fogged-in, devil's club-infested, moss-encrusted conglomeration of cliffs and trees and swamp is like any other. Why not drill right here? We'll tell them that we drilled. We'll have the core to prove it. Nobody will ever know we didn't make it to the Poco Plata claims."

They unloaded and set up the drill, drove random holes into the virgin rock, and put a drill right into the richest silver deposit ever found in that area—thus proving that silver, as well as gold, is where you find it.

When Chris arrived in Ashcroft, he got a room in the hotel. He had a poor night. He missed his wife and the bed seemed as big and empty as a tennis court.

Next morning he cursed as the starter groaned, grunted and died. He coasted life into the motor and started up the long twisty hill towards Highland Valley. Although he now had to pay attention to the road and watch for 30-ton trucks carrying copper concentrate, he was still mulling over the business of finding a mine. He grinned ruefully as he remembered that he had once found a rich gold mine and that only a small detail of timing had prevented him from cashing in on it.

It was when he had first joined Midas Explorations. He had spent the first winter in the office and library, reading government reports and mining journals, looking for inspiration. The area assigned to him was southwestern British Columbia and he had gone back to the early literature, reading Selwyn and Dawson, working his way forward to the newer reports by Camsell, Cockfield and Rice. The best of these, in the opinion of many, were the reports of the remarkable George M. Dawson.

Dawson, as the result of an accident in childhood, had not grown properly; when mature he was a hunchbacked dwarf, standing only about 4 feet tall. Of a wealthy family, he was well educated. He joined the Geological Survey of Canada in whose employ he soon proved to be one of the great geologists of his day. He described the geology of many areas throughout British Columbia and the Yukon, his reports spanning the years from the 1870s to the 1900s. He ended his career as chief geologist. Dawson City is named after him. He studied not only the geology of many regions, but also reported on the botany of his study areas and on the ethnography of the Indians. His report on the Haidas of the Queen Charlotte Islands is considered a classic. Because of his disability, he did much of his field-work on horseback, penetrating trackless valleys and ascending peaks rarely reached today except by helicopter. It is said that when one of his mounts was sold it would be found to be useless as a saddle horse because whenever it saw a rock outcrop it would go to it and stop, waiting patiently for its rider to examine the rock and record the geological particulars.

The young Chris was reading Dawson's 1879 report

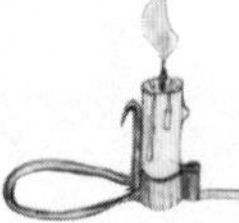

on his explorations in southern British Columbia, interpreting Dawson's observations in light of modern knowledge, looking for ideas for the coming field season. He came to a section that described a mountain composed of gently sloping alternating layers of limestone, marble and gabbro so spectacular that it was referred to as Striped Mountain. The lower slopes of the mountain were of granite which had been injected into the overlying marbles. Chris immediately recognized the geological setting as the classic environment for a certain kind of ore deposit, and, when he read further on that the rocks were locally rusty from decomposing pyrite, felt the thrill of discovery—he knew that he had found a place of obvious potential and that it must be examined.

Where is this mountain? he asked himself. He flicked back through the pages—O ho! Thirty miles east of Vermilion Forks. But where the hell is Vermilion Forks?

Reading back and forth, looking at maps, scaling off distances, he finally concluded that Vermilion Forks must be the old name for the town of Princeton. So far so good. On a modern topographic map, with a shaking hand, he scaled off thirty miles along the Similkameen valley, arriving at the village of Hedley, which lies at the foot of a mountain composed largely of varicoloured layers of limestone, marble, and gabbro. That mountain, it turned out, was the site of a gold mine which paid millions of dollars in dividends in the twenties and thirties.

Using impeccable reasoning, Chris had discovered a gold mine. But he was sixty years too late! His disappointment was tempered by the realization that his methods had been vindicated and his conclusions had been sound. He also found some comfort in the notion that since geologists deal with rocks hundreds of million years old in an earth that has been around for several billion years, a race lost by a mere sixty years could reasonably be considered a draw!

He was aroused from these reflections by the flashing multicoloured lights of an overtaking police car. He pulled over and the other car wheeled in behind him. He watched in his mirror as the door opened and a Mountie emerged clutching a notebook and pushing her cap down on her golden curls. She came to his window, as grim and business-like as a sexy-looking blonde with a giant revolver slapping her ample hip can be.

"May I see your driver's license?"

Chris asked mildly, "What's the trouble?"

"Seventy kilometres an hour in a fifty kilometre zone."

"Where did it start?"

"Half a mile back." She obviously wasn't yet thoroughly metricized. "Posted in plain sight. I'm going to have to give you a ticket."

"Gosh. This is going to jump my car insurance—I got a ticket for a left turn the other day."

She looked him over, glanced into the back of the car at his hard-hat, scruffy boots and working clothes. He didn't look like a desperate criminal. Relenting a little, she said, "Well, I could make it an official warning. Greenall Road, Vancouver? I've a cousin lives near there. O.K., drive carefully—you won't be as lucky next time. You should get your lights tended to. Your tail-lights are flickering. Dirty fuse or loose wire. Maybe a short."

"Thanks. I've been having trouble with a low battery. I may have a short. I'll have it looked at in town."

In a few minutes, Chris arrived at the new mining town of Logan Lake, drew up in the shady parking lot behind

the hotel, and checked into a room.

The village nestled in the valley at a discreet distance from the nearest of the giant open-pit mines scattered around the countryside. Discreet? Why discreet? One of the worst, one of the most unforgiveable errors a mining engineer can make is to site a town or a mill or a smelter on top of an ore-body. There have been many mining areas where, after twenty years of operation, the engineers have discovered that they had overlooked a large ore-body, one that just happened to be lying right under the city hall. Such placements generally result not only in the dismantling, removal and reconstruction of the city hall, cathedral, hotel, brothel or, more likely, half of the town, but also in the firing of the responsible engineer.

That evening in the hotel pub, Chris joined the engineers from Foundation Metals and Ashcroft Resources, the companies sharing ownership of the Cougar Lake deposit with Magnalode. These were old friends and as they sipped their beer, news of new projects alternated with good-natured banter.

"Chris, why did you people let Chino Copper get away from you? Did old Marlo Geech outsmart you?"

"The cores were very discouraging when we backed off. Well, the overall grade was marginal. Actually it didn't look too bad—there were a couple of high-grade sections—but Toronto was committed to the Quebec nickel-copper project and was short of money. But that's nothing compared to Carcross Amalgamated. What happened? You had a clear option on the whole damn thing and the assays were great."

"Yeah, but at the time when we had to make up our minds, the price of copper was on the way down and we couldn't see putting a hundred million smackers into 75 miles of road, a townsite and a mill. What are the new owners going to do?"

And so it went for a couple of hours. When they called it a day, Chris strolled out to the parking lot to retrieve a duffel bag from the car trunk. As Chris left the pub, Ben Richards got up from his table and followed him out. He watched him relock his car and disappear into the hotel.

◊◊◊

One AM. Ben slipped out of his pick-up and walked over to Chris' Ford. He extracted a narrow length of spring steel from his shopping bag and in a few seconds had the driver's door open. No traffic at all. The only sound the muffled beat of music from the pub. He silently raised the hood and, using a tiny flashlight, threaded a 6-foot length of high tension cable through the space beside the clutch pedal and under the floor mat, to end under the driver's seat. He fitted a detonator cap, the size of a pencil stub, onto the end of the wire, inserted the cap into one of three banana-sized sticks of dynamite, and taped the package to the stanchion supporting the driver's seat. He pulled one of the spark-plug leads from the distributor and plugged into its place the forward end of the new cable. Satisfied, he lowered the hood and locked the door. That'll fix the bastard.

Next day, Chris and the other engineers rode in a rusty Jeep to the Cougar Lake copper property, about 6 miles from Logan Lake village. The deposit was of the porphyry copper type: a cubic mile or so of the diorite country rock was sparsely mineralized with copper sulfides. These tiny brassy grains, resembling in colour the common pyrite or fool's gold, occurred along cracks in

the dusty diorite of the exploration trenches.The intensity of mineralization ranged widely. Some football-sized chunks contained no copper; some domino-sized chips ran 5 percent copper. How to sample such a deposit and arrive at an average grade?

The answer was to take as large a sample as was practical so that the local differences in grade would be averaged out. But the sample had to be assayed and one couldn't send a thousand-ton sample to an assayer.

The procedure that Chris and the other engineers finally agreed to was this: drill and blast trenches, about a foot wide and a foot deep, into the fresh mineralized rock on parallel lines running across the deposit. Carefully record the positions of the excavated material. Feed it by batches into crushers and grinders in a small temporary mill erected on the property. Pass the crushed material, now sand-size, through a succession of splitters, each like a giant funnel with two spouts.At each splitter the mineral-rich sand would be randomly divided into two equal fractions, one of which would be discarded. Repeat this splitting process again and again until each of the original half-ton samples is reduced to a few pounds that are representative of the original large sample. Send hundreds of these reduced samples to the assayer and plot the results on detailed maps.

In this way, they would gain a reasonable idea of the grade of the copper mineralization at the exposed surface of the mineralized body.This information would be supplemented by the results from drilling. Some drills would yield 4-inch thick cores providing a complete record of the kind of rock traversed, and on assay, the copper content of the rock. Other drills would pulverize the rock, and the cuttings or sludge blown or washed to the surface would be assayed.

They finished their work at noon of the third day, agreed on their strategy, and dispersed to their various headquarters to obtain formal approval and to prepare concrete plans and schedules.

Chris checked out of the hotel, happy to be going home. The garden was probably drying out—the boys no doubt spending their holidays at the beach instead of watering his hanging baskets and his parsnips.

He climbed into his car, fastened the seat-belt, turned the key and was rewarded by a soft click.

Damn and blast. I should have had that battery looked at.

Chris went back to the hotel, phoned for a service truck and was promised one in fifteen minutes. He returned to his car in a foul mood. He leaned back against the door and watched a small plane moving in and out of the clouds. His eyes narrowed as its engine faltered, but in a moment it had resumed its steady throb and flew on, disappearing behind the hills.

A brightly painted tow truck wheeled around the corner and stopped nose-to-nose with Chris' car. A bored-looking young fellow, blackened hands, greasy brown coveralls, climbed down. Up with the hood, jumper cables extended and clipped on. He nodded to Chris.

"Give her a try—I think she'll go now," he said, idly patting the spark-plug leads to see that they were all snug. "Wait a second. You've got a loose wire here, this should plug in here—but—what the devil?" He was following the extra wire back, under the fire-wall, under the car, through the floor, peering with his flashlight under the seat. Chris leaned in to see what he was doing.

"Jesus—get back! There's dynamite under your seat! I'll call the cops—keep everybody away."

In ten minutes two Mounties arrived. Afterwards, they

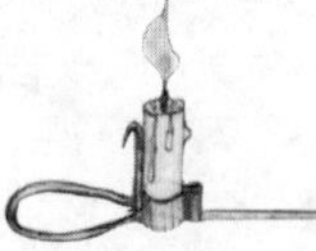

explained to a shaken Chris that if his engine had turned over, an induced high voltage, instead of travelling to a spark-plug, would have gone to the dynamite and he would have been blown sky-high. The Mounties were puzzled.

"We've never had anything like this before. Any enemies? Wife trouble? Girlfriend trouble?"

Chris explained that he lived in Vancouver, had only been here a couple of days, and that there was no one out to get him, as far as he knew.

The other Mountie spoke up. "Could it be a mistake? We've had that nasty strike—miners at Damascus Copper have been off work for three months. Some crazy miner might have mistaken him for a scab. Or management."

"Maybe," the first Mountie conceded. "Easy enough for some hot-head to get his hands on some dynamite. But what about drugs? Could be that someone's trying to establish a monopoly. There've been a few beatings, and that knifing. Anyhow, I think you're right, it's probably a case of mistaken identity. We'll dust the car for prints and we'll need a formal statement from Mr. Bancroft down at the office." He turned to Chris. "You'd better figure on not getting away until tomorrow. And you've got to get that battery attended to."

Next morning the parking lot was deserted. As Chris nervously unlocked his car, cautiously peering under the driver's seat for signs of a renewed bombing attempt, Ben appeared from behind an adjacent car and pushed a revolver against Chris' ribs.

"Reach in and unlock the rear door. Slowly. Get into the driver's seat, slowly. Fasten your seat belt."

As Chris followed instructions, Ben edged into the back seat and carefully slid over the back of the bench seat to sit beside Chris, keeping his gun low and out of sight.

"Back out slowly, head out of town towards Ashcroft." Chris was baffled and scared.

"What's going on? What do you want?" he stuttered.

"Don't give me that crap, you son-of-a-bitch," snarled Ben. "You stole Cougar Lake. Killed my dad. Now you're going to pay. Just keep driving. Keep your eyes on the road." The voice was vaguely familiar. Chris stole a quick glance at the man's face.

"I've never seen you before in my life! You've got the wrong man."

"You work for Magnalode, don't you?"

"Indirectly. I work for Kingfisher."

"Same thing."

Chris glanced again at his companion. Christ, it's him! The crazy aluminum mine prospector—with a moustache. He suddenly realized that this must be the guy who had almost succeeded in dynamiting his car. He began to sweat—this was going to be a one-way trip.

As they wound their way out of town, traffic was light. Ahead, Chris could see the stretch where he had been stopped for speeding. He gradually accelerated until they were cruising along at a comfortable 70 miles an hour. Ben looked at him, questioning, but Chris stared straight ahead. He was lucky; in his rear view mirror he saw a familiar sedan with a red cherry on the roof pull out of its hiding place beside the highway and gradually overtake them. No flashing light yet—she was getting his exact speed. Finally the blinking light. Chris paid no attention—he didn't want to risk getting another warning, he wanted to be arrested. He accelerated slightly, going over the centre-line. Ben looked at him just as the

siren sounded. Chris braked slowly and pulled over onto the shoulder. In his mirror, he saw his blonde policewoman pull in behind him, stop and get out, rearranging her holster with one hand, clutching her notepad in the other. She came up to the driver's window and recognized him.

"Some people never learn, do they? Your license please." Chris was conscious of the revolver sticking into his side. Slowly and cautiously, he reached for his wallet and extracted his library card.

"License. License." Chris took back his card, fumbled around for a bit, and pulled out a credit card. He gave her an insane grin, winked, and finally extracted his license. He handed it to her with a sick smirk. Her face set, her patience seemingly exhausted, she growled: "Would you please get out of the car?" She stood back as Chris slipped through the door. He managed another wink and a grimace.

"You've been drinking. Have to give you a breathalyser test. Walk back to my vehicle. If you can." She steadied his arm as he turned. Chris was bucked up to see her wink at him and saw that she was surreptitiously undoing the flap on her holster and, at the same time, keeping an eye on his passenger who was moving gradually sideways into the driver's seat. Chris signalled the Mountie, rolling his eyes to the right, but she continued to steady him until she saw that his passenger had made it to the driver's seat and had one hand on the wheel and the other occupied with the ignition key. With one bound she was at the window, her revolver at Ben's head. She opened the door slowly as Chris ran around to the passenger side of the car and retrieved Ben's gun.

It was now a simple matter to handcuff him, his hands

joined through the window of the back door. After she called for reinforcements on the radio, she stood with Chris by the police car, talking in low tones. Ben was silent.

"He came to the Kingfisher office once," Chris said. "He's a lunatic. Threw a rock at me—could've killed me. And he's probably the guy who tried to dynamite my car last night."

"You're kidding. Well, we'll see what we can find out about him back at the office. Here comes Jamie."

Chris followed the police cars back to Logan Lake to tell his story and to make his second formal statement to the Logan Lake police. He set off for home next morning, comfortable in the knowledge that the maniac was safely in custody.

CHAPTER 19

A CLOSE THING!

Bill put down his pencil and straightened up from the map on the rough table as Gus entered the tent.

"How's it going?"

"Not great," answered Bill. "I think I wasted the first hole—missed the granite." They both looked discouraged.

The first drill hole had been sited on the diorite and directed so as to penetrate through the contact and into the granite. Bill had thought it important to test the contact zone and had assumed that the contact surface between the two rock types dipped about vertically.After 200 feet of drilling had been wasted in barren diorite, Bill had stopped the drill and re-assessed the geological structure. Clearly the granite-diorite contact was dipping at a low angle.The first drill hole, if extended, might not hit the granite at all.They would have to relocate the drill and probe in a different direction. He was beginning to wonder if they had made the right gamble.

"We'll move the drill up the hill into the limestone area and poke a hole in the opposite direction. From there we're bound to hit the granite."

"How much more drilling have we got left before we

go broke?" Gus asked.

Bill winced. "About 800 feet. We'll collar it outside the granite plug, in the limestone, and figure on hitting the granite contact at about 100 feet. I want to be sure of testing the contact zone. The granite plug must be plunging west and this new hole ought to give us a good section through most of it. Let's tell the driller."

They walked to the drill, stepping around the core-boxes which held 200 feet of unmineralized and worthless diorite. The driller was changing the transmission oil.

"We'll move the drill to a new site for the second hole," Bill told him. "We'll move the tent up there too. I want to keep a close eye on the core. Let's walk up there and I'll show you the spot."

Bill drove a stake showing the location and direction of the new hole and the driller went off to prepare for the move. Gus' small tractor would drag the machine to the new site.

Next day, work started on the new hole. At first, penetrating only drift, the hole was drilled oversize to accommodate a pipe or casing. This was driven down the hole to bedrock to keep soil and gravel from caving into the hole. Drilling then continued through the casing and into the limestone. Bill's projection showed that the drill should very soon cut through into granite and he and Gus anxiously scanned the core as each section was dumped into a core-box.

At first the core was of limestone, as expected. At greater depth it was succeeded by a sugary-textured marble. Bill was relieved—the transition from limestone to marble showed that the granite contact was being approached. At the 60-foot mark, the marble was speckled

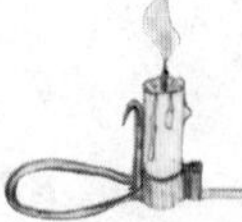

with calcium-rich silicate minerals. These were formed by the reaction of emanations from the cooling and crystallizing granite magma with the calcium carbonate of the marble. Bill noted these with satisfaction and was not surprised when the drill passed into granite at 105 feet.

Now they grabbed each piece of core as it was dumped into the core-box. Bill dipped each length into a bucket of water, washing the mud off and then peering at it anxiously with his hand-lens. He found the odd flake of metallic grey molybdenite but the percentage was low.

Three days later, with the drill at 550 feet, the moly had become scarcer and Bill's glum look told the story. The following evening, when the driller knocked off for the day, the hole was down to 700 feet and, if anything, the moly was scarcer than before.

That afternoon, Julie had appeared at the camp. She had invested most of her savings in the venture and joined the men whenever she could get a few days away from the office. She could see at once that things were not going well. They held a council of war. Gus was philosophical about it.

"Well, let's drill the last 100 feet. If we don't see anything better than what we've been getting we'll give it up. You can't win 'em all!"

Bill was feeling very low. Barring a miracle, his bright idea was going to cost them all their savings and he felt he had let them down. Julie, perhaps seeing the larger picture, telling herself that she had Bill and a job, consoled him.

"It's not the end of the world. And it was fun. And exciting. Anyhow, nothing ventured, nothing gained."

"Well, we aren't going into debt. Still, it probably was a dumb business from the start."

They agreed that they would deepen the hole by 100

feet and, if there was no improvement, they would stop the drill.

Next morning they watched the driller resume his work and waited on tenterhooks for the first core. When it spilled out into the box, they were disappointed. Although Bill could point to the odd flake of molybdenite, the grade was far too low to be of economic interest. They watched with sinking hearts as the deeper core showed even less mineralization. Finally, Bill gave the word to stop the drill.

Late that afternoon, after the driller had dismantled his equipment and dragged his machine away, Julie joined Bill at the core-boxes. He showed her the sparse moly and shook his head. She began to look at the core in the other boxes.

"What's this stuff? It's different from the granite."

"Limestone—probably was a coral reef three hundred million years ago."

"Seems to be whiter, coarser, here," she said, pointing to the marble.

"That's because we are getting closer to a hot granite contact. The limestone was baked by the granite magma." In his morose state, Bill was not the usual enthusiastic explainer.

"Well, what are these bits and spots?" Julie persisted.

Bill answered without enthusiasm. "Minerals. The green one is diopside and the fibrous white one is tremolite. They develop close to the contact. Calcium-magnesium silicate minerals. Worthless."

"What's this one?" This time, Bill bent over to look more closely.

"Dunno." He estimated its hardness by scratching it

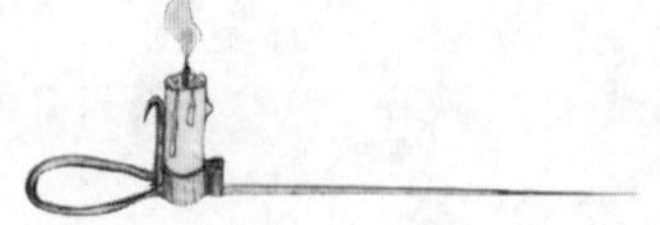

with the tip of his knife blade.

Minerals range in hardness from talc, which can be scratched with the thumb-nail, to diamond, the hardest of natural minerals. Quartz will scratch a knife blade. Calcite, the mineral of limestone and marble, is easily scratched with a knife.

"Too hard for calcite. These contact rocks can have all sorts of weird minerals. I don't know what it is. Would have to make some tests. Anyway, it's not what we're looking for."

"But Bill, here's more of it. In fact, it's all through the core in this box. It looks sort of greasy."

Bill had been about to tell Julie to forget it when her words jogged a memory. He examined the mineral with his hand-lens, scratched it again, and finally leaned back on his heels, a look of suppressed excitement on his face. He took a 2-inch piece of marble core rich in the unknown mineral in his left hand, and a similar-sized piece of limestone core in the other, and hefted them. He traded left for right and hefted again. And again. The piece with the unknown mineral was clearly heavier, denser than the unmineralized limestone.

He shouted over to the tent. "Gus, have you got a mineral-light down at the cabin?"

"Yeah, but I haven't touched it for years. It's on the book shelf. Needs a battery. There's a new one beside the radio."

"I'll nip down and get it. I'll be back before dark," Bill said, and without any explanation to Julie, set off down the trail, almost running. Julie was a bit miffed at being dismissed in this fashion and looked enquiringly at Gus. Gus shrugged his shoulders.

Bill arrived back just at dusk. He was carrying Gus' ancient ultraviolet lamp, which resembled a large angular flashlight. Gus and Julie had had some sandwiches and tea and offered some to Bill, but he shook his head and without a word picked his way out to the core-boxes now in complete darkness. He found the box with the contact rocks where Julie had noticed the strange mineral. He turned off his flashlight and switched on the ultraviolet lamp. Julie's puzzling crystals leapt out, fluorescing a ghostly bluish white. He found the same fluorescing mineral through a core length of about 40 feet, its abundance peaking close to the granite contact. The granite showed none of the mineral.

The others had followed him out to the core-boxes, Gus having some idea what was going on but Julie completely mystified. Bill straightened up, let out a whoop, grabbed Julie around the waist and whirled her around in the dark until they fell.

"Julie, you did it!" he shouted. "You found it! You saved us!" Bill hugged her, kissing her, then giggling hysterically, then kissing her again. Julie pushed Bill away and he fumbled for the flashlight.

"Found what?" she demanded. "Tell me!"

"The rock is loaded with scheelite!" Bill shouted.

Gus had brought the Coleman from the tent. He picked up a length of granite core.

"No, no," Bill explained. "Not in the granite. It's in the limestone, in the marble. We drilled right through it and I'm an idiot. If Julie hadn't made me look at it, we'd never have found it."

Completely mystified, Julie asked, "What the dickens is scheelite? Is it worth anything?"

"Scheelite is the ore mineral of tungsten. Sure it's worth something—lots if you have a decent-sized body of it. Thousands of tons are used in the steel industry. Light

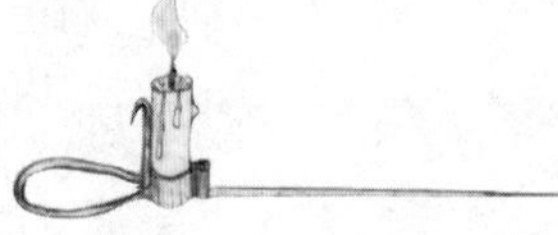

bulb filaments are made of it."

Bill went on to explain that scheelite was very often overlooked in rocks because to the naked eye it had no very distinctive properties, looking, on casual inspection, not very different from common rock-forming minerals like feldspar. But scheelite had a high specific gravity and specimens of tungsten ore were noticeably heavy for their size. And under ultra-violet light, scheelite fluoresced with a characteristic bluish white. A careful prospector would check the rocks at granite-limestone contacts, the geological environment in which most scheelite was found.

The next day they were up at dawn, locating more of the marble and contact rock in the scattered outcrops. The following night was one they would never forget. They followed the inadequate flashlight from outcrop to outcrop, stumbling over rocks, slipping on the damp grass, testing with the magic light, finding more and more of the fluorescing scheelite. They had a few disquieting moments when they found that the seed capsules of certain wild plants and also a few insects showed a white fluorescence and that other minerals, like zircon and calcite, fluoresced with their own distinctive colours when exposed to the ultraviolet rays. But there seemed no doubt that they had found a large and continuous scheelite deposit. Late that night, there was a great celebration in Gus' cabin.

The following noon, Bill and Julie set off for Vancouver. Bill had decided to drop in on the Prof. He had some technical questions to ask about tungsten ores and he had seen a volume on scheelite deposits on his bookshelf. Julie had not yet met him, but she had heard a lot about him.

CHAPTER 20

BEN AND THE PROF

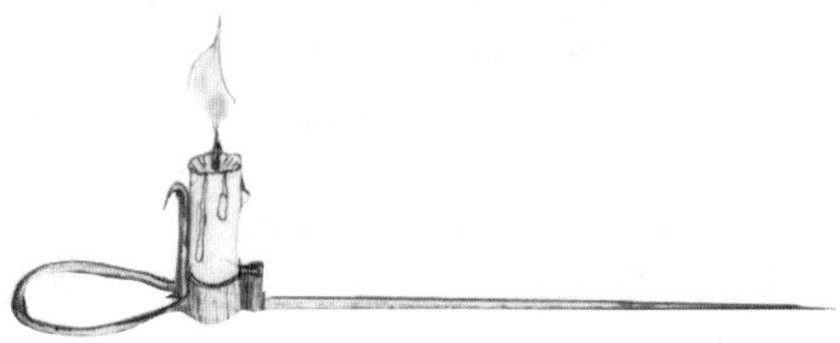

After going through the formalities of signing Ben in, the Mounties emptied his pockets, took away his belt and shoelaces, and led him downstairs to the windowless cell-block. Ben seemed very small, even harmless, and certainly no threat as he walked between the two burly Mounties. There were three cells and he was placed in the middle one. He seemed docile, pitiable, and resigned to his capture. They brought him his supper and disappeared up the stairs.

A quick look around showed Ben that he was alone. He needed a weapon. He examined his cell. The only furniture was a welded steel cot with a mattress of striped twill. He rolled back the thin mattress and examined the bed. Nothing. He glanced at the steel bucket sitting in the corner, then peered through the bars into the adjacent cells. Nothing. He stretched out on the mattress, hands clasped behind his head.

His eyes wandered over the heavily painted ceiling covered with layers of thick ochre-coloured paint. In the oblique light from the bulb in the corridor, brush marks, swirls, ridges and overlaps stood out like miniature mountain ranges. A little lake, perfectly circular, about three inch-

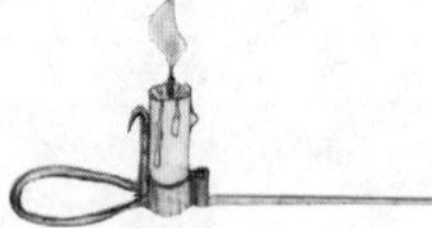

es in diameter, nestled among the mountains. A lake? He looked more closely. A disc, held by two screws, covered an unused electrical outlet. It had been painted over many times and was barely visible. He sat up.

His eye lit on the bucket. He prised the bail from the bucket—a strap of thin steel—and bent it back and forth until it snapped. The broken ends were twisted. He placed a deformed end under the leg of the bed on the concrete floor and put his weight on it. Then he lifted the bed and pounded the metal flat. Satisfied, he stood on the bed, and with his makeshift screwdriver, scraped the paint from the slots and methodically loosened and removed the screws. Blinking away the falling paint flakes, he worked the disc loose and peered upwards at two coiled wires.

He pulled one of the wires until it extended about a foot from the ceiling. He wrapped it around his fist and pulled hard, sawing it back and forth, gaining a few inches. Then he put his whole weight on it. A nail or screw, perhaps holding an insulator, yielded somewhere between ceiling and floor and he gained a few feet. He repeated the procedure with the other wire. He bent a wire back and forth. The wire became hot and finally the copper yielded and the wire pulled free. He was quicker with the second wire.

Ben knotted the two pieces of wire together to form a stiff loop, doubled the wire around his right hand and twisted it three times to form a device something like the frame of a tennis racket.

He practiced with it, stabbing it through the bars, thrusting, turning, and withdrawing.

He spent a sleepless night.

At eight, a Mountie brought him his breakfast.

"'Bout time. I'm starved," Ben said with a shy grin, his

right hand held against his side. The Mountie slid the tray on the pass-through in the barred door.

As he turned away, Ben moved like lightning, slipping the wire loop through the bars and, with a quick half-turn, over the Mountie's head and around his throat. He hauled back with maniacal strength, crashing the Mountie's head against the steel bars. He got a foot up against the door as a fulcrum, using his body weight and hauling back with both hands. The cable almost disappeared into the flesh of the Mountie's throat. The holstered gun hung uselessly as the Mountie clawed weakly at the garrotte. He struggled for less than a minute and then went limp. Ben took no chances, gritting his teeth as the whole weight of the unconscious Mountie bore on his unprotected hands. Finally he released his hold and the body crumpled.

Ben stretched out on the floor, wrinkling his nose at the combined stink of urine, disinfectant, and cement dust, and dragged the body against the bars. Working awkwardly with one hand, he was able to loosen buckles, tug the holster to his side, and finally release the revolver. He checked the pants pockets that he could reach. No key. He extracted a pocket knife.

He began moving the body past the cell door and to his left. He had to lever it painfully, a bit at a time, lying on his right side, nudging it around the corner and partly into the unoccupied cell farthest from the stairs. He got the bulk of it out of sight but the head and shoulders were still visible. He covered the projecting mound with his grey blanket, then paused to get his breath.

He looked up at the light, a naked 100 watt bulb in the middle of the corridor ceiling, about 5 feet from his cell door. The light illuminated the partly concealed dead

Mountie and, through the bars, Ben's own cell. He cut a long strip from the mattress ticking, tied it to the trigger guard of the revolver, rove the strip over the top bar of the door and adjusted the length. A quick push and the revolver swung in an arc out into the corridor and against the ceiling. Short by a foot. Paying out more line, he swung the revolver again and smiled as the light bulb imploded. Now the corridor was dimly lit by a single bulb halfway up the stairs. The dead Mountie was almost invisible. Ben retrieved the gun and slipped it into his waistband.

He cut up the mattress ticking and twisted and braided a crude rope which he hooked over a wire stub projecting from the ceiling. He draped the other end around his neck and stood in the semi-darkness, his back to the corridor, standing on the end of the steel bed. Ten minutes later he heard a call, then steps on the concrete stairs. He canted his head to one side and stood still. Someone approached the cell, paused, and shouted: "Give me a hand, the creep's hung himself."

Ben heard the door mechanism click, waited a few seconds, then dropped to the floor with gun extended and faced two sheepish Mounties.

"Turn around, hands high. Grab the bars. Now slowly separate—that's enough. Put your right leg through the bars and hook your toe around the bar. One funny move and you're dead."

After handcuffing them to the bars, Ben gagged them and tied their feet. He took pistols, wallets and keys, locked the cell door, and crept up the stairs. At the top he was able to see that the office was empty. He went behind the desk and smashed the radio equipment, pulling out wires, tearing loose the microphone and bashing the dials. He ripped out the telephones. He eased out into the parking lot through the rear door and selected an unmarked police car. He drove to the parking lot behind the just-stirring hotel, deftly exchanged the license plates from his pick-up with those of the car and drove west.

In mid-afternoon, Ben reached Lytton and turned into the Esso station for gas. A battered Beetle pulled into the parking lot on the other side of the pumps. Bill and Julie climbed out, stretched, and made for the coffee shop. Ben ducked behind the car. He watched them give their order and disappear into the washrooms. Quickly he paid for his gas, drove to the far end of the parking lot and waited. When Bill and Julie pulled out, Ben followed.

It was easy to keep up with the under-powered Volkswagen. At Hope, they continued straight on to the west, on the north side of the river. Now it was dusk and Ben followed more closely. A few miles east of Agassiz, the Beetle slowed, turned left on a lane, and disappeared towards the river. Ben pulled off to the side of the highway and waited a few minutes. He heard a dog bark and distant conversation. A door closed. He drove slowly down the lane. The Beetle was parked beside a house.

Ben stopped, switched off the ignition, and got out of the car, closing the door silently. He walked up to the house. Standing on the front steps, he could hear talking and laughing. After drawing the heavy police-issue revolver, he knocked. Frantic barking warned him that there was a dog inside.

The Prof opened the door and looked questioningly at him. Ben pushed him back. The dog leapt, locking his jaws on Ben's left arm but Ben crushed his skull with a single blow. The dog fell to the floor, jerked spasmodically, and was still. Ben waved the Prof into the living room where

Bill and Julie had just gotten to their feet. He lined the three of them against the wall.

There they stood, backs to the bookshelf, Julie between the two men. Ben sized up his captives, appearing to be uncertain as to his next move. He focussed on Bill.

Using the gun as a pointer, Ben waved Bill a little to the left. The Prof saw the gun turn and realized that, unless he acted, Bill was done for. At that moment, the house began to rock. The windows rattled and the kettle chattered on the stove. Julie screamed. Ben looked wildly around the room. Seeing his chance, the Prof leapt at the intruder just as the gun steadied. He was aware of a flash and a bang, and felt a blow to his chest but managed to grab the man's gun arm and hang on. At the same time, Bill lunged, wrapping his arms around Ben's upper arms and body, his greater weight and strength twisting Ben around and forcing him down. The Prof was spun loose and crashed against the wall. Bill and Ben writhed on the floor, Bill trying to get control of the gun hand. The train whistle blared. As they rolled, Ben was momentarily on top. He managed to partially free the gun and began to force it around towards Bill's side.

Julie, frantic, was looking for a weapon—fire tongs, a chunk of amethyst—her eyes swept across the top of the bookshelf. She grabbed, turned, and struck. As if in a dream, Bill saw Ben's eyes open wide, his chest arch and the gun fall from his hand. Bill stared up at Julie's distorted face.

He pushed Ben's body off his chest and it rolled partway onto its back, coming to rest in a twisted propped-up position. He gingerly retrieved the gun; one look showed him the fellow was dead. Julie stood, ashen-faced, shaking, staring at the body. Bill ran to the phone, read the emergency number taped to the wall, and, almost incoherent, mouth dry, tongue out of control, blurted into the mouth- piece: "Shooting at Wegner's place, hurry, just off the highway, by the river, bleeding badly, 10 miles east of Agassiz. Hurry!"

Bill checked the Prof, who was still breathing although his clothes were soaked with blood. Bill could see that he had received a fatal chest wound. He tried to make him comfortable with the help of Julie who seemed to have recovered some of her colour and had stopped shaking.

The Prof's eyes opened. His voice was very low as he looked at Bill.

"Don't step on any cockroaches."

Did he wink? Bill wasn't sure. The Prof's face grew pale and his eyes closed. Then he was gone.

Bill went over to the body on the floor. He rolled the body over and saw the haft of the miner's candle-holder standing in his back—the stiletto had passed through Ben's heart. Julie, watching him from a chair, gave an hysterical half-laugh, half-sob: "I didn't think I could do it!" she said.

They heard the howl of sirens and within minutes the Mounties were at the door, followed by a couple of paramedics. A quick examination confirmed that the Prof was dead.

As he was carried out, Bill gave the Mounties an account of what had happened. The Mounties conferred and one went out to his car to use the radio. On his return he reported: "Vancouver says that a Ben Richards had been arrested in Logan Lake. He escaped custody a few hours ago. Killed one of our constables. There is a general alert out for him. I guess this is him. Revolver looks like R.C.M.P. issue. Headed for Vancouver and for some reason

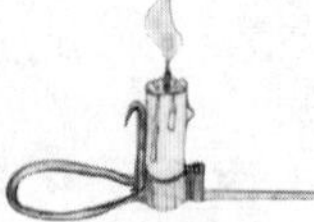

decided to get off the highway—maybe he was looking for a place to hole up for a few days." He examined a candle-holder, the twin of the one with which Julie had stabbed Ben.

"Never seen one of these before," he remarked, and looked at Julie with a mixture of interest and respect.

"I never want to see one again!" she replied.

As they followed the police car and ambulance into Agassiz, Julie said to Bill: "We've seen that guy before. In the office. Screamed at Chris, threw a rock at him. What's going on?"

"You're right. The moustache fooled me. Why was he after us? Or maybe the Prof. Maybe Chris will know."

She thought for a moment. "What was that business about the cockroaches?"

"Oh, the Prof used to rant on about religion. Used to make fun of reincarnation."

◊ ◊ ◊

A few days later, on a cool late-August evening, Chris answered the door.

"Sgt. Fortier. Come in." They sat in the living room. "What's new?" asked Chris.

"We have received some more information about your kidnapper, Ben Richards. He was brought up in Ashcroft. Apparently his father owned valuable mining claims in Highland Valley. He lost them, lost everything and committed suicide. The son hated the big mining companies, especially Magnalode. Magnalode owns the Cougar Lake copper deposit. He claimed the mineral deposit was stolen from his father. That, I believe, is your company?"

"Well, actually my company is Kingfisher," Chris said, "but we're a subsidiary of Magnalode. Richards came into the office once. A crazy man. Almost had a seizure when he found out that we were part of Magnalode."

"So it appears that is why he tried to kill you and your young associates. There is also a good possibility that he killed the mining recorder in Ashcroft who had a hand in arbitrating disputes about ownership of claims at the time."

"Well, that explains a lot," Chris said. There was a long silence.

"What about the woman in the bush across the street?" Chris asked. "Made any headway on that one?"

"That is an enigma," admitted Fortier. "We can see no motive, no connection with anything. Perhaps a drunk driver, simple hit-and-run, he panicked and strangled her and hid her." He shook his head.

Elaine came into the room. "Time for our walk. Oh, I'm sorry, I didn't know you had company."

Chris introduced her to Fortier.

The sergeant stared at her. He forced himself to ask, "Where did you buy that coat?"

"At Marty's, just down on Tenth Avenue," she said. "Why do you ask?"

"When did you buy it?"

"Last May."

"Did they have more than one for sale?"

"They had two—do you like it?" She smiled and turned

to show the whole coat.

He saw, in his mind's eye, the green-and-white-checked coat caked with mud and alder leaves and crossed by glistening slug trails. The coat on the woman found in the bush. The coat just like the one that Chris' wife was wearing.

He explained to Chris and Elaine why the woman had been murdered.

CHAPTER 21

MILOS

The Greek islands are particularly delightful in the autumn. Most of the tourists have gone. The weather is bright and the oppressive summer heat is past. The sea temperature remains high well into October and the swimming is at its best. True, there's a fair amount of plastic and other rubbish left from the hordes of summer visitors and many of the small hotels fold their beach umbrellas, stack away their deck chairs and close their doors in early autumn. But the grapes are ripe, sweet, juicy and abundant.

Bill and Julie had left Athens after a couple of uncomfortable days. It had been noisy, hot, the air dirty, the streets littered and Bill had had his pocket picked on their one venture onto the subway. Jet lag now behind them and taking advice from a geological friend, they had travelled by ferry to Milos, a small island a little off the beaten path, and they were now housed in a small hotel above the ferry landing. Their windows looked across the broad harbour to the hills scarred by pumice mines—Milos is a volcanic island. There were few guests, only two other couples, both elderly.

The swimming in the warm, clear, salty water had been

wonderful. They were the only swimmers on their small beach and they became objects of special interest. An unusual pair: she, trim, sepia-skinned, in her scanty bikini; he, tall, bony, milk-white skinned, flame-headed. The sun-browned fishermen looked up from their nets and watched the exotic couple, half amused and half envious. The black-clad widows watched stony-faced, and their growled remarks had a bitter edge.

They sat at a table under a canvas awning at one of the two tavernas on the only street, a glass of white Demestica and a large Amstel beer sitting in front of them as they chose their dinner from the multilingual menu. Behind them, half a dozen chickens and a lamb turned slowly on a spit. The menu, even in translation, still held some mystery.

"One of these days I'm going to order *featguts* just to see what it is," she giggled. They settled on roast lamb and chips.

A black and orange vase, holding a few wilting wild flowers, was a copy of an ancient amphora, decorated with half a dozen gods, thespians, olympians or perhaps just ordinary Athenian citizens, chasing and being chased in perpetuity. Tremendous thighs. Thighs like those of professional soccer players. Not surprising, Bill thought, they used their legs in 500 B.C.

As they ate, they watched the ferry creep in, drop anchor, go astern into the dock, and disgorge one battered truck and half a dozen passengers, each carrying bundles or cartons.

The warm darkness surrounded their candle-lit table. He left a pile of 100-drachma notes, and they stumbled over irregular paving blocks the few hundred feet to their hotel. They crowded into the tiny elevator and pushed the button for their floor. The door to the lobby closed. No door on the cage. He cautiously buffed his nails on the speeding wall. A bouncing stop. Carefully down the dark hall. He turned the heavy latch key with the half-inch wards, turned it again, and they stepped into the cool, simply furnished interior. He reached out and crushed her in his arms.

◊ ◊ ◊

A lot had happened in the days after their surreal nocturnal hunt for scheelite on Gus' hillside. The deaths of the Prof and of Ben had been front-page news for a few days. Julie and Bill had given evidence at the inquest. At the Kingfisher office, Isaac had received an inquiry from head office in Toronto as to whether he could spare an experienced geologist. They were suddenly desperately shorthanded because they had acquired a couple of promising showings north of Sudbury. Jay had grabbed at the opportunity and Isaac was glad to see him go. Soon after Jay's departure, Isaac had gotten in touch with Bill and offered him his old job. Bill had accepted, his only conditions being that he start work in a month and that Julie be given a month's leave.

Amalgamated Minerals had optioned their tungsten property. And if the local Indians didn't discover that Gus' mining claims covered sacred burial grounds, if the environmentalists could be persuaded that mining would not endanger the last remaining habitat of the three-toed tree toad, if the government didn't proclaim a new park that enclosed Gus' claims, if the lawyers didn't

argue that Kingfisher had not, in fact, relinquished its claims to Gus, if the scheelite mineralization persisted to reasonable depths, and if the price of tungsten didn't plummet because of a world-wide glut, mining could begin in a year or two.

Then the red-winged blackbirds would rise from the bulrushes as the earth shook in dull concussion. The quail would scatter and the killdeer protest as giant trucks ground along the dusty road. But when the tungsten was mined out, in ten or fifteen years, the mine area would be restored. Aspen and pine would grow over the scars, and deer and bear would return. The beaver would rebuild their dam, the shrieks of loons would echo around the lake, and in a hundred years few would know that the mine had ever existed. Or that Gus, Bill and Julie had ever walked beside the lake.

Acknowledgements

The writer thanks many friends on whom he foisted early versions of the story. Some of these are Bert Price, Don McTaggart, Prof. Ronald Hatch, and Joe and Sharon Nagel. George Payerle's advice and encouragement were greatly appreciated. Alex Jones, Joe Montgomery and Ted Affleck gave useful advice on the mysteries of stock promotion.

Stephen Herrero's book on bears, Cruise and Griffiths' on stock market scams, Vogt and Hyman's on witching, and Bancroft's on the early history of British Columbia were useful references. E.A.Haggan's account of placer mining in the Cariboo District, in the Mining and Engineering Record, 1925, provided material not generally known.

The writer is deeply indebted to Jo Blackmore of Elton-Wolf Publishing and to her hard-working and demanding editors, Paul Vanderham and Suzanne Bastedo who guided the author through many revisions. Warren Denny designed the book and cover. The painting on the cover is by Katharine Dickinson.

The writer's wife Margaret good humouredly endured the writer's frustrations and saved him from many a folly.